David Wishart

David Wishart studied Classics at Edinburgh University. He than taught Latin and Greek in school for four years and after this retrained as a teacher of EFL. He lived and worked abroad for eleven years, working in Kuwait, Greece and Saudi Arabia, and now lives with his family in Scotland.

David Wishart's previous novels, I, VIRGIL and OVID, are also available from Sceptre Books.

D1424586

T17296

Nero

DAVID WISHART

SCEPTRE

British Library Cataloguing in Publication Data

Wishart, David, 1952–
  Nero
  1. Nero, Emperor of Rome – Fiction 2. English fiction – 20th
  century
  I. Title
  823.9'14 [F]

  ISBN 0 340 66702 8

Typeset by Palimpsest Book Production Limited,
Polmont, Stirlingshire
Printed and bound in Great Britain by
Caledonian International Book Manufacturing Ltd, Glasgow

Hodder and Stoughton
A division of Hodder Headline PLC
338 Euston Road
London NW1 3BH

To Joyce Collins, who deserves a dedication but has never had one; and to Doctors Peter and Jean Aungle, with my thanks for their help with Lucius

AUTHOR'S NOTE

The main characters in *Nero* are historical, although – as Petronius himself admits in Chapter Four – I have interpreted them subjectively. This, to be fair, is not much different to the practice of the ancient authorities themselves, who more often than not had their own axes to grind (and their own knives to bury).

Nero committed suicide in 68, two years after the story closes: those interested – and the account makes interesting reading – will find the details in Suetonius's *Nero* 47–50. The emperor's almost-final words were, 'What a loss I am to the arts!' ('*Qualis artifex pereo!*')

Tacitus's account of Petronius, however, is short enough to give in abbreviated form, and it may be interesting to compare it with my purely fictional version. The first name Gaius (represented only by the letter C in the text) is probably a copyist's error:

> I should perhaps say a few words about Gaius Petronius. He spent his days asleep and his nights working and at his pleasures; so gaining a reputation not as others do by energy but by its opposite. None the less, he was not considered dissipated or profligate . . . but a voluptuary of some refinement. He was unconventional in speech and actions and manner . . . and people liked this, ascribing his unconventionality to a straightforward character. Yet as governor of Bithynia and later consul he showed himself an able and active administrator.
>
> Having reverted to a dissolute (or ostensibly dissolute) lifestyle he was admitted into Nero's circle of intimates as his Adviser on Taste; and the emperor would consider

nothing enjoyable or refined unless Petronius approved it. This brought him the hatred of Tigellinus, who considered him a rival and indeed a superior where the science of pleasure was concerned. Accordingly . . . he accused him of collusion with Scaevinus [a member of the Piso plot], bribing one of his slaves to incriminate him. Petronius was allowed no opportunity to defend himself, and most of his slaves were arrested.

At the time, Nero was in Campania. Petronius, on his way to meet him, got as far as Cumae, where he was stopped. He did not hesitate, [but] instead of throwing himself into death headlong he slit his wrists so that he could die at leisure by applying tourniquets and slackening them off. Meanwhile he talked with his friends, but not seriously or like someone who wants to be remembered for his strength of character, and listened while they recited not dissertations on wisdom or immortality but frivolous songs and light verses . . . He dined splendidly and had a nap, so that even though his death was forced it might appear natural. In his will he did not, as most did, flatter Nero or Tigellinus . . . but wrote down an account of the emperor's crimes, giving the names of his male and female bedmates and the details of any novel obscene practice involved. This he sent to Nero under seal . . .

Nero was unsure how information on his night-time activities could have become public knowledge; but then he thought of Silia, a senator's wife . . . who had been a recipient of the imperial favours and was a close friend of Petronius's. She was accordingly exiled for failing to keep her mouth shut . . .
(Tacitus, *Annals*, XVI, 18/19)

The Tacitus extract reveals one important liberty I have taken with historical facts: my story ignores Petronius's governorship and subsequent brief consulate, both of which belong in the early 60s. This was necessary, of course, for the sake of the plot: the former would have taken him out of Rome and away from events for at least a year, and the latter identified him a little too closely for my liking with the establishment. The only other major historical anomaly I am guilty of (as far as I know!) occurs in Chapter Five with the introduction of Junia Calvina. Junia was actually in exile at the time and remained so until after the death of Agrippina; but I needed her as a character.

One more confession, of lesser importance: the real Arruntius's first name was Paullus, which would have caused confusion on the introduction of St Paul. He was not (again as far as I know) the real Silia's husband, and 'my' Arruntius's character and inclinations are complete inventions.

Finally, my thanks to Roy Pinkerton of Edinburgh University (who is certainly *not* responsible for any remaining factual errors!); to my wife Rona, and to Teresa Roby and her staff, for being so patient over books from their respective libraries.

Dramatis Personae ∫

The story takes place between 50 and 66: all dates are AD. Purely fictional characters are given in lower case.

ACTE, Claudia: Nero's freedwoman mistress.

AGRIPPINA, Julia: 'the Bitch.' Nero's mother, and the Emperor Claudius's third wife.

ANICETUS: an ex-tutor of Nero's, and his Commander of the Fleet at Misenum.

ARRUNTIUS, Gnaeus (actual first name Paullus): Silia's husband. A right-wing senator who had been involved in the murder of the Emperor Caligula.

BASSUS, Laecanius: consul (with Crassus Frugi) at the time of the Great Fire.

BRITANNICUS: Claudius's son (born 41) by Messalina.

BURRUS, Afranius: with Seneca, Nero's tutor and later adviser. Commander of the Praetorians.

CALIGULA: the Emperor Gaius (Caligula is a nickname); Claudius's predecessor, Agrippina's brother, and Nero's uncle. Murdered 41.

CASSIUS LONGINUS: a right-wing senator.

Chryse: Acte's maid.

CLAUDIUS: 'the Idiot.' Emperor, Nero's predecessor and adoptive father. Poisoned 54.

Crito: Petronius's head slave.

Dion: Petronius's secretary.

JUNIA CALVINA: Silia's friend, a noblewoman descended from Augustus. Her brothers and nephew (the Junii Silani) were among the most prominent of Nero's (and Agrippina's) victims.

Justin: Paullus's servant.

Lalage: Silia's maid.

MESSALINA: Claudius's second wife, and the mother of his son Britannicus. Executed 48 for adultery and treason.

NARCISSUS: Claudius's freedman private secretary.

NERO: emperor (54–68), born 37 as Lucius Domitius Ahenobarbus. Son of Agrippina and Gnaeus Domitius Ahenobarbus. Adopted (50) by the Emperor Claudius, after which time his correct name became Nero Claudius Caesar Drusus Germanicus.

OCTAVIA: daughter of Claudius. Nero's first wife.

OTHO, Marcus Salvius: Nero's erstwhile friend, sometime husband of Poppaea. Returned to support Galba after Nero's death (68) and was briefly emperor after him (Jan–April 69).

PARIS: ballet-dancer and mime artist; one of Nero's favourites.

PAULLUS: Paul of Tarsus (St Paul). He spent some time at Rome in the 60s and was later beheaded there on Nero's orders. Letters exist purporting to be a correspondence between him and Seneca, but these are almost certainly later Christian forgeries.

PEDANIUS: City Prefect murdered by one of his slaves.

Persicus, Fabius: a senator friend of Petronius's.

PETRONIUS (Titus Petronius Niger): the narrator. Nero's unofficial Adviser on Taste (*Arbiter Elegentiae*), usually identified with the author of the *Satyricon*, a picaresque novel of low life in first-century Italy.

PISO, Gaius Calpurnius: prominent right-wing senator involved in the plot against Nero.

POPPAEA SABINA ('Poppy'): wife of Otho, then of Nero. Their only child, Claudia, died in infancy.

RUFUS, Faenius: after Burrus's death, co-commander with Tigellinus of the Praetorians. Executed after the Piso plot.

SENECA, Lucius Annaeus: born Corduba, Spain, circa 5 BC. Philosopher, writer, playwright and statesman. With Burrus, Nero's tutor and adviser.

SENECIO: a freedman favourite of Nero's. Executed after the Piso plot.

SILIA: Arruntius's wife, and Petronius's mistress. Exiled (66) to Marseilles.

TERPNUS: a famous Greek musician and singer.

THRASEA PAETUS: an individualistic senator, moderate but opposed to Nero. Forced into suicide 66.

TIGELLINUS, Ofonius ('Tiggy'): Nero's protégé and latterly principal adviser. After Burrus's death, co-commander of the Praetorians (with Faenius Rufus). Forced into suicide under Otho (69).

Xanthus: Petronius's table slave.

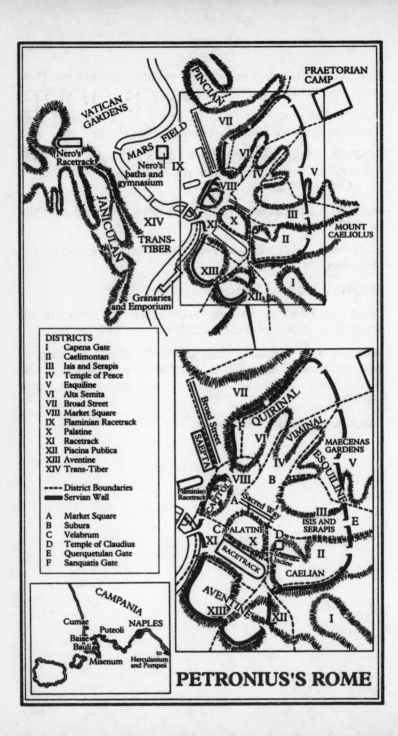

DISTRICTS
I Capena Gate
II Caelimontan
III Isis and Serapis
IV Temple of Peace
V Esquiline
VI Alta Semita
VII Broad Street
VIII Market Square
IX Flaminian Racetrack
X Palatine
XI Racetrack
XII Piscina Publica
XIII Aventine
XIV Trans-Tiber

--- District Boundaries
▬▬ Servian Wall

A Market Square
B Subura
C Velabrum
D Temple of Claudius
E Querquetulan Gate
F Sanquatis Gate

PETRONIUS'S ROME

PROLOGUE:
Cumae, June AD 66

A piece of advice before we start. Don't believe those fools who preach that death is a friend, or, worse, like Paullus and his crew of fanatics, the happy gateway to a better and fuller existence. It's nothing of the sort. Death, gentle reader, is nothing but a necessary bore, and you can tell it I said so. There, now.

I, Titus Petronius Niger, aesthete, author and erstwhile Adviser on Taste to Nero Claudius Caesar (the gods rot the little bugger) have reached a climacteric in my existence; I might say two climacterics, for although autobiography and suicide aren't normal bedfellows they're both pretty final, and I've no intention of rushing either to oblige anyone; certainly not by poking a sword through my own gut, which may be the traditional recourse of the Roman gentleman but is, in my view, hopelessly crude, not to say extremely messy and hell on the upholstery. No. I will bleed to death in comfort, like a civilised being. If done in a leisurely fashion by tightening and loosening the wrist-tourniquets (as I will do it), opening one's veins allows one to hang up one's clogs at a decent pace. If I really have to die before my time (and needs must, ho hum, when the emperor drives, even when the emperor is poor loopy Lucius) then I intend to savour every minute of the process. Even if it kills me.

Dion is smiling. Dion is my secretary and, currently, my right-hand man. That, my dears, should you need such things pointing out to you, is a pun, albeit one in execrable taste. What you're reading now is all Dion's work, and Titus Petronius Niger is merely a voice: refreshed, let it be said, by the fine wines and exquisite delicacies which lade the groaning table beside his couch. Nevertheless, when the time comes for us to part I will endeavour to sign my own name across the page before I finally dispense with the tourniquets and at last allow greedy nature to run (oh, my!) her liquid course.

A disagreeable prospect, you will admit; but then we have a long way to go together first. Oh yes, my gentle friends. Lucius's men will not arrive to inspect my corpse before morning. The night is still young, these Baian crayfish are excellent, and Dion is supplied with plenty of ink and paper. So.

What exactly is this great work that we're embarked on? Not, as you might expect, a hatchet job on the man responsible for my death, the quondam Lucius Domitius Ahenobarbus, whom history will remember (unless she's lucky enough to forget him altogether) as Nero Claudius Caesar, Rome's fifth emperor (not counting old Julius), darling of the muses and self-styled theatrical genius. Oh, and of course the world's most illustrious pyromaniac; I doubt if history will forget *that* little nugget of scandal. Certainly Lucius – I'll call him that, by the way, since it's all the nomenclature the poor dear deserves – provides scope and to spare for character assassination, and at present, as you'll readily understand, my feelings towards him aren't exactly friendly. All the same, I can't bring myself to hate the lad, however much of a monster he's become; in fact if truth be told I feel more sorry for him than anything else (a sentiment that would have the crack-brained old Jewish humbug Paullus nodding in approval). After all, it isn't altogether poor Lucius's fault that he's in the wrong job, and he has tried his best. Being three tiles short of a watertight roof hasn't helped much, either.

So, my dears, this is no kick in the imperial teeth. Call it a most lamentable comedy. Or possibly a mirthful tragedy. And because Lucius is who he is, and I am who I am, there will also, I'm sorry to say, be a fair amount of dirt to be dug . . .

Dion is frowning, and I don't much blame him. Dion may be a slave, but the lad is no mean judge of style, and I am rambling. Petronius, you bore, you grow inelegant. Stop it at once and begin your tale.

Heigh ho and off we go. End of prologue. Let me introduce you to my coy mistress Silia.

AD 50

We met in the Danaid Porch. Perhaps you know it, part of Apollo's temple on the Palatine? Its statues of the forty-nine married ladies who killed their husbands on the wedding night have made it the most popular place of assignation in Rome for (let's not be hypocritical about this) would-be adulterers and adulteresses like ourselves. She was standing with her maid studying the artwork, I was lurking beside one of the pillars a few feet away, studying her breasts.

By any standards she was beautiful: late twenties (my own age), dark hair carefully coiffeured and masked by the thinnest of veils, a perfect profile and a body richly curved beneath an impeccably arranged Coan silk mantle. She had seen me, of course, in her turn, and we watched each other covertly for a while, sizing each other up as one does on these occasions. After a decent interval I moved in for the kill.

She glanced directly at me and remarked to her maid: 'A poor thing, Lalage, isn't she? Condemned to eternal torment just for getting rid of a boring husband.'

An invitation if I ever heard one. The maid giggled. I moved closer.

'Your poor thing would hardly have had enough time to be bored, lady.' I leaned across and set my hand next to hers on the statue's cheek, noting as I did so the ring on her third finger. 'Hours, at most.'

She smiled at me. Her teeth were pearls.

'Oh, that's quite enough time for it,' she said. 'Husbands are like tunnyfish, darling, they go off terribly quickly. Especially if they aren't fresh to begin with.'

We both laughed. In that exchange the contract had been, so to speak, proposed, drawn up and signed by both parties. Negotiations in the Danaid Porch are like that, short and sweet and to the point, with no time wasted on inessentials. Patting the stone face in farewell, she turned to her maid.

'Lalage, walk behind us, please,' she said. 'And not too closely, there's a dear.'

We made love in her bedroom, on top of a silk coverlet thickly embroidered with gold and purple beasts: it had come from China along the spice route, and must have cost a fortune. I taught her the lips and tongue trick I'd learned from a courtesan in Damascus (once, or so she told me, the mistress of Herod Agrippa himself. If so then the Jewish king had taste); she provided me with a delightful variation on the Alexandrian String of Pearls which she claimed to have invented – no mean feat, if true. All in all a pleasantly exhausting afternoon, and highly educational. Afterwards we bathed in rose water, and Lalage brought us cups of snow-cooled wine and a dish of dried figs. Then I watched while Silia dressed and the maid repaired her hair.

'You will stay for dinner, won't you?' She was holding still as the girl applied Egyptian cosmetic to her eyelashes with a fine brush. 'Gnaeus won't be back until late.'

'Gnaeus?'

'Don't be obtuse, dear. My husband.'

'Oh.' Oh yes, of course. The ring on the finger, the skull at the feast. The inevitable skull. One can no more avoid the Gnaeuses of this world than one can expect a Suburan cookhouse not to have cockroaches in the kitchen. 'Tell me about Gnaeus.'

'He's a darling,' Silia said, flicking the lashes to dry them and inspecting the effect in the mirror. 'You'd like him.'

'No doubt. But mutual compatibility wasn't exactly what I had in mind.'

She laughed. 'Titus, dear, don't look so worried. We have an arrangement. Besides, he's into boys at the moment. Or rather one boy in particular. A pretty little thing called Theorus.'

'Oh, *that* Gnaeus!' I had the man placed now: Gnaeus Arruntius, a paunchy middle-aged roué who'd been one of Caligula's set. Not a bad sort, although badly gone to seed since he'd helped the conspirators ventilate the godling's belly nine years previously and given us all over to idiot Claudius. He had, if I remembered rightly, an appalling taste in hair oil.

'Indeed.' Silia held her cheek out for the maid to powder, and the air was suddenly full of the delicious scent of perfumed talc. 'I really can't imagine what he sees in Theorus. The child's a pain, and he's costing poor Gnaeus a fortune.'

'So I've heard.' I sipped my wine and savoured its hint of myrtle. 'But then boys always do, my dear. Even to hire one's pricey.'

Silia laughed. 'Oh, I know! It's an absolute scandal!' Her freshly made-up eyes sparkled. 'Speaking of which, Smaractus has some nice little Syrians just in.'

'Does he, now?' That was interesting: Smaractus's was one of the city's oldest-established houses, with a name for quality. 'Since when?'

'They arrived this morning. We could have one later if you're not too tired.'

'You promised me a meal.'

'I don't think we have much for dessert.'

'You'd have to hurry, madam. The dinner's nearly ready.' Lalage was packing away the cosmetics. 'It's sows' wombs with crackling, spare ribs and trotters.'

'Ah, well, maybe some other time.' Silia sighed. 'The best ones'll have gone by now anyway.'

To tell the truth, I wasn't too disappointed. I find Syrians over-rated and consequently overpriced. Hiring one, as I would have felt obliged to do if Silia had insisted, would have been a chore rather than a pleasure and spoiled what promised to be a charming evening. Besides, the String of Pearls gives one an appetite. I was looking forward to the sows' wombs; indeed, at that moment I could have eaten a horse. Served perhaps with a caraway-oregano sauce, with just a touch of lovage to give it depth.

* * *

We'd polished off the main course and were tucking in to the nuts and fruit when Silia's husband walked in. I almost swallowed my wine-cup.

Silia was marvellous. Not an eyelid did she bat.

'Gnaeus, dear,' she said with a smile. 'I thought you had a late meeting.'

'We broke up early. Blaesus's gout was playing him up.' Arruntius stretched out on the third couch. I had been right about the hair oil. The scent put me in mind of perfumed goat-sick. 'Evening, Petronius. You've just dropped by, have you?'

Not trusting my voice, I nodded and buried my face in my wine. Arrangement or not, the situation was acutely embarrassing. I was well and truly caught, and genuinely complacent husbands are rare as Arabian truffles in November.

Silia passed him a plate of cinnamon cakes.

'Titus and I were just discussing the imperial adoption, darling,' she said smoothly. A lie, of course, but a plausible one: the whole of Rome was talking about our new princeling. 'Lucius Domitius is such a nice boy. Or I suppose we should call him Nero Caesar now.'

Arruntius ignored the cakes and selected an apple. His heavy jaws closed on it with an audible crunch. He chewed and spoke between swallows.

'Nero's all right. Wet as hell, mind, but a nice enough lad. It's his mother I can't stand. Agrippina's a horror. God knows why Claudius married her. You'd've thought the old idiot would've learned his lesson.'

We were alone, of course, but I still glanced over my shoulder to make sure no one was listening. Arruntius noticed, and laughed.

'Come on, Petronius! I'm no traitor, and I'll say what I like in my own house. The woman's pure poison. We were better off with Messalina. At least with her we knew where we stood. Or lay, rather. Am I wrong?'

Claudius's last wife had been executed two years previously for adultery. Her eventual successor Agrippina was presently engaged in devouring the emperor as a female spider devours its mate. Arruntius wasn't wrong, but all the same he'd spoken a bit too frankly for my taste. I drank my wine and said nothing.

'Mind, it's the other kid I feel most sorry for.' Arruntius was digging between two teeth with a fingernail for a fragment of apple peel. 'Young Britannicus.' Britannicus was Messalina's – and Claudius's – nine-year-old son. 'With a stepmother like that the lad's in trouble. Deep trouble.'

'You think so?' I said.

'I'll give him two years. Maybe three. Certainly he'll never put on his adult mantle.' Arruntius spoke quite dispassionately; we might've been talking about the Blues' chances at the next racetrack meet. 'A pity. He's the best of the bunch.'

'Gnaeus.' Silia had been listening to all this with perfect equanimity. 'Do have a cup of wine, dear, and be a little more civilised. I'm sure Titus appreciates politics just as little as I do.'

Arruntius set the apple core down with a smile.

'All right, darling,' he said. 'Perhaps we could talk about Titus himself.' He turned to me. 'Just why did you drop by, Petronius?'

Oh, Priapus! The front door was miles away, I wasn't particularly fast on my feet, and besides I had for the past hour been getting quietly but thoroughly stewed. My brain (and other parts of me) went suddenly numb.

'I . . . ah . . .'

While I stammered incoherently Arruntius leaned over and punched me gently in the ribs.

'Joke, boy,' he chuckled.

I subsided in some confusion. Silia was watching with grave amusement.

'And how is Theorus, darling?' she said, slitting a pear.

Arruntius settled back on his couch with a grunt.

'Thriving,' he said. 'And getting greedy as hell, the little brat.'

'Such a shame. But then I've always thought he looked a grabber. His eyes are too close together.'

'Nonsense.' Arruntius picked up his wine-cup – filled with the last of our post-coital snow-cooled wine – drank and made a face. 'What is this stuff, Silia? Rats' piss?'

'Ariusian, dear. Ten years old. Don't you like it?'

'Who bought it?'

'No one, darling. It was a gift from one of your clients. The man with the ships.'

'Oh, yes?' Heaving himself up on his couch, Arruntius bellowed, 'Philip!'

The head table slave put his head round the door. He looked grey, as well he might: I wasn't the only one to distrust husband and wife arrangements.

Arruntius handed him the jug. 'Take this Greek muck away and bring us some decent Setinian. You hear me?' Philip shot off as if he had been greased. 'My apologies, Petronius. Bastard clients think they can palm off any old rubbish on a patron these days.'

'What was your meeting about?' I asked. The numbness was wearing off and I was feeling more myself again.

Arruntius settled down again and kneaded his belly – like Claudius he was subject to heartburn. 'Drafting a speech of congratulation to the emperor on the new addition to his family. Just pro forma, but you've got to go through the motions.'

'What's he like? The boy, I mean.' I'd only seen Lucius once from the crowd at a public ceremony three years before. He'd been nine then, unassuming and a martyr to spots.

Arruntius belched.

'A pretty enough lad. Nice in his own way but nervous as hell and wouldn't say boo to a goose. He's not a patch on his father.'

'Hardly a point against the boy, dear,' Silia sniffed.

'You think not? At least he had character.'

'Ahenobarbus was a vicious, arrogant brute.'

'That's what I said. He had character.' Arruntius grinned; a fragment of apple peel clung to his left incisor. 'A bit of red blood in his veins. The man was a good old-fashioned damn-your-eyes Roman. Nero's been surrounded by women all his life and it's made him soft. Not good to be too much tied to the bloody apron strings. What he wants is toughening. A few good bouts in double-weighted armour with an ex-gladiator who won't take any nonsense, that's what he needs, and if he doesn't get them pretty quick he'll suffer for it later. We all will. You mark my words.'

A remarkably profound observation, you must agree in retrospect – but then Arruntius wasn't the bluff ingénu he appeared, and he'd mixed enough with the imperial family to know what was what. He was quite right, of course. We did suffer for it, although given Lucius's background it constantly amazes me that he grew up as sane as he did. Which isn't saying much, but you know what I mean.

Just then Philip reappeared with the wine, and Arruntius held out his cup.

'Some Setinian, Petronius?' he said when the slave had filled it. 'Come on, boy, your cup's empty! The evening's young, you're beautiful and we may as well make the most of both.'

I credit myself with a fair degree of insouciance, but – as I'm sure you can readily understand – I was finding this cosy domesticity far too wearing on the nerves for comfort. Even if Arruntius's latter inducement wasn't wholly serious. I stayed only as long as politeness demanded. Then I made my excuses and left.

2

Two days later, Arruntius being in Baiae negotiating for a yacht, I took Silia to the race-meeting given by Claudius in his new son's honour. We arrived just in time for the start – terribly late, in other words; but Silia being a senator's wife we were entitled to use the special rows. We settled down with our nuts and dried fruit next to a distinctly camel-like senator and his family, just as the trumpets blared and the imperial party stepped into the box. Claudius, as he always did, looked like he'd been bundled into his mantle and rolled all the way from the palace. Agrippina, on the other hand, was splendid; *queenly* would perhaps be a better adjective.

'Just look at that gold embroidery, Titus!' Silia murmured in awestruck tones. 'Who does she think she is?'

The senatorial camel, overhearing, looked profoundly shocked. Silia ignored him.

'The Empress of Rome, darling,' I said drily. 'Or hadn't you heard?'

'Yes, I know, dear, but really! It is a bit much. She'll be wanting her own official carriage next.'

I saw what she meant, and I was rather taken aback myself. I am no republican – the god Augustus forbid, as my pious old nanny used to say – but I'm not a royalist either, should such a fabulous animal exist any more in Rome, and all Agrippina lacked of regalia was the crown. Beside her poor old Claudius, even if he was wearing his President of Games mantle, looked downright dowdy.

The cheering started as he stepped forward to the front of the box, his arm tight round the shoulders of a scared-looking youngster. Lucius, of course; the newly adopted son who, technically anyway, was sharing the burden and glory of this morning's entertainment.

'Where's Britannicus?' I whispered in Silia's perfumed ear. Claudius's natural son was conspicuous by his absence.

'Perhaps he's ill. The child is asthmatic, after all.' Silia giggled. 'Or is it epileptic? I can never quite remember the difference. The thing where you have fits and roll around the floor foaming at the mouth.'

'That's poetic inspiration, darling.'

'Don't be silly, Titus!'

I glanced up again at the vacant space. 'Perhaps he wasn't invited.'

Silia frowned; she saw the implications of the remark. 'Oh, no! Oh, the poor lamb!'

'The poor lamb has a stepmother now. And you do know what they say about stepmothers.'

She shivered and looked back towards the box.

'Agrippina's certainly terribly pleased with herself. Like a cat that's just got its claws into someone's pet sparrow. And isn't Lucius simply scrumptious? All sort of gauche and innocent and virginal.'

He was certainly a good-looking lad, although I'd have drawn the line at scrumptious: he still had his spots, for one thing. Perhaps Arruntius's 'pretty' described him, although it was an insipid prettiness that personally I found unattractive. He had the red Ahenobarban hair, bright and bristly as copper wire, a prominent brow and deep-set eyes; but on the demerit side his chin was weak, his ears stuck out like the handles of a wine jar, and his whole attitude suggested a continual apology for existing. Not, as Arruntius had said, a patch on his father, who'd been a fine figure of a man before the drink got him. Still, looks aren't everything, and Lucius was after all the new crown prince. The mob cheered while the Idiot beamed and slavered over him, and his mother looked on fondly in the background.

Claudius handed the boy a white cloth. The cheering swelled to an ear-hurting roar.

'Oh, how nice!' Silia said. 'The emperor's letting him drop the napkin!'

Lucius raised the white square high above his head and dropped it on to the sand below. The starting gates flew open and the chariots sprang out.

They were running two to a team, with both Reds as favourites – hardly surprising, since Red had swept the board that season, winning three races out of five with the other three colours sharing the remainder. Not that any individual race was a foregone conclusion by any means. In chariot-racing things can change in an instant. A bit of bad luck, an error of judgment, and the whole contest is thrown open; which is what makes it exciting. Not to mention the added spice of a little possible bloodshed.

This time the Reds led from the start. They were two lengths ahead of the field when the first driver cracked a wheel against the turning post. His partner reined in and swerved, missing the crippled chariot but allowing the leading Green to slip past him. From then on it was a two-car race: the second Green was out as well with a broken spoke while Blue and White could have been using plough-oxen for all the speed their drivers could manage. By the sixth lap Red and Green were neck and neck with Blue and White a dozen yards behind, and when they came to the final turn the whole racetrack was on its feet yelling itself hoarse. I was myself, and so was Silia.

Then I became aware that someone, somewhere, was shrieking: a strange, sharp, almost female sound unlike and apart from the deep animal roar of the crowd. I glanced across at the imperial box. Lucius was on his feet and pounding the ivory rail in front of him with his fist. His pasty, scared face was transformed and glowing with an excitement that in an older boy I would have described as sexual.

Suddenly, Silia squealed and gripped my arm, and I looked back at the race. The Red charioteer – a nose in front of the Green and on the outside – had pulled in hard on his rein and was sliding round the post in a scattering of sand, leaving the Green no more than a narrow gap to make his own turn. Red wheel-hub caught Green wheel and the Green chariot swerved with a sickening crunch into the central barrier. Its driver, jerked from the wreckage by the leather reins tied round his waist, smashed head-first against the suddenly bloody marble.

From high up and to my right came a scream – a quick scream like a woman's, and quickly choked off. I looked back at the imperial box. Lucius was standing frozen, his jaw sagging. Then he suddenly put his hand to his mouth and turned away. As he ducked beneath the rail and disappeared from view I saw the stream of vomit jet from his mouth.

Tut! *Not* the behaviour of a President of Games, even a twelve-year-old associate president. I wondered if anyone else had noticed the lad losing his breakfast. Not his new father, that was certain: the Idiot's liking for spilled blood was excelled only by his own timidity, and his whole attention was fixed on the shambles opposite. Not Agrippina either: she was watching as well, quite dispassionately. Only me, so far as I could tell; although of course there could well have been a few hundred others on the terraces. I hoped not, for the boy's sake and reputation. These accidents happen, and although some people mayn't find them very pleasant one must take them in one's stride. And one certainly doesn't expect the President of Games to be squeamish, however young he is.

Red came in first, of course, romping home with the two Blues trailing by twenty yards. In the interval before the next race slaves removed the mangled corpse and sponged the blood from the marble barrier. I looked towards the box, but Lucius wasn't there any more.

I told Silia what I'd seen on the way home (we were travelling by litter, side by side, with the curtains open).

Silia thought it was sweet.

'*Sweet?*' I was, as you can imagine, shocked.

'Of course it's sweet, dear,' she said calmly, plumping her cushions. 'The poor lamb's obviously terribly sensitive. Don't you think that's sweet?'

This was too much. I don't often get angry, especially over matters that don't directly concern me, but I'm afraid I lost my temper a little.

'Silia,' I said, 'I don't know about you but I haven't been sick at the sight of blood since I was ten. And at the racetrack, for heaven's sake!'

Her hands paused. 'What has that got to do with it?'

'Don't be obtuse, darling. If it'd been the midday games there might've been some excuse.' Midday at the games is carnage pure and simple, with unarmed criminals facing armed opponents. 'At the racetrack it's ridiculous. The boy's almost thirteen, two years away from his adult's mantle. And if he's going to be the next emperor . . .'

'He might not be. Britannicus is Claudius's son.'

'Do you honestly think Britannicus'll succeed, with the Bitch in charge?' She frowned and said nothing. 'Well, then. We've just seen the future master of the world toss his guts up. How can anyone that weak-stomached hope to be emperor?'

'I don't see what being weak-stomached has to do with it, dear. A dislike of bloodshed is quite a laudable characteristic in a ruler. Not to say rare.'

I sighed. 'Silia, I am most terribly sorry, but that's nonsense. How can an emperor make life and death decisions if he lets his sentiments rule his judgment? Your husband was right. The boy's far too soft for his own good. Or for Rome's.'

'Well, yes.' She frowned again. 'I do see what you mean. But I still think it's sweet. It'll make a change to have someone decent in charge of things who doesn't take pleasure in killing for killing's sake. Someone who isn't a misanthrope or barking mad or a suspicious old pedant like the last three emperors we've had. Just an ordinary, normal person. Now do stop being silly, Titus. You're giving me a headache, and we don't want that this afternoon, do we?'

She said that, Dion! Her actual words, I swear it!

Just an ordinary, normal person.

Ha!

Ah, well. It's all part of life's rich tapestry. You've got to laugh, haven't you, ducks?

Lucius, an *ordinary, normal person* . . .

O Jupiter best and greatest! O Isis and Serapis! Oh, my aching ribs!

An ordinary, normal person!

Xanthus, my boy. Fetch over that bowl, if you would, and undo these cords for a moment or so.

A pause, readers, for bleeding. Then perhaps another figpecker, and a little more of that excellent Faustinian.

3

AD 51

Not that Lucius had to wait another two years for his adult mantle, oh no. Crown princes never do, especially those with pushy mothers. He put it on nine months before his fourteenth birthday (the earliest legal date); and while the ten-year-old Britannicus was quietly edged to the sidelines his jug-eared, spotty elder stepbrother was showered with public honours. A lesser woman might've been satisfied with that much, but not Agrippina. The poor Idiot was browbeaten into replacing anyone likely to support his real son's interests with men of her own choice. Most of them were nonentities. One was different.

I first met Afranius Burrus, the new Commander of the Praetorians, at a party to celebrate my cousin Turpilianus's appointment as City Judge. A staid affair, and not my style at all: darling Turpy wouldn't be seen dead at a decent party, let alone at a far more enjoyable indecent one, and a thoroughgoing orgy is simply wasted on the man. He wouldn't even let me bring Silia because, and I quote his very words, 'Your relationship with the lady, Titus, isn't altogether honourable.'

Oh, Serapis! I especially liked the *altogether*, and so did Silia when she heard. Turpilianus, as you may have guessed, is a prig, or possibly a prick, of the first water. You can choose between the terms yourself, if you like, but I know which I prefer. Burrus on the other hand was straight as a builder's rule . . .

Oh dear, oh dear! Coming from me that does sound so terribly disapproving, but it's most emphatically not meant to be. I've always had a high regard for people who practise virtue rather than preach it, and Burrus was one of them. I liked him from the start, which was more than I can say for Lucius's other mentor Seneca, who was a preacher if I ever met one. If anyone could have hauled Lucius by his silly jug ears on to the straight and narrow it was Burrus. It was a sad pity he died.

We were couch-mates at the party. I discovered early on in the evening that he collected old Greek pottery, and we had a most enjoyable argument that kept just on the right side of acrimony: he liked Corinthian ware, I find it gaudy. Neither of us was prepared to give an inch and we both enjoyed ourselves immensely. That broke the ice, although Burrus could talk intelligently to anyone and on most subjects; a skill unique in my experience among professional soldiers, even those who come late to the profession as he did.

To keep the conversation going I asked him how he was getting on with his young pupil.

'It's too early to say.' Burrus spread his large hands and shrugged. 'But I'd be better pleased if the empress'd keep her nose out of the boy's business.'

'Really?' I was surprised, not at the sentiment (everybody by that time was gut-sick of Agrippina) but at the fact that Burrus had expressed a critical view to a comparative stranger. It was my first experience of the man's refreshing bluntness. Also of his good sense.

'Really. He's a fine lad with a lot of promise,' (where had I heard that one before?) 'but he's no will of his own and he's soft as a girl.'

The slaves were serving dessert. I had ours serve me some cold stewed quinces (God knows where Turpilianus had got them from or what they cost, but they were excellent) while I told Burrus the racetrack story. He nodded.

'I wasn't there myself that day but I'll believe you. That's young Nero all over. Too nice for his own good, and can't leave go of the tit.' He frowned, perhaps remembering belatedly the need for tact. 'No offence to the empress, of course.'

'Of course not,' I said. 'Perish the thought. A truly remarkable woman and a most caring mother.'

'A paragon.' He matched me dryness for dryness. 'All the same the best thing she can do now is step back and let us get on with the job. Then we might knock some of those fancy ideas out of the lad's head before they get a proper grip. Start to make a man of him.'

I scented a piece of juicy gossip.

'Fancy ideas?'

'His obsession with chariot-driving, for one. Oh, I know. Every lad worth his salt since Romulus has wanted to be a charioteer. I wanted it myself. But by eight or nine years old any normal boy's grown out of it. Nero's almost fourteen, and he's still obsessed, he even plays with toy chariots in his room. It isn't natural.' He stirred the quinces round with his spoon. 'Besides, it's not respectable.'

There spoke the true antique Roman. I helped myself to a handful of dates rolled in honey and poppy seeds from a passing tray.

'His father liked chariots too. Perhaps they're in the blood.'

Burrus's frown deepened. 'Yes, well, the son keeps it in proportion, thank Jupiter. So far, at least.' Ahenobarbus's driving had been notorious. On one occasion he had intentionally ridden down a child on the Appian Way. 'But then there's this Greek business, and that's worse.'

I pricked up my ears. 'Greek business?'

We were interrupted, infuriatingly, by the wine slave, a most unprepossessing Gaul with bare legs like hairy tree-trunks. I had him fill our cups to the brim. City Judge or not, Turpy was stingy as hell, and although he served good wine it was well watered and sparse as desert dew. (They say he served beer to his guests when he governed Britain a dozen or so years later. I can believe it. He and Britain were made for each other.)

When the cups were full Burrus waved the man away.

'Don't mistake me, Petronius,' he said. 'I've got every respect for the Greeks. We owe them for every scrap of culture we've got. But when all's said and done it's us Romans who'll civilise the world. The Greeks're past their prime. Decadent. Men like you and me, we take them or leave them, and with a pinch of salt. We don't think they're the gods' only gift to humanity.'

That was another thing I liked about Burrus. He automatically credited one with his own standards. I took my inclusion as the compliment he meant it to be.

'And Nero does?' I said.

'Nero does. Speaks the language like a native. Even thinks like them, from what I can see. But that's not the half of it.' He glared into his wine-cup and added quietly: 'The boy sings.'

Oh, Serapis! This was gossip and to spare! In my surprise and delight I almost swallowed a date-stone. A singing crown prince was something new in the world.

Seeing my expression (and misinterpreting it completely) Burrus gave a sour nod.

'That's right. Appalling, isn't it? Sings and plays the lyre. Composes poetry. Writes playlets. You name it, he does it, everything bar press flowers. A proper little Greekling. He turns my stomach at times, and I'm not ashamed to admit it.'

'But this is serious!' I was trying desperately not to laugh; it would've offended him terribly.

'Of course it is.' Burrus took a swallow of wine. 'Maybe I'm misjudging the boy, but it's worrying all the same. I've had him out on the exercise ground with a training sword and he's got no more idea of fighting than flying. No fire, no aggression, nothing. He's like a pudding. You see what I mean about fancy ideas? They're all right in a dilettante like you, Petronius, no offence meant . . .'

'None taken. I appreciate your frankness.'

'. . . but not in an imperial. Rome'll never stand for it.'

Just then there was a stir at the top end of the dining-room: cousin Turpy was getting up to make a speech. We listened respectfully to the new City Judge's orotund phrases and I marvelled at what, seemingly, Rome would stand for from those she called to high office. Jupiter knows how long he spoke, but I must have nodded off.

When I woke up the slaves were clearing the tables and surreptitiously finishing off the wine (not much of that, to be sure). Burrus, along with most of the other guests, had gone home, and I had the most almighty crick in the back of my neck.

Unobtrusively I slipped out, having wrapped a few more of the dates up in my napkin for later; and, the night being less than half spent, went in search of more congenial company.

That little conversation had been quite an eye-opener. In principle I agreed with everything Burrus had said (or most of it, anyway). Of course I did. But all the same young Nero Caesar sounded quite interesting. At least the lad promised to be different.

4

Dion, my aspiring editor, tells me that before we go any further I must introduce you to Seneca: philosopher, statesman, speculator and (this not least) hack tragedian.

First a warning. I didn't like the man (surprise!), so you must, as archers say, allow for the wind. Though Aeolus knows the old fart was full of wind in his own right, both literally and metaphorically, so . . .

All right, Dion! All right, point taken, that was cheap, and not really fair. He did his best, I admit, according to his lights, and the material he had to work with wasn't too promising. But I'm not all that sure these disgustingly gory tragedies of his weren't at least partly responsible for shaking poor Lucius's beans loose. And the man was a hypocrite and a crawler of the first order, you can't get past that, my boy.

Dion disagrees. Dion, bless his little cotton drawers, has the greatest respect for Seneca, both as a philosopher and as an all-round sincere human being. Serapis knows why, but there you are. I much preferred Paullus myself (we'll come to him eventually, if I live that long). The old Jew may have been barking mad but at least he was honest and, so far as I'm aware, practised what he preached, whereas that pious canting fraud was nine-tenths humbug.

A potted biography, to bring us up to date and because he really is important, as you'll see. Seneca was a provincial, born at Cordova. Having pursued a frighteningly thorough course of education he came at last to Rome where he bored the pants off everyone in the courts. Exiled to Corsica after Caligula's death for furkling one of the imperial sisters, he spent the next eight years composing grovelling philosophical exhortations to anyone and everyone he thought could arrange his recall. Fortunately no one did. Finally, the year of the imperial nuptials, he was brought back by Agrippina as tutor to the young Lucius. The rest, as they say, is history, although . . .

Dion's pen has snapped (good secretary that he is, he carries a replacement behind his ear). He objects to the furkling, saying it was a trumped-up charge, and to the inclusion of the word grovelling. All I can say is that I knew Seneca, and he didn't, and that you may form your own conclusions. Enough, boy. Shut up and get writing.

The appointment was political, of course. Seneca was an academic high-flyer who had no love for Claudius, and Agrippina expected, reasonably enough, that he would be pathetically grateful; more, that a fifty-three-year-old furkler would be more than susceptible to his benefactress's abundant physical charms. With him providing the brain, and Burrus the brawn, behind her devoted young princeling, Agrippina must have reckoned she was on to a winner. Especially since she'd already pulled the bones out of the opposition and stitched the Idiot up so tight he couldn't so much as scratch himself without her permission.

Ah, well. To paraphrase Aeschylus, whom the gods wish to destroy they first make smug bitches. Enough, for the present, about Seneca.

The sun has gone, and Xanthus is lighting the lamps. Heigh ho, Petronius, you garrulous oaf, at this rate you'll never reach Lucius's principate, and no doubt the Praetorians will be hammering on your door at dawn to make sure you're decently stiff. Get on with it, skip the next three years and let Claudius tuck into his dish of mushrooms without further ado.

Agrippina went from bad to worse. Among others whose deaths she arranged was that of her sister-in-law Lepida. Lepida was accused of attempting the empress's life by magic and of allowing the gangs of slave workers on her Calabrian estate to run riot – a neat touch this, and designed to frighten the wollocks off the timid Claudius. So the Idiot signed the warrant for her execution, which was duly carried out. Unfortunately for him, when informed of Lepida's death he was foolish enough to pass a comment to the effect that Agrippina's own days were numbered. A nod is as good as a wink to a blind horse and, to mix metaphors, the Idiot's goose was cooked. Agrippina availed herself of the services of a certain Locusta, who provided her with a subtle poison which she added to a dish of mushrooms served that evening to Claudius at dinner.

The Idiot was saved by an involuntary bowel movement. On the pretext of making him vomit, his doctor Xenophon (who was also in the plot) administered a faster-acting poison. In moments Claudius was bereft of life, his family of a loving husband and father, and the Roman state (ah, me!) of its chiefest ornament.

Hail, Nero. Xanthus, the basin, please.

5

AD 54

We, meaning Rome, didn't find out about the death until the next day. Personally I was quite delighted. Lucius deserved his chance, although Agrippina was another matter; and unfortunately you can't have the sea-urchin, as the saying goes, and leave the prickles.

Evidently the Senate thought so too. They were heartily sick of Claudius, and Lucius promised to be a great improvement, but getting the lad out of Agrippina's clutches would be a major job. Not being a senator I missed his maiden speech, but later at the Pullian Street baths I bumped into one of the nobility's brightest and best, a friend of mine called Fabius Persicus. He'd just, he told me, got back from the relevant meeting at the palace.

'The palace?' I was surprised. The Senate only meets in the Senate House or in some other public, consecrated place. 'Why the palace?'

Persicus leaned forward so that the slave could scrape his back.

'You may well ask,' he grunted. 'The Bitch is feeling her oats.'

'Bitches don't eat oats, dear.'

'Oh, ha ha!' He was scowling. 'Very funny, Petronius.'

'I try. I can even ask the same question twice if I don't get an answer the first time. Why the palace?'

'Because even with the Idiot gone Agrippina still thinks she's the bloody co-head of state, that's why. Only being a woman she isn't allowed into the Senate House.'

This was even more surprising.

'Agrippina was at the meeting?'

He shook his head. 'No. But there was a curtain at the far end of the room and I'll bet you a dozen of Faustinian to a cup of vinegar she was on the other side of it.'

'Naughty.'

'It's worse than naughty. It's insulting.' He stretched his neck sideways and winced as the scraper's blunt edge caught his right earlobe. I expected him to cuff the slave but he didn't; the lad – a pretty enough thing in a sulky way – evidently had other talents which made up for his clumsiness. 'Jupiter knows why Nero allowed it.'

'He knew?'

'Of course he knew. How could he not? Still, she's got what she wanted, the lad's emperor. Maybe she'll draw her claws in now and let him get on with things.'

I sat back against a pillar: I'd had my scrape earlier, and I quite enjoy watching others suffer. Persicus turned over. The slave poured oil on to his chest and rubbed it in exactly as if he were basting a chicken. I wondered if Persicus had promoted him out of his kitchen.

'How was he himself?' I asked.

'Nero? Oh, Nero did fine. More than fine. A bit nervous, but that's understandable. At least he can string a sentence together without tripping over his tongue or spraying you with spit like the Idiot. What's more he talked straight sense. Believe me, that's another thing that hasn't been too common lately.'

All this sounded most promising. Persicus was an honest, conscientious man (well, fairly honest and conscientious) who said what he thought. And he spoke for the best of the Senate.

'So you think he'll do?'

'He'll do. So long as he can shake himself loose from the tit.' The point of the scraper snagged a rib, and he winced. 'Jupiter! You watch what you're doing, you little bastard!'

If the boy had been mine I'd've sent him arse over tip into

the pool, 'other talents' or not, especially since he only smiled in apology. He had nice teeth, though.

'Will he? Shake loose, I mean?'

'You pray that he does, boy! Pure sweetness and light, that's our future, if he lives up to his promises. No secret trials, no corruption, no favourites. No fuck-all of what we've been used to these last thirteen years.' Persicus grinned suddenly. 'Hey! Smile, Petronius! You're on the threshold of the Golden Age!'

'Oh, my dear! I've heard that one before!'

'This time it could be true. We'll have another god on the team. Maybe he can swing it, if he doesn't trip over himself as usual.'

'Oh, and who's that?'

'Guess.'

I laughed. 'Claudius? You're deifying *Claudius*?'

'Got it in one, boy. And don't spread it around either because it's not official.' He sat up. The incompetent bath slave collected the tools of his trade and ambled off, drawing more than one appreciative glance from the loungers by the cold plunge. 'The Bitch wants to build him a temple on the Caelian. Only thing is, the engineers have to lick the hydraulics problems first.'

I frowned. 'What hydraulics problems?'

Persicus chuckled, his eyes on the boy's retreating buttocks. 'How to make a cult statue that shits itself and drools at the same time. What else would they be?'

Golden Age or not, there were ominous signs that Agrippina had no intention of pulling her claws in. First to go was Narcissus, Claudius's all-powerful secretary and the empress's principal opponent. Not many tears were shed for him: the old fraud had been feathering his nest at public expense for years, and being an ex-slave and, worse, a Greek he was persona definitely non grata with the Senate. However, towards the end of the month when I went round to Silia's to pick her up for a birthday party I found her friend Junia Calvina doing a Niobe all over the marble floor.

'I'm sorry, dear.' Silia had her arm round the sobbing girl's shoulders. 'I can't go. Junia's had a bit of bad news.'

A bit of bad news was putting it mildly; Junia was large and cheerful, and not normally given to hysterics. I sat down on a folding chair while she continued to deliquesce and Silia explained. The two had been shopping for trinkets in the Saepta when a young fool by the name of Passienus had come up and commiserated with the girl over the death of her brother who, as far as she knew, was alive and well and governing Asia. Junia had promptly gone to pieces, and Silia had been obliged to ferry her home and feed her doughnuts.

'It wasn't Passienus's fault, Titus.' The waterworks were slowing by now, but Junia's plump face was flushed and puffy. 'Not really. He thought he was being ever so kind and daring because Marcus was poisoned by imperial agents.'

'He was what?'

'P-poisoned. By agents of the emperor.'

I couldn't believe my ears. It was too melodramatic for words. Marcus Silanus was one of the most ineffectual men I'd ever met, and about as dangerous to the state as a pet rabbit. If the situation hadn't been so serious I'd've laughed.

'The emperor had him killed? Lucius did?'

'Don't be silly, dear.' Silia was still patting Julia's hand. 'The men were acting on orders from Agrippina.'

'They admitted that?'

'Of course not. But they implied it. And Agrippina's practically co-ruler these days, as you well know.'

I still didn't believe it. 'Julia, you're certain? That it was an official killing?'

'Oh, yes.' She dabbed at her shiny nose with a handkerchief. 'They murdered him quite openly, at a dinner party.'

'But why on earth should Agrippina want to kill your brother?' I was being tactful: a more natural question would've been, 'Why on earth would she bother?' Marcus Silanus had all the rage and fire of an undercooked blancmange.

'Because we're descended from Augustus, of course.' The handkerchief came up again and Junia blew. Hard. The walls echoed. 'That horrible woman's jealous.'

'Ah.' I sat back. Of course. That explained everything. Now she'd got her son on to the throne Agrippina was eliminating other possible claimants. The fact that she'd begun with poor Marcus Silanus, who couldn't have mounted a decent rebellion to save himself or drummed up enough support for the presidency of a glee club, didn't augur well for the future: Silanus wasn't by any means the only descendant of Augustus around.

The Bitch was feeling her oats right enough.

'You go on to the party, Titus.' Silia looked up. 'We'll be fine here.'

'No, darling.' I shook my head. 'I'm not especially bothered. Honestly.' I wasn't. The couple who were giving the birthday bash (they were both men, filthy-rich business acquaintances of mine) had as much culture as my door slave. Less: he could count *and* read, and he didn't wear cheap make-up. I moved over to the couch next to Junia and poured a cup of wine from the flask on the table.

'There's only Decimus and me in the family left now.' Junia was sniffling in earnest again. 'Plus little Lucius, of course.' Lucius was her nephew, Silanus's son and heir. 'We'll be next, I just know we will.'

'Don't be silly, Junia!' Silia snapped. 'Agrippina may be a nasty piece of work but when all's said and done she's only the emperor's mother. She can't tell him what to do, he won't allow it. Nor will the Senate.'

Junia shook her head violently; a single teardrop landed on my wrist.

'Nero won't stand up to Agrippina,' she said. 'He's soft as a worm.'

She was right, of course, and personally I wouldn't have given tuppence for the Silanus family's chances of seeing the new year in. However, now wasn't the time for pragmatism. I put the wine-cup to Junia's lips and tilted. The wine was neat, and there was plenty of it. She choked and swallowed. Silia patted her on the back.

'Listen, Junia darling,' I said firmly when the spluttering had stopped, 'the emperor may be a worm, but worms do turn. Especially imperial worms new to the job. Agrippina won't have everything her own way much longer. Now drink up like a good girl, have another doughnut and give us a smile.'

She did, eventually; Junia was a splendid girl (though rather overlarge and bouncy for my taste) and as I've said already she wasn't usually prone to the horrors. Members of the old aristocratic families seldom are; they take death by politics in their stride. A few more cups of neat Setinian and a little jollying along and she was enough herself again to be sent home giggling; by which time if Agrippina had walked past she would've spat in the Bitch's eye.

She wouldn't have missed, either.

6

It was late by the time Junia left, and we'd had more than enough wine ourselves, so we went straight to bed. Unhappily, however, Silia was in no mood for fornication.

'It really is too bad, Titus,' she said. 'Junia was in a terrible state, and she's absolutely right about the emperor. Someone should do something about that woman.'

I sighed. Politics is always trying when one's mind is on erections rather than elections.

'What would you suggest?' I said. 'A scorpion in the imperial drawers?'

'Don't be flippant. I'm serious.'

I was serious myself; neat Setinian always makes me feel randy.

'Darling, Junia has my sympathy. Rome has my sympathy. But there is not a great deal that I personally can do about the situation. Certainly not at this time of night. So . . .'

Silia pushed my questing hand away.

'Titus, do listen!' she snapped. 'This is important! I didn't like to say so in front of poor Junia, but things are going to get worse. You know they are. And by that time it'll be too late.'

'Agrippina isn't the only one with influence over young Lucius, dear.' Priapus! What the hell was I doing in my mistress's bed at two in the morning discussing Julia Agrippina? 'There's always Seneca and Burrus.'

She snorted. 'Agrippina will make mincemeat of those two. So long as she has that poor boy under her thumb she can do anything she likes with him, exactly as she did with Claudius.'

Outside the window an owl hooted. Not the most propitious of omens, and entirely apposite; the blankets were now humped up into an impenetrable barrier. Seemingly all nature was against me. I gave up with as good a grace as I could manage.

'Silia,' I said gently, 'Lucius is only seventeen, he's been under his mother's thumb since he was born, he's had no father to put backbone into him and as a result he's as wet as a half-wrung dishrag. What do you expect? Give him a few months as emperor and he'll dry out enough to tell Mummy to get lost. Now go to sleep, please.'

She lay quiet for a long time. I closed my eyes and tried not to think of sex. Then, suddenly, she said: 'Do you think he's a virgin?'

I sat up so fast that I bumped my head on the brass cupid bed-end.

'What?'

Silia had propped herself up on one elbow and was staring at me wide-eyed. 'Titus, please do pay attention. It's a simple enough question. Do you think that Lucius is a virgin?'

Oh, Serapis! Too much, my lord, too much! I rubbed my scalp, feeling for the rising bruise.

'For God's sake, woman! The boy's been married to the Idiot's daughter Octavia for a year! Of course he isn't a bloody virgin!'

'Don't shout, dear. You'll wake the slaves. I don't mean a technical virgin. I mean a real one.'

'Silia, it's the middle of the night and I am not up to splitting philosophical hairs.'

'How old were you when you had your first girl?'

Plato in a bathrobe! 'Darling, I'm sorry but you've lost me completely. I don't see the connection. And anyway I'm afraid that piece of information is really none of your business.'

'Fourteen?' She ignored me. 'Fifteen?'

I rested my aching head against the offending cupid and closed my eyes. First no sex, now no sleep and questions no gentleman should be expected to answer; certainly not in another woman's bed. Such is *not* Petronius's idea of the perfect way to finish an evening.

I wondered if it was too late to go to the party after all.

'Titus, I asked you a question.'

'Fourteen. She was the daughter of my father's bailiff. Now honestly, I'd rather not discuss the matter.'

'And did your mother choose her for you?'

Despite myself I laughed. 'She thought I was off fishing, darling. Which I was, in a way.'

'There you are, then.'

'There I am what?'

'Titus, don't be obtuse! Lucius's was an arranged marriage, and from all accounts he can't stand the girl.'

I saw, finally, what she was driving at.

'So you're saying all our emperor needs to boost his self-esteem is a roll on the potting-shed floor with the girl of his dreams? Silia, don't be ridiculous!'

She sniffed. 'Why should it be ridiculous? What the poor boy needs is a nice girl of his own choosing who honestly thinks he's marvellous and who'll give him a bit of confidence.'

'Any girl who thought Lucius was marvellous would be certifiable.'

'Nonsense. He's a charming boy, underneath his spots. And I know just the girl. Woman, rather.'

'If you know her already how can she be of his own choosing?'

'Don't quibble, dear, it's vulgar.'

'Silia, listen to me!' I was becoming seriously alarmed. 'You cannot mess with the imperial family!'

'Who,' she snapped back, 'is messing?'

'You are, darling. Or you would be. Besides, it really is none of your business.'

She sighed. 'Titus, you're being terribly tiresome. Of course it isn't my business. But someone has to do something. If that dreadful woman isn't stopped soon poor Junia and several other friends of mine will almost certainly end up dead or exiled. That I will not have.'

'I'm sure Seneca and Burrus are perfectly capable of . . .'

She placed a finger over my lips. It smelled of perfume.

'Seneca and Burrus are men. The poor lambs haven't a hope of stopping her. And you haven't met Acte.' Her lips brushed my forehead and I felt the Setinian stirring. 'Now go to sleep, dear. I'm tired.'

She lay down and turned her back towards me. The owl hooted again, mournfully. Probably a male locked out of his nest for the night, stewed on Setinian.

Bugger. I went to sleep. Eventually.

7

Future historians will no doubt describe Acte as a beautiful young siren, common as muck but with the face and figure of a goddess, sitting on her rock and tempting Lucius down from the Palatine not with her song but by the shimmer of her glorious upturned rosy-nippled breasts and peerless thighs; a nymph of the Aventine with long, unbound hair spilling over her bare shoulders and reaching past her narrow waist to her generous hips and silky purse.

Wrong, my dears. Wrong, wrong, wrong. She wasn't like that at all. If she had been, Lucius – at this stage of his career, at least – would've run a mile.

Silia introduced us in the tiny room three floors above an Egyptian glassware shop near Pompey's Theatre, where the woman had her theatrical costumes business.

'Claudia Acte,' she said. 'Acte, this is my friend Petronius Niger.'

We shook hands (her idea, not mine, and she almost broke my fingers). I wasn't bowled over, to put it mildly. She was Asiatic Greek, thirty if a day, dumpy as a sack of flour, with thick black eyebrows like mating earwigs, coarse-grained skin and a face that wouldn't've launched a rowing boat on the Tiber, let alone started the Trojan War. She even, I noticed with distaste, had a wart. The world to choose from, I thought, and Lucius is expected to fancy *this*?

None the less, I was polite. It wasn't her fault she was ugly, poor soul.

'Claudia Acte?' I said. 'You're an imperial freedwoman?'

'That's right.' Her voice was pleasant, at least: honey-rich and dark. 'I bought my freedom from the Divine Claudius three years ago. He set me up here.'

I was looking round as she spoke. The flat was hardly what I'd been expecting either, although I suppose one could say any attempt at decoration in a tenement shows eccentricity. The window shutters were brightly painted with flowers and trailing plants, with real plants in earthenware pots and fish-pickle jars full of flowering weeds resting on the sill. Theatrical masks hung from nails on the bare brick walls. I assumed these were part of Acte's stock, but curiously every one was cracked or split, so perhaps they were supposed to be decorative. If so then they were remarkably effective, forming a sort of three-dimensional mural. The room itself, of course, was tiny. Most of the floorspace was taken up by a workbench covered with bits of cloth, coloured threads and pots of glass jewels. On top of all the rest lay a woman's dark blue cloak; obviously part of the costume that Acte had been working on when we arrived. I picked it up and examined it. The material was cheap and very plain, but from a distance it would look quite impressive. Unusually for a stage costume, it was well cut and the stitches were small.

'Electra?' I asked.

She shook her head. 'Phaedra.'

'Really?' I raised my eyebrows. In the Greek myth Phaedra's passion for her stepson had brought the young man to his death. 'Hardly flashy enough for a seductress, I'd've thought.'

'Phaedra was no seductress. She was only a woman who couldn't help herself. That's what makes her tragic.'

My eyebrows went up another notch: one doesn't expect literary criticism from a seamstress.

'It's very well made,' I said. 'Too well made for a play.'

'Actors act better in a real costume. Or one that feels real. Ask anyone in the business and they'll tell you the same.'

'Acte comes from a theatrical family, Titus.' I was probably looking as bemused as I felt, because Silia was smiling.

I laid the cloak back down. 'Your father was on the stage?'

'Sure.' Acte's plump face broke into a not-unattractive grin; her teeth were healthy, white and even. 'Both grandfathers, and their fathers as well. We go all the way back to Thespis, Dad used to say. And Ma played the double-flute.'

'In Rome?'

'Miletus, although we travelled around. My parents sold me to a Syrian merchant. He brought me to Rome.'

'How old were you?'

'Seven or eight. They'd had three bad seasons in a row, so they were cleaned out.' Her voice was matter-of-fact. 'A few years later I got left to the emperor as part of a job lot in the guy's will, and that was that.'

'Talk to him about Nero, dear.' Silia was trying on a wire tiara crusted with glass emeralds and examining herself in a small bronze mirror.

Acte picked up the cloak I'd been looking at and rubbed the material gently between thumb and forefinger. Despite their strength her fingers looked surprisingly delicate. 'Lucius? Lucius is a lovely boy. He'd make a good actor if they'd just leave him alone. Maybe even a great one.'

I laughed, then wished I hadn't because she turned on me with eyes sharp as a pair of dressmaker's pins.

'I mean it,' she said. 'And I know, believe me. I've seen the best. We used to talk a lot, before I bought myself out, when his mother wasn't around.' She laid the cloak back down on the workbench. 'Talk theatre. Proper Old Greek theatre, not this modern tat. Euripides. Sophocles. Even Aeschylus. That boy's got the heart for a play, and heart's rare. Everything else comes with practice, but never heart, you've either got it or you haven't. You know he had me crying once?'

'Really?' I was genuinely surprised. The woman looked nail-hard. She would have to be, after the life she'd led.

'Yeah, really. We were talking about Hecuba – Euripides's Hecuba – when he suddenly starts giving me the old woman's first speech. You know it?'

'"Levin of Zeus!"' I quoted. '"Black Night! What fears and phantoms have roused me from my sleep?"'

She nodded. 'That's it. When it's done well it sends the ice up my spine, has done ever since I was a kid and heard my father speak it in the Samos Theatre. I knew then he was good, really good, even if he didn't have the voice. That comes with training, but like I said the heart you're born with, and you can't fake it or hide it.' She faced me, her eyes level. 'That boy's a natural actor, Petronius. As an emperor he's wasted.'

This time I didn't laugh. I didn't dare.

Silia had been listening closely. Now she put down the tiara.

'How would you like to work at the palace, Acte?' she said.

The woman frowned and turned towards her. 'Doing what, for example?'

'Does it matter?'

'Sure it matters. I've done my time as a slave, lady. This place may not look much, but it's mine. I'm my own mistress, I can pay the rent and still eat regular. What more would I want?'

'To help Lucius, perhaps.'

The frown deepened. 'He's the emperor. He doesn't need help from me.'

'Doesn't he?' Silia sat down on the bench. 'Tell me one thing, dear. Do you think he'll make a good job of it?'

'No chance.' Acte shook her head. 'With his temperament he hasn't got a hope.'

First theatrical criticism, now a political assessment. Delivered with equal aplomb. Not your average freedwoman, this. I raised my eyebrows again, but Silia didn't seem surprised, either at the answer or at the tone.

'Oh, don't get me wrong. He'll mean well,' Acte went on. 'Like I say, the kid's got a lovely nature. But he's desperate to be liked and he's terrified of making mistakes. He'll do what other people tell him to do just because they *are* other people and he thinks they know better than he does. Especially older women.'

'People like his mother?' Silia said.

'You said it, lady, not me.' Acte turned away from her, picked up the tiara from the workbench and began methodically to twist it out of shape. 'I don't name names behind people's backs.'

'But that's who you meant, isn't it?'

Acte's head came up.

'Look!' she said sharply. 'Stop cross-examining me, right? I don't know politics. I don't know anything but theatre and stitching costumes together. Yes, I'm fond of Lucius. I'm sorry for him and I don't like his mother. But that's where it stops. If the people at the top think she's good for Rome then I'd be a fool to say any different.'

'But they don't,' I said. 'Quite the reverse.'

Silia shot me a warning glance. 'No one's trying to put words in your mouth, Acte.'

'Okay. That's fine by me.' The strong slim fingers tugged at the wire. 'So let's keep it that way.'

'You can help Lucius, if you really want to. In fact, dear, you're the only one who can.'

Acte laughed. 'Oh, yeah. Sure. So Afranius Burrus keeps telling me when we split a bowl of porridge together.'

'That's not what I meant at all. Of course not. Lucius doesn't need anyone else telling him what to do. He does need a friend. Someone he can talk to.'

'I told you.' Acte set the tiara down, or what was left of it. 'The boy's an emperor now. Emperors don't ask ex-slaves for advice.'

'Stuff and nonsense!' Silia snapped. 'Your former master Claudius did it all the time!'

'I'm no bumlicker like Narcissus. I fry my own fish in my own pan, lady. And I don't need any favours.'

Silia was becoming seriously annoyed. I knew the signs – the spreading flush, the tight lips, the slight tapping of the left foot. 'I said a friend, dear, not a hanger-on. The poor boy will have enough of Narcissus's sort.'

Acte was quiet for a long time. She picked up the tiara and pulled it carefully back into shape while Silia glared at her. Then, suddenly, she stood up.

'Okay,' she said. 'Okay, but no promises. You say I can help. Tell me how.'

Silia told her. In the end she took surprisingly little persuading: Jupiter knows what the woman saw in him, but as you've probably realised yourself reading between the lines Acte was seriously smitten even then with young Lucius. Silia had a word with Crispinilla the imperial wardrobe mistress (they used the same perfumier), poor ugly Acte was duly drafted on to the palace's domestic staff, and we sat back to await results.

The effect was even better than we'd hoped for. By the end of the month Lucius was head over heels in love . . .

Oh dear, oh dear! This is beginning to sound dreadfully unconvincing, like one of those gushy, ghastly Alexandrian novelettes where clean-limbed young strangers (who turn out to be princes in disguise) sweep dewy-eyed heroines off their feet and carry them away on their Arab chargers to an eternity of expurgated wedded bliss. Don't blame me, please; it's honestly not my fault. That's how things went, even although the heroine was rather a sight and the princely hero had spots and bad breath. Human nature is a curious beast, and there is no accounting for taste. I use the word loosely, of course.

The dewy-eyed part, however, was literally true. When Acte came round to Silia's to report just after the Kalends she was sickeningly primaveral. Even her wart glowed.

'He's marvellous,' she told us. 'Just as nice as I remembered him. Kind and considerate and sensitive and . . .'

'Have a grape.' I held out the bowl.

Silia looked daggers at me. 'Stop it, Titus,' she said. 'I think it's lovely. So terribly romantic. Do go on, dear.'

'. . . and he wants me to marry him.'

'Serapis!' I almost dropped the dish. 'You're not serious!'

Acte looked at me. Her eyes were like deep pools in which reflected starlight lurked (they were! I swear they were!).

'Why not?' she snapped. 'Why shouldn't he?'

'For one thing, darling, he's already married to Octavia.'

'But he doesn't like the little wimp. He's never even slept with her.'

'There, Titus!' Silia gave a smug, self-satisfied smile. 'I knew he was a virgin.'

'Does Agrippina know about this?' I was, I admit it, in shock. Self-confidence was one thing. Divorcing an imperial wife, however wimpish, to marry an ex-slave who made theatrical costumes for a living was not the behaviour one expected of an emperor.

'Of course she doesn't! Agrippina doesn't even know we're . . . seeing each other.' Acte blushed; she actually blushed!

'This is your fault Silia.' I rounded on her. 'I warned you about interfering. You've created a monster.'

Silia gently removed the fruit bowl from my nerveless fingers and replaced it on the table.

'Don't talk nonsense, dear,' she said.

'It isn't nonsense! The Senate'll never stand for it for a start!' I turned back to Acte. 'And what about Burrus and Seneca? What do they have to say about these impending nuptials of yours?'

'They don't know either. It's our secret. They just think Lucius and I are' – she paused and lowered her eyes modestly – 'cohabiting.'

This was too much. 'Cohabiting? You're cohabiting crazy, both of you!' I glared at Silia. 'All three of you!'

'Titus, dear, you're being a bore.'

'You think this isn't serious? What happens when Agrippina finds out?'

'Oh, we've talked about that.' Acte was calm. 'Lucius says he's the emperor, not her, and if she makes trouble he'll tell her where she gets off.'

Oh, Serapis! I goggled at her, beyond speech.

'I really don't see why you're making all this fuss, darling.' Silia smoothed out a non-existent crease in her mantle. 'We wanted the boy to have more self-confidence. Now he does, thanks to Acte here. And I'm sure Seneca and Burrus are simply thrilled that he's facing up to that terrible woman at last. They are, aren't they, dear?'

'Sure.' Acte glowed. 'They're doing handstands.'

'You see, Titus?' Silia turned back to me smugly. 'Everything is going just splendidly. I told you it'd work, didn't I? Now stop scowling and don't be such a sourpuss.'

And if this had indeed been a gushy, ghastly Alexandrian novelette we'd leave it there, with young love and virtue triumphant, evil vanquished and sourpusses censured; but life, I'm afraid, isn't like that. Life, sadly, is a bowl, not of cherries, but of pickles.

Let's hear it for the sourpusses.

8

Sourpusses, however, were not much in evidence at first. When I next stumbled into Persicus down at our mutual baths he was ecstatic over the new regime; in fact, he hailed me from the other side of the cold plunge.

'Hey, Petronius! You know any good poets?'

I went over. The sulky slave with the chicken-baster's hands wasn't in evidence; traded in, no doubt, for a later model.

'No, but if you're really interested I do a nice line in dirty drinking songs,' I said.

'Then widen your field, boy!' A grin. 'Start writing encomiums.'

'I didn't know you even knew the word, darling.' Bitchy, but I'd had a hard night. Never have bear meat on top of ostrich-brain fricassee.

He laughed. 'Yeah? Well, we've got ourselves an emperor for a change.'

'So I've noticed. Mind you there's already been Augustus, Tiberius, Caligula . . .'

'Stuff it.' He threw his towel at me. 'You know what I mean. The lad's doing well. They're saying down at the Senate House that he's old Augustus born again only without the starch.'

'They would say anything.'

He shook his head decisively. 'Not in private. They mean it, Titus. That's some commendation, even if they do know Burrus and Seneca are pulling the strings. The kid's got to listen to somebody, and at least now it's not Agrippina. She is out – but I mean seriously!'

'And how is our dowager empress taking it?' We sat down with our backs against a pillar.

'How do you think? Like a rhino with migraine.' He frowned. 'Hey, you know this Acte woman?'

'No.' I wasn't going to let Persicus in on that little secret, oh no. Good at his job he might be and a splendid young man all round, but he was also the loosest mouth in Rome. 'No, I've never even seen her.'

'Me neither. I don't move in these circles, and he keeps her well under wraps. But she must be something really special the way she's hooked the boy away from Mummy.'

'They say she was Mithridates's mistress.' I put in my two-pennyworth of false gossip: Mithridates was one of the leading eastern client-kings and randy as a drunken camel. 'They also say she wore him out in a month.'

Persicus whistled. 'No kidding? Jupiter's balls! That makes sense, because when the Bitch caught them together she went up the wall.'

'Agrippina caught them?' My stomach turned over. 'You mean, she's found out?' It'd been inevitable from the start, of course, but even so . . .

Persicus grinned. 'She walked in on them this morning, in Nero's bedroom. The kid just lay there petrified like he'd been caught with his hand in the honey jar, but Acte told her to piss off.'

'And did she?'

'She did. She was spitting blood. But she went right enough.'

'Persicus, how do you know all this?'

'Oh, it's true, don't you worry!' He was practically crowing. 'I got it on the slave network. The story was all over the palace by noon. The Bitch is on the skids, Petronius. A month or two more and she'll be history.'

'If Acte lives that long.' I was frowning. Now the secret was out I didn't rate her chances better than marginal.

'Agrippina wouldn't dare touch a hair of the lady's head, not with Nero up there on his cloud. She's got more sense.'

'You think she'll just give up? Let her have him?' If Persicus thought that then the odds were pretty fair.

He stared at me. 'Give up? The Bitch? No chance. Three in a bed isn't her bag.' I must've looked blank because he laughed. 'Hey, Petronius! You didn't know? Agrippina's been screwing her blue-eyed bunny rabbit for years. No wonder she's jealous.'

'It's a lie!' Acte was furious when I told her later, in Silia's boudoir. 'Lucius has never slept with his mother!'

'Are you sure, dear?' Silia was holding still while Lalage worked on her eyebrows with a pair of tweezers.

She shifted uncomfortably on the couch's edge. 'Of course I am.'

'Persicus may be an oaf, Acte,' I said. 'But he's a well-informed oaf. He's seldom wrong where gossip's concerned.'

She reddened. 'Yes, okay,' she said quietly. 'He wants to, I know that, it's obvious from the way he looks at her sometimes. And she leads him on, she always has done. But that's as far as it goes.'

'If they are having sex together it'd certainly explain a lot.' I was watching Lalage. The girl had the most endearing habit of putting her tongue between her teeth when she concentrated. Nice eyes, too. 'And Agrippina isn't exactly scrupulous.'

'I wouldn't be especially surprised either,' Silia said calmly. 'Agrippina's had enough personal experience to consider incest almost a commonplace.'

I caught the reference, of course, although Acte obviously didn't: she only looked offended. If gossip was to be believed (and I always make it a point to believe good gossip) Agrippina's late brother Caligula had bedded all three of his sisters. Sleeping with one's sister, however, was one thing – the old Egyptians did it all the time, and there are other reputable precedents – but mother and son did seem to be taking things a little too far. I said as much.

'Titus, dear, you really can be most incredibly naïve at times.' Silia sniffed. 'Agrippina will do anything for power. And Acte admits that the lad is sexually attracted.'

Acte's good-natured face bunched into a scowl. 'She's got him so he doesn't know which end's up.'

'Oh, how dreadfully embarrassing for him,' I said.

Acte turned on me. 'Look, don't joke about this, Petronius. It's serious, and it's complicated.'

'Complicated?'

'Deep down Lucius hates Agrippina's guts, but as far as he's concerned she's everything. He might break with her, but if she broke with him it'd be the end of the world. You understand?'

'Oh, yes. I understand. In fact, I'm ahead of you.' I was, and it was worrying. Very worrying. What Acte was saying was that if push came to shove and Agrippina presented Lucius with an ultimatum the boy would cave in; in which case Acte would be quietly disposed of, Silia and I badly compromised and Agrippina in a stronger position than ever. This was what we got for meddling, and it served us right.

'You don't know the half of it.' Acte took a deep breath. 'She . . . caught us together one day. You know?'

I nodded. 'Persicus did mention that as well, dear.'

She stared at me. I thought she was going to blush, but she didn't. Instead she said, slowly and sourly: 'Hey, your friend's a real mine of information, isn't he?'

'The biggest in Rome.'

'He tell you she hit the roof?'

'Yes.'

'Damn right she did! I've been around, and I've never heard language like that, nowhere, not even on the Ostian barges. The woman's crazy, Petronius. I swear she didn't know what she was saying.'

'Wait a moment, Acte.' Silia laid a hand on the maid's arm. 'Lalage, that's enough for now. This isn't for your sensitive ears.' The girl (sensitive ears, my foot! She was enjoying every minute of this) picked up the cosmetic box and left the room with a flounce. 'I'm sorry, dear. Carry on, please.'

Acte frowned. 'Anyway, when she's finished Lucius is great. I was really proud of him. He's shaking like a leaf but he tells her very firm and quiet she can't talk to him like that, that he's a grown man now and the emperor and he can handle his own life.' She paused. 'Then she says . . . the empress says . . . "Britannicus wouldn't hurt his mother like this. He's a good boy."'

I almost laughed, even though I knew it wasn't funny. And it wasn't. Not at all. That much was obvious from Acte's expression.

'Lucius goes chalk-white,' she went on. 'He doesn't say any-thing, but mother, that hits him hard, and the bitch knows it. She looks straight at him and she says real slow and cold: "Britannicus wouldn't hurt his mummy like this, Lucius. Britannicus is a better boy than you are. Better in every way. Britannicus is Mummy's pet lamb now." I tell her to go and she goes. Then Lucius just . . . curls up.'

'What?'

'Curls up, Petronius. Like this.' Acte lay down on her side and brought her knees up almost to her chin, hugging them hard. Then she sat up again. 'He looked dead, only he was breathing okay and his eyes were open. It took me hours to bring him round.'

'Jupiter!' I whispered.

'The boy isn't normal,' Silia said decisively. 'He needs a doctor.'

'He needs a priest,' I said.

Acte turned on us furiously. 'Look, just lay off, will you? I told you, Lucius is just scared. He's shit-scared of life without his mother. It's not his fault.'

'It's not a matter of fault.' I was still shaken. Silia was right, behaviour like that wasn't normal. 'The boy's emperor. The last thing Rome needs is another Caligula.'

Acte got to her feet; she was almost crying. 'I wish I'd kept this to myself now! Lucius isn't mad! He was okay after we'd talked it over, really he was. It just hit him hard at the time, you know? It could happen to anyone.'

'Of course it could,' I said neutrally. 'Anyone at all.'

'You've never even met him! You don't know what he's like! He's . . .'

'Sensitive. Yes, you've told us that several times. And, Acte, I don't have to meet him. As Silia says, the boy isn't normal. I only hope his abnormality doesn't become too . . . embarrassing.'

'Fuck that!' The tears were obvious now. 'And fuck you as well, both of you! I wish I'd never told you! If you met him you'd know at once he was okay!' She looked from one of us to the other, her chin with its wart jutting out aggressively. 'He's an artist and he's . . . all right, yes, he's sensitive!'

Neither of us spoke or met her eyes. I don't know about Silia, but I couldn't have trusted myself to do either. Acte stormed out. In the distance we heard the front door slam.

Three days later an invitation arrived to have dinner at the palace. Obviously we were being given an opportunity to judge Lucius for ourselves.

Not the best evening to choose, as it transpired, by any means; but of course poor Acte couldn't have known that at the time.

9

We arrived at the palace in great style, thanks to the matching set of gleaming Nubian chair slaves I'd borrowed from Persicus. It was my first ever imperial dinner party, and I must admit to feeling a little nervous: even although I had no respect for Lucius personally the lad was emperor and, whether I liked it or not, the most powerful man in the world. Arruntius being a senator and from a respectable family, I had assumed that Silia was used to moving in such exalted circles and would know the score. As it turned out, she wasn't and didn't; and she chose the moment when, invitation in hand, we were approaching the guard at the gate to disillusion me.

'It's all Gnaeus's fault, Titus,' she explained. 'As usual. We've never been welcome at the palace since the poor silly dear helped murder Caligula.' She sniffed. 'Personally I would have thought Claudius would have been grateful, but there you are.'

I handed the invitation to the huge German, who checked the official seal and gave it back.

'Do you think my mantle's all right?' I murmured as we passed through.

'Very smart, dear. You look most distinguished.'

'Then I have failed lamentably as a reprobate.'

A slave in green livery led us through the entrance hall and along a well-lit corridor towards a pair of cedarwood doors studded with ornamental brasswork. He knocked and the doors swung open on to the imperial dining-room.

We were honoured, it seemed. There couldn't have been more than a dozen people there, and from the small number of empty places we were among the last to arrive. A slave led us to one of the side tables near the imperial dais. We put on our party slippers, reclined, and another slave poured perfumed water over our hands.

Lucius lay on a purple and gilt couch. He was wearing a gorgeously ornate tunic in the Greek style, his copper-red hair bound with a gold charioteer's ribbon. Beside him, Acte looked splendid (make-up carefully applied can do wonders), although she was far more plainly dressed than he was.

When she saw us she grinned and elbowed the Ruler of the World in the ribs. Obviously we were back in favour.

'Darling,' she said, 'you're not being very welcoming. Say hello to my friends.'

The boy turned. He still had that fragile prettiness I remembered from the racetrack, enhanced by delicately rouged cheekbones and mascara'd eyelashes. The eyes themselves were bright and restless, shifting towards my face and away again.

'Sir.' I inclined my head formally. Beside me Silia did the same.

'Petronius.' His voice was a thin, nervous tenor. 'Lady Silia. How lovely to see you both. Acte's told me so much about you.'

He stopped: a pause, I assumed, but he gave a little giggle and turned away. Even Acte looked surprised. She whispered something to him, but he shook his head and glanced towards the closed doors. Both movements had a sharpness I found both odd and disturbing. Acte, now, was frowning.

The slaves were serving the hors d'oeuvres. I knew most of the guests by name, of course, and some more intimately. They were a mixed bag. At the table next to ours Salvius Otho, Annaeus Serenus and the two Terentia sisters were squeezed together like amorous sardines on to the one couch. Otho was surreptitiously feeling up the younger Terentia's thigh, and Serenus already looked stewed. Diagonally across from us Burrus was in deep conversation with an elderly senator whom I didn't know; he caught my eye and nodded. At the table between him and the dais were another senatorial couple, Calpurnius Piso and his wife Licinia. They were listening to a much older man with a fringe of iron-grey hair and the jowly, bag-eyed face of a pregnant toad. Piso looked bored, and I didn't blame him:

Annaeus Seneca in full spate wasn't the most entertaining of couch-mates.

Silia brushed my arm and I leaned against her. She put her lips to my ear.

'Look at Britannicus, dear,' she whispered. 'What a shame, the poor lamb!'

I turned in the direction her eyes indicated. Near the back of the room, out on its own and in the shadow of a pillar, was a small table at which Claudius's natural son reclined. Next to him lay a boy of his own age whom I didn't recognise. His coarse peasant features contrasted with the fine wool of an expensive mantle. The two were in deep conversation, ignoring the rest of the dinner party.

'Who's the other lad?' I murmured.

'Flavius Vespasian's son Titus.'

'Vespasian?'

'The African governor. Such a nice little boy, Acte tells me, and simply devoted to Britannicus. A pity his father's such a clodhopper.'

I must say now that I have no memory whatsoever of what we ate, drank or said at that first meal at the palace; but then there was, as you'll see shortly, a very good reason for that. What I do remember is Lucius calling over one of the servants at the dessert stage and whispering something in his ear; then, when Acte looked startled, giving the same tense little giggle I'd heard him use earlier. And, of course, I remember the subsequent arrival of Agrippina.

Her mantle was in the Alexandrian style, so stiff with gold leaf and pearls that it might've been made for a queen (perhaps it was). She was carefully made up and coiffeured, her eyelids lacquered with pearl-dust and her lips artificially reddened. At her entrance conversation faltered and faded away to nothing. Seeing her standing in the doorway I felt, myself, that someone had stepped over my grave. Beautiful Agrippina undoubtedly was, but for all her white breasts and faultless figure she carried a scent of rottenness.

Lucius stood up. He swayed slightly, holding out his hands towards her as if they were close enough to touch. His eyes were glassy. I wondered if he was drunk, but his speech was quite clear.

'I'm afraid you've missed dinner, Mother,' he called out. 'Such a shame. Still, it's lovely to see you. Come up here, darling. Sit by me and Acte.'

I looked at Acte. She was rigid, her eyes on Lucius.

'I'm sorry. I had a headache.' Agrippina hadn't moved.

Lucius gave his nervous, high-pitched giggle.

'Perhaps you should talk to Xenophon, then,' he said. 'He has such a nice bedside manner. And they say he's never willingly lost a patient.'

Agrippina's face froze: Xenophon, as I think I've mentioned, was the doctor who'd poisoned Claudius. Slowly, and without a word, she walked the length of the silent room, mounted the dais and reclined on the edge of Lucius's couch as far from Acte as she could. The two women ignored each other.

'You must be absolutely ravenous, Mummy.' Lucius's eyes had never left her face. 'We can't have that, can we?' He reached behind him and snapped his fingers. A slave brought forward a steaming salver and took up a position by the empress's right shoulder. 'Mushrooms. The food of the gods. One nibble, my dear, and who knows what lovely things mightn't happen?'

Someone – I think it was Otho – smothered a laugh. One of the Terentias giggled. There were no other sounds. All eyes were on Agrippina and the dish of mushrooms.

'I'm not hungry, darling,' she said at last. 'Really.'

Lucius frowned. 'But I had them prepared specially. And I'll be terribly upset if you don't eat. We all will.' He snatched the spoon from the slave, scooped a mushroom from the dish and held it level with her lips. 'Please? Just a tiny one? Just one, for your little Lucius?'

I didn't like Agrippina, but I had to admit the woman had courage. Staring straight into Lucius's eyes, she opened her mouth. Lucius smiled, popped the mushroom in and closed her mouth gently with his free hand.

She chewed and swallowed. The silence now was absolute.

Nothing happened. I thought I saw Agrippina sag a little on her couch, but I may have been mistaken. The exhalation of breath from the other diners was almost palpable.

'There, Mother. That wasn't so bad, was it?' Lucius was still smiling. He threw down the spoon and turned to face the room at large, 'And now darling Seneca is going to entertain us with a reading of his latest work. Seneca!'

All eyes except mine went to the jowly figure lying next to Piso. I was still watching Agrippina. Her eyes were closed, and under her make-up her face was grey.

Seneca, when I turned back to him, was looking distinctly embarrassed, his jowls red as a chicken's wattles.

'Oh, my dear boy!' he murmured. 'Oh, now, really! Perhaps under the circumstances it would be better to . . . ah . . . postpone . . . ah . . .'

'Nonsense!' Lucius was acting like a man in a high fever. His eyes were bright, his face was flushed and he was almost gabbling. 'Do come on, darling! We're all agog! Simply agog! Besides, you promised.'

A slave stepped forward with a book-roll. Seneca took it from him as though it were a live viper and undid the fastenings. Then he looked up and cleared his throat.

'My voice isn't . . .' He paused. 'Honestly, my dear fellow, do excuse me. To tell the truth I really am a little hoarse this evening.'

'Oh, you!' Lucius gave him a dazzling smile. 'You've the best reading voice in Rome, hoarse or not. Besides – he glanced slyly at Agrippina – 'Mother is simply dying to hear it. Aren't you, Mummy?'

Agrippina didn't answer.

'Ah. Very well. If that is your wish, then naturally . . .' Seneca looked even more unhappy. He cleared his throat a third time, took a swallow of wine, and unrolled the book. 'It's called . . . ah . . . I call it the "Pumpkinification".'

The elder Terentia giggled. Seneca glared at her, cleared his throat yet again, and began to read: '"I would like to set down for the edification of future generations an account of what took place in heaven on the thirteenth of October, of this the first year of our Golden Age . . ."'

Agrippina gasped. Seneca stopped abruptly; so abruptly that I distinctly heard his jaw click.

'Is something wrong, Mother?' Lucius was solicitous. 'A touch of wind from the mushroom, perhaps?'

'No. No, darling.' She was visibly fighting for self-control. 'It's just a twinge of that headache I mentioned.'

'Then perhaps I should send for Xenophon after all. Or even Locusta . . .'

'That won't be necessary,' she snapped. 'Darling.'

'Well, then.' Lucius beamed at Seneca and raised an eyebrow. Seneca swallowed and continued with his recitation. He was now an interesting shade of puce.

You know the piece, of course. It's a satire on Claudius's deification, a fictional account of the Idiot's arrival in heaven and the contemptuous treatment he receives there. It was, I had to admit, slickly penned, wickedly clever and, in places, achingly funny. It was also far and away the most gratuitously vicious attack on a human being I'd ever encountered. I'd no time for the Idiot in life, but Seneca's "Pumpkinification" sickened me. It was like kicking a corpse. You ask me why I have such a low opinion of the old hypocrite. Go and read that little squib, my friends, and you'll have your answer.

The reading finished amid an embarrassed silence. Everyone was watching Agrippina, who had sat through it with a face like chiselled marble. As Seneca hastily put the roll away in the fold of his mantle, Lucius began to applaud, slowly and with deliberation. No one else moved.

'Lovely, darling! Absolutely lovely!' he said; then, turning to Agrippina: 'Wasn't it lovely, Mummy?' And, before she could answer: 'Now I think we should toast my divine stepfather's memory.'

Slaves stepped forward to fill the cups. There was still no talking. Lucius stood up and peered towards the back of the dining-room, shading his eyes as if trying to make out something in the far distance.

'Cooee!'' he shouted. 'Britannicus! Oh, Britannicus! Briti-briti-tannicus!'

There was no answer. Britannicus ignored him, pretending to be deep in conversation with the African governor's son. Acte, I noticed, was close to tears.

Lucius beamed. He turned to the head wine slave.

'Make sure his wine's well watered,' he said loudly. 'The poor child's obviously had too much already, it's gone to his ears. But now let's have that toast.' Snatching the man's jug he slopped wine into a goblet and pressed it into Agrippina's unwilling hands. 'There, Mother,' he said. 'You propose it for us. To the Pumpkinified . . . oh, I am *so* sorry, my dear! To the Divine Claudius!'

Agrippina stood up. Her eyes were on her son's. She raised the goblet.

'To your predecessor and father, the former emperor,' she said calmly. 'To the Divine Claudius.' She took the barest sip.

'Oh do come on, Mother!' Lucius's voice was bright and jagged as a new sawblade. 'You can do better than that, a hardened drinker like you! You don't think the wine might be – oh, my! – poisoned, surely?'

She stared at him for a long time. Then, slowly, her eyes on his, she drained the cup and set it down empty on the table. We all waited for her to fall.

Someone at the back of the room – the African governor's son – shouted. Along with everyone else, I turned to see Britannicus writhing like a hooked gudgeon on the floor beside his couch.

'It's all right, darlings!' Lucius's voice was shrill with excitement. 'It's all right! The child's an epileptic! He's an epileptic! I tell you it's *all right*!'

We were all on our feet now, staring at the writhing figure, but no one made any other movement. Silia's hand gripped my wrist, the nails digging hard into the flesh, and she was murmuring, over and over again, 'Oh, gods! Oh, gods!' Finally the boy stopped moving. There was a horrible rattling sound, followed by a long silence. Everyone, now, was looking at the emperor.

Slowly, he lay back down on his couch. His eyes glittered and he was breathing in short, shallow gasps as if he had just achieved a sexual orgasm.

'Oh dear, oh dear!' he said softly to Agrippina. 'Mummy's own little boy seems to have choked. So who's her darling now, then, we wonder?'

Their eyes locked for a long, silent moment. Then the empress swept down from the dais and out of the room.

I glanced across at Seneca and Burrus. They looked grey and old. Acte's head was on her arm, and she was weeping.

Two days later, when Acte finally showed her face by arrangement at Silia's, I still hadn't got the horror out of my bones.

'He's very upset,' she said. They were her first words, before she had even sat down.

Silia and I both stared at her. '*He's* upset?' I said. 'Serapis!'

Acte rubbed her puffy eyes. She looked terrible, and I doubt whether in these two days she'd slept at all. 'Of course he is! He didn't enjoy doing it, you know. He felt really bad later.'

I couldn't trust myself to comment. Getting up from the folding stool where I'd been sitting when the slave brought her in I began to pace the room.

'Do sit down, Titus,' Silia said from her chair by the pool. 'You're making me giddy.'

'He was frightened.' Acte was glaring at me. 'He always lashes out when he's frightened. It's not his fault.'

'Even frightened people draw the line at murder, dear,' I said. 'Sane ones, anyway.'

'Lucius is sane!' Acte snapped. Then she dropped her gaze. Her long slim fingers twisted together. 'Well . . .'

'Exactly.' I pulled up the stool. 'Admit it. The boy's barking mad.'

There was a long silence.

'It took him ages to admit he was responsible,' Acte said at last in a low voice. 'To me, I mean. To everyone else he's still insisting Britannicus had a fit or swallowed the poison by accident. Seneca and Burrus say they believe him, but you can see they're just being . . . careful.'

'Indeed,' I said drily. '"Careful" is right. Where was the poison, by the way?'

'In the water jug.'

'Ah. Clever.' That explained Lucius's instructions to the wine slave about further diluting the boy's wine. Everyone else's would've had the correct amount of water already mixed in. 'I'm surprised he didn't kill the other lad while he was at it. The governor's son.'

'Oh, but he wouldn't! Lucius isn't a murderer!'

'Oh, Serapis!' I turned away from her in disgust.

'What about Agrippina, dear?' Silia said quickly.

'She's keeping her distance.' Acte picked absently at a broken nail. 'But that's another thing. Lucius is terribly worried that she's angry with him.'

'He's what?' I genuinely couldn't believe my ears. 'Oh, my dear girl! Oh, how simply marvellous!'

Acte had the grace to look embarrassed. 'Petronius, you don't understand! What his mother thinks is important to him, very important. He's afraid she doesn't love him any more.'

I took a deep breath. 'Let's get this straight, darling. The emperor insults Agrippina in public, pretends he's poisoning her, actually *does* poison her stepson in front of her eyes, and the poor dear's afraid that she mightn't love him any more?'

'That's right.'

'So what the hell does he expect? A round of applause?'

Silia held up a hand. 'Let Acte explain, Titus.'

Acte frowned. 'Yeah, I know it sounds . . . odd, but like I said you don't understand because you don't know Lucius like I do. After everyone left he was okay. Really high, you know? So . . .'

'"Okay" means the same as "really high" in your vocabulary, does it? I see.'

'Titus!'

Acte shot me a sideways glance. 'He kept saying, "Now she'll *have* to love me," and "Wouldn't Uncle Gaius have been proud?"' Oh, Jupiter! 'But then when I finally got him to bed he just lay curled up, saying she wouldn't love him any more because he was bad.'

'For God's sake!' I leaned back, forgetting in my anger that

I was sitting on a stool, and almost overbalanced. 'Lucius is a grown man! That's the kind of language I'd expect from a six-year-old!'

'That's the point I'm trying to make, Petronius,' Acte said patiently. 'He is a child, in many ways.'

'He's the fucking ruler of the world, darling, and don't you forget it! And I don't like that bit about Gaius, either.' Gaius – Caligula – had murdered his quondam co-heir Gemellus. If Lucius took to regarding Caligula as a model of behaviour then we were in the shit up to our eyeballs.

'It's not his fault!' Acte snapped. 'It's the empress! She has him tied up in knots!'

'I agree, Titus,' Silia said.

I stared at her. 'You what?'

'Oh, I'm not defending him. What he did was inexcusable. But that woman is a spiritual Lamia.'

Despite my anger, I saw her point. Lamia is the nursery bogey who steals children from their cradles, eats their flesh and sucks their blood. It was a fair parallel to draw. If Lucius was turning into a monster then a large part of the blame was Agrippina's. Even so . . .

I got up and poured myself a cup of wine.

'What has he done with the body?' I asked: Britannicus's death had still not been officially announced.

'He had it burned.' Acte's voice was toneless. 'We buried the ashes in the palace cellars. Petronius, he's suffering, don't you understand?'

I drank my wine and said nothing; frankly, I couldn't trust myself. Whatever sympathy I could muster most certainly did not extend to poor dear Lucius. The little bastard was a disaster waiting to happen and we'd be far better off without him.

'I'm afraid, Titus, that in this instance I'm on Acte's side. Lucius deserves his chance,' said Silia. 'Dreadful though this whole thing is I think it may turn out to be for the best in the end.'

I sighed.

'I'm sorry, my dear, but I disagree. The boy's mad and bad both. Unfortunately he's also Emperor of Rome. Let's just hope Seneca and Burrus can keep him in bounds.'

Acte squared her jaw.

'Of course we can,' she said.

'Bully for you, darling.' I drained my wine-cup. 'Personally I intend to keep my head down.'

I did. By the gods I did. Not that it had any effect.

I was coming out of my banker's in the Market Square when I bumped into Arruntius – literally – as he hurried away from a huddle of broad-stripers near the old Speakers Platform. Whatever they'd been discussing (and they'd been discussing something, that was clear, not just passing the time of day), the matter was serious. Arruntius was scowling. I apologised.

'Morning, Petronius.' He didn't sound too friendly, but then I had trodden fairly decisively on his foot. 'What brings you out of the woodwork so early?'

I shrugged. 'A poor investment. I'm cutting my losses before they cut me.'

'Know the feeling.' His scowl lifted a little – cash-flow problems are always a shared bond – but he still looked grave. We fell into step together as he walked towards the Temple of the Divine Julius.

'You've heard the news?' he said at last.

'What news?'

'About the prosecution.'

'No. What prosecution?'

'It's all over the Square. That stupid cow Silana. Jupiter grant Silia's not mixed up in it somewhere, although I wouldn't put it past her.'

'Silia?' I felt the first prickle of unease. Junia Silana was Silia's sister-in-law, or had been until her brother had been executed for adultery with the infamous Messalina. They were still close friends. 'Arruntius, just tell me, please. What's happened?'

'Silana's taking on the empress. A treason charge.'

I stopped dead. 'Silana's accusing Agrippina of treason?'

'Not directly, she's using a couple of freedmen stooges. But it's common knowledge. Last night all hell broke loose up at the palace.'

'What makes you think Silia might be involved?'

'You tell me!' he snapped. The scowl was back with a vengeance. 'You're the bastard who got her mixed up in politics!'

That was unfair and he knew it; if anything it was the other way round. However, a gentleman does not criticise a lady, especially if she is his mistress and he's talking to her husband, so I let it pass. Arruntius was clearly not himself; not that the real Arruntius was much better, mind.

I caught at his arm and steered him towards the porch of Castor's Temple. Like him I was worried, seriously so. He was right, of course. This was just the sort of dangerous, high-handed, crack-brained scheme Silia might well come up with, and although Silana was no demure Roman matron she was not, to put it kindly, overburdened with brains. I parked us by a pillar and began the serious grilling.

'All right, then,' I said. 'Now tell me the whole story.'

'You honestly don't know?'

'Honestly.'

Arruntius shook his head. 'I don't know all the details myself.'

'Oh, come on, Arruntius! Whatever you've got!'

'You know Silana's hated the empress's guts since that business with young Africanus?'

I nodded. The affair had provided a juicy bit of scandal several years before. Silana, never the chastest woman in Rome, had sunk her well-manicured claws into a certain young nobleman called Sextius Africanus. Agrippina had used her influence to break off the liaison (rumour had it because she wanted the good-looking boy for herself) and Silana, up to then Agrippina's closest friend, had never either forgotten or forgiven.

'Well,' Arruntius went on, 'what with Agrippina in disgrace Silana's taking the chance to get her own back. According to her the empress is planning a coup, with Rubellius Plautus as co-partner.'

I laughed. 'Plautus? Arruntius, you cannot be serious!' Rubellius Plautus was a boringly sensible young prig with a strong sense of duty to the state. It would not have surprised me if he had SPQR embroidered on to his drawers. 'Even the emperor wouldn't believe godrotting Plautus, darling!'

'You want to bet?' Arruntius was looking sour. 'It's plausible enough. Agrippina's been touting for support for months among the top families. Plautus's mother was Tiberius's granddaughter, he's got the blood and the connections. And last I heard the emperor wasn't exactly noted for his level-headedness.'

A fair point. I remembered what Acte had said about Lucius lashing out when he was frightened. And Lucius, it was becoming horribly apparent, was very easily frightened indeed.

'So what's the problem?' I said. 'It's terribly hard luck on Plautus, of course, but if Silana manages to get rid of Agrippina she'll've done everyone a favour.'

'If is right. I wouldn't count my chickens, Petronius. Only someone as peabrained as Silana would underestimate Agrippina.'

'There's your answer, then. Silia is not a peabrain.'

'Let's hope she isn't,' he grunted and moved away from the pillar. 'You seem to know more about my wife than I do. Now I'm sorry, Petronius, but I've important business. Will you be seeing her today?'

'Silia? I might.' In fact we'd arranged to meet later that morning at Argyrio's, the jeweller's in the Saepta, to browse through his latest acquisitions.

'Good. Then tell her what I've told you. And even if she isn't involved tell her that if she's any remaining vestige of sense she'll drop her good old pal straight down the nearest drain-hole.'

'But it was all Silana's idea, dear, honestly!' Silia was wearing her most innocent expression; the one I didn't trust an inch. 'I was so proud of her for thinking of it, because she isn't very . . . well, poor Silana isn't exactly cerebral, if you know what I mean.' She held up a pair of ruby earrings. 'What do you think of these, Titus? Aren't they lovely?'

'Far too ornate, darling. And ridiculously overpriced.'

'True.' She handed them over to Argyrio, who was holding the stacked trinket-tray on the other side of the counter and smiling vacantly at the air between us: deafness was a common complaint in the Saepta's upmarket shops. 'Put them on my husband's bill, please, Argyrio.'

'Certainly, madam,' he said; the deafness was, after all, selective.

Silia scanned the tray. 'Oh, look!' She picked up a cameo brooch with Lucius's face in profile and held it up to the light; such light as there was in the shop when the doorway was almost blocked by the two gigantic Nubians whom Argyrio used to protect his stock from sneak-thieves and bogus customers. 'Isn't it a good likeness, poor lamb? He's such a pretty boy! Mind you, he'll go terribly jowly like his father in a couple of years. You can see the signs already.'

'So.' I took the brooch from her and put it back: imperial portrait jewellery is so tacky, I always think, however well done. 'You had nothing to do with this ridiculous scheme.'

'Of course not!' She paused. 'Well, not much. And I wouldn't exactly call it ridiculous. It really is quite plausible.'

Plausible. Arruntius's adjective.

'It may be plausible, dear, but is it true?'

'Oh, Titus, please don't be tiresome, there's a dear! What does truth have to do with it?'

I sighed. 'Because if the accusation's false, as I assume it is, then Arruntius is right. Silana will never make the charge stick, and Agrippina will be in a stronger position than ever.'

'Nonsense. She's only just clinging on by her fingernails as it is. A charge of treason will be the last little push that sends her over the edge.'

'You think Lucius would exile his own mother without firm proof? *Especially* his mother?'

'But of course he would! Frankly, dear, I think he'd welcome the excuse. They've hardly exchanged a word for months, not since he sent her out of the palace to live in that poky old place of her grandmother's. Lucius is growing up at last, he isn't the boy he was.'

'That's certainly true. In fact why should he stop at exile? He already has one family killing to his credit, and there's nothing like murder for giving one confidence.'

'Titus!' Silia was frowning, and making frantic signalling movements with her eyes. I glanced at Argyrio, who was already at the far end of the counter straightening a necklace. Even selective deafness, it seemed, had its limits, and I'd just overstepped them.

'I'm sorry,' I murmured.

'So you should be! Anyone would think you were defending the woman.'

'Of course I'm not defending her! But I am worried, especially after that talk with Arruntius.'

'Oh, don't pay any attention to Gnaeus! The poor dear hasn't an optimistic bone in his body.'

I didn't laugh. 'That may be true, darling, but Agrippina's still dangerous, and she's slippery as a greased eel. You're no match for her, and poor Silana certainly isn't. So it's all down to which way Lucius jumps.' A thought struck me. 'What does Acte have to say?'

'How should I know?' Silia still sounded petulant; I could see that I'd have to buy her that hideous imperial cameo after all. 'I haven't seen the woman for over a month.'

I beckoned to Argyrio. He came, rubbing his palms together and exuding an expensive scent of musk.

'Then perhaps you should,' I said.

12

Getting into the palace was even more difficult than usual. Arruntius was right, all hell was loose and security had been doubled. Luckily Silia spotted a freedman she knew who was willing to carry a message to Acte. She came to the gate personally and took us through.

I hadn't seen her myself for two or three months, not since Britannicus's death in fact. Then, she'd looked terrible, and she didn't look all that much better now. Life with Lucius couldn't be easy, especially for someone not brought up to the stresses of political life. If nothing else I admired the woman's dedication.

'Come on up,' she said. 'Lucius is with Seneca. We won't be disturbed.' She led us along a marble-lined corridor and then through a door fitted flush with the panelling. 'This is the back way. It's more private.'

'A change from your old city tenement, darling,' I said, to make conversation.

'Yeah.' Her voice was brittle as glass. 'Which do you think I prefer? One guess.'

I didn't reply; the answer was in that voice. Another short corridor led to a flight of wooden stairs, unpolished, intended for servants rather than (the word came unbidden) inmates. Then we were through a second door, and back to the world of marble and wall-paintings. A female slave – a girl of about thirteen – appeared. She looked frightened.

'That's okay, Chryse,' Acte said. 'Leave us in private, will you?'

The girl nodded and left. Acte opened one of the several doors that led off the small landing.

'Welcome to the sanctum,' she said. 'Make yourselves at home.'

I'd expected, I think, a high-grade courtesan's suite, all soft colours, luxurious furniture and erotic decor, but the room was tiny, almost as small as Acte's tenement workshop; in fact I recognised the workbench and some of the masks. A tailor's dummy stood in one corner with a half-made costume draped over it.

Acte saw me looking. 'It makes me feel comfortable. Basically I'm a slob. Sit down. No couches, I'm afraid, just chairs. They take up less space.'

We sat. Acte perched on the edge of the workbench.

'I'm glad you've come,' she said. 'In fact I was going to come to you. I need advice, fast.'

'What about?'

'She's got away with it.' I didn't have to ask who 'she' was. The Empress Agrippina. 'Petronius, it was horrible! She walked all over him!'

'Tell us. From the beginning.'

'We were having dinner last night. Seneca was there, but not Burrus, he was over at the Guards camp. Lucius was drunk – he often is these days – but he was in a good mood. Then Paris came in.' Paris was a ballet-dancer, and one of the emperor's favourites. 'He was in a terrible state, or he pretended to be. Me, I think he was putting it on.'

I nodded. Being a professional actor, Paris could mimic any emotion you cared to name, but Acte was no fool. She would have spotted the deception at once.

'So what happened?'

'He told Lucius that his mother was plotting to kill him. No frills, just that. It took a while to get through to Lucius because like I say the poor kid was drunk, but when it did he blew up. He'd a dinner knife in his hand and I swear he would've killed the guy if I hadn't hung on to his arm. Seneca grabbed him too and we got him settled enough to listen. Then Paris got down to details. Seemingly Lucius was to be murdered by his own guard at the next games, Agrippina would marry young Plautus and make him emperor. The Senate were for him, half the legionary commanders.' She paused. 'Burrus, too.'

Something cold touched my spine. With Burrus gone Lucius might well be uncontrollable.

'What about Seneca?' I asked. 'What was he doing while all this was going on?'

Acte's mouth twisted in a pale smile. 'I thought he'd mess his pants, but he was great. I mean, *great*. He turned sort of slow and pompous, the way he does, and it was just what Lucius needed.' Her actor's voice deepened. '"Now don't be hasty, my dear boy, don't be hasty. Great men are never hasty. Remember that Alexander always thought before he acted, and he was merciful. Good rulers are always merciful." Great, like I say. He calmed Lucius down. We couldn't have done it without him.'

Silia shifted on her chair. 'Well personally, my dear,' she said coolly, 'I think it was a pity he interfered.'

'You weren't there.' Acte frowned. 'Sure, I want the empress dead. She'd bury me quick enough. But Lucius was frightening. Believe me, lady, he wouldn't've stopped at Agrippina or Plautus, or even Burrus, not by a long chalk. We'd've had the treason trials all over again. That what you want?'

Silia didn't reply, and nor did I. To anyone who had lived through them, only one answer was possible.

'So Seneca calmed the emperor down,' I said.

Acte shifted on the bench. 'Yeah. He persuaded Lucius to let things lie till he'd heard her side of the story. She was round first thing this morning.'

'And proceeded, as you say, to walk all over the poor boy.' Silia was pointedly not looking at Acte. 'Oh how very unfortunate for you both!'

'Look, just lay off me, will you?' Acte snapped. 'It wasn't my fault. And Agrippina may be the worst kind of bitch but at least this time she was within her rights.'

'You mean she hasn't been trying to regain her influence these last few months?' Silia said sweetly. 'My dear, I agree the specific charges were fictitious, but the empress is no innocent where conspiracy is concerned. Rome would be better off without her, and I'm sorry we seem to have missed our chance.'

'Don't you have any concern for justice at all, lady?'

Silia held her gaze.

'Not in this instance, no,' she said in a level voice. 'Justice in this case is a luxury we can't afford.'

Acte had her mouth open to reply, but I got in first.

'Let's leave the philosophical questions aside, darlings.' I said. 'Acte, just tell us what happened, please.'

Acte took a deep breath. 'Oh, she denied everything, told Lucius the accusation waş false and she'd been slandered. Played the doting mother. Sure, I know, it was pure garbage, but she knew what she was doing. She had the poor kid bawling inside five minutes. By the end he was begging her for the chance to make it up to her.'

I thought of my conversation with Arruntius. He'd been right, of course: Agrippina might be out of favour, but she was still a very dangerous woman. And evidently, despite the efforts of Seneca, Burrus and Acte, her hold on Lucius was as strong as ever. It didn't bode well for Rome. It did not bode well at all.

'So she's off the hook,' I said.

'Yeah.' Acte nodded. 'Silana's being exiled. Her front-men who brought the charge as well.'

'And Paris?'

'Not Paris. He's too good a dancer.' I laughed, and she glared at me. 'I'm serious, Petronius. That's important to Lucius. He'd hate to lose someone with Paris's talents because of a little mistake.'

'A just decision,' Silia said drily.

This time Acte didn't rise to the bait. 'I told you before,' she said. 'Lucius isn't a vengeful person. And he's got his own priorities.'

'So it would appear. Still, it's nice to see he's not totally under his mother's thumb.'

Acte scowled. She had my sympathy: I was becoming a little annoyed with Silia myself.

'Silia, dear,' I said. 'You do realise that this whole sorry mess is completely your fault?'

She looked at me blankly. 'I beg your pardon?'

'If you and Silana hadn't cooked up your ridiculous scheme in the first place, darling, then Agrippina wouldn't be back in favour.' I looked at Acte. 'She is back in favour, isn't she?'

Acte nodded. 'Not as much as before, but yeah, she's come out well. That's why I need advice.'

'But, Titus, I told you!' Silia had the grace to look guilty. 'The accusation was all Silana's idea!'

'Nonsense, darling. Silana's as thick as two short planks. And you can count yourself lucky that . . .'

Which was as far as I got, because just then the door opened and Lucius walked in.

13

The emperor wore a saffron Greek tunic, longer and far more lavishly embroidered than the usual Roman version. The way he moved and the way he held himself suggested drunkenness; not falling or aggressive drunkenness, but pleasant intoxication. He stood in the doorway beaming at us.

'Lucius, love.' Acte got up quickly from the bench where she was sitting – we were on our feet, too – and tucked his arm under hers. 'You remember my friends, the Lady Silia and Titus Petronius?'

'Yes, of course.' The emperor gave an even wider smile. 'Of course! How lovely to see you again, darlings. Did you enjoy my little dinner party?'

The question sounded so natural that it chilled me. I looked at Acte. Her face was pale under her make-up.

'Very much, sir,' I said.

The smile didn't waver. 'How nice. I'm so glad. You must come again. Acte will arrange it.' He hugged her and planted a kiss above her cheekbone.

I laid my hand on Silia's elbow and began to edge past him towards the door. Lucius stopped me.

'Oh, no, no, no!' His free hand, laden with gold rings, waved us back towards our chairs. 'Don't rush off, my dears, I won't hear of it. We so rarely have visitors, real visitors. Sit down, please.'

We sat. Lucius threw himself into the last vacant chair and hitched his leg over the arm. The tunic rode up exposing the pasty-white skin of his naked thigh, dotted with thick red hairs. The silence was painful. Finally Acte broke it.

'Petronius was just saying I should count myself lucky living here in the palace, love.'

'What, this place?' His brows came down. 'Oh, it's adequate, I suppose, but I wouldn't call it grand. One day I'll build you a proper house, dear. Somewhere fit for a human being to live in.'

Acte's tired face relaxed in a smile.

'That's nonsense,' she said. 'This is big enough for anyone, and much too grand for me.'

He reached over and hugged her. 'Isn't she lovely, Titus?'

'Quite adorable,' I said, blandly ignoring the use of my first name.

'I'm serious.' Acte kissed the tip of his nose. 'It's like living in a mausoleum with all this marble around.'

'But it won't be just marble, darling. We'll have gardens, real ones, not the table-napkin vegetable plot we've got just now. Perhaps a lake or two with a few islands. You'd like that, wouldn't you?' He turned his still-smiling face on me. 'You see my lovely girl, Titus? Not like the others. They're all on the make, all my other so-called friends. Seneca's had millions out of me already, the greedy old pig, and as for Mother, she is really grasping, Titus, I mean really!' He frowned. 'Not that I mind, of course. And you don't mind my calling you Titus, do you?'

'Not at all. I'm flattered.'

'Only if Acte likes you then you must be nice.' He kissed the tip of her broad nose and let her go. 'Very nice. Good. Then that's settled. I feel that we're going to be great friends. Great friends.' Oh, Serapis! This I didn't need! 'You have natural good taste, Titus. I can tell.'

'Thank you, sir.'

'You too, Silia.' His smile embraced us both. 'I consider both of you to be very special friends indeed. Don't think I don't know who I have to thank for bringing Acte here.'

So much for subterfuge. I glanced at Silia, who had coloured to the roots of her impeccably styled wig. For the first time I began to have a sneaking respect for young Lucius. The lad wasn't as daft as he looked.

He turned back to me. 'And you enjoy the theatre, of course. Anyone with real taste must.'

'Oh, I do. Very much. Such as it is in Rome.'

'Right. Right.' He nodded. 'Here it's a nonsense. All pirates and padded phalluses and stale old jokes. Roman theatre's dead. There're no greats and never have been. Except for darling Seneca, naturally.'

'Naturally.' I kept my face straight. Seneca had yet to notch up an actual performance for one of his interminably boring melodramas, but those I had read showed he was no Euripides.

'Of course the poor old dear's no Euripides.' My surprise must have been evident in my expression, because Lucius smiled at me in a most disconcerting way. I wondered if he had somehow caught my thoughts; he could, I was already beginning to realise, be very perceptive as well as very charming. 'But at least he tries. It's a pity he's such a' – he giggled – 'oh, such a terrible *Roman*.'

I nodded. 'I agree. All that blood and guts. Not to mention the . . .' I stopped myself just in time: I'd been about to say 'incest', but that would've been tactless in the extreme. 'Not to mention the other unsavoury features.'

'Oh, I don't mind the blood. It's only pretend, only stage blood, and it is rather . . . exciting in a way, Titus, don't you think?' His eyes glazed over for the barest instant and then were clear again. 'But the Greeks, now, the Greeks are simply splendid, aren't they? Look at her! She could never be Roman.'

He pointed over my shoulder, to something that hung on the wall behind me. I turned to see one of Acte's decorative masks. It was old, made of thin wood and horsehair: the face of a tragic heroine. The artist had painted lines of exhaustion and privation at the corners of the mouth and on the forehead. Its blank, empty eye-sockets stared back at me.

'Electra.' Lucius was smiling. 'Isn't she simply gorgeous? She belonged to Acte's father. Didn't she, darling?'

'That's right.' Acte's voice was curiously brittle. 'Dad gave me her as a keepsake. He was too old to play Electra by then anyway.' She spoke, I thought, with a certain bitterness.

Lucius swung back to me. 'You know Euripides's *Electra*, Titus?'

'In outline, yes. But not well.'

'Oh, but you must read it, my dear! It's a simply marvellous play!' He jumped to his feet and lifted the mask from its nail. 'Let me show you what you're missing! Acte, darling, you take Orestes!'

With his back towards me he fitted the mask over his face and head. Then he turned. His shoulders dropped into the actor's stance. The mask's eye-sockets were no longer empty; they glared at us across the room with an almost feral intensity. Suddenly Lucius was no longer the emperor, or even a gushing, half-drunken youth, but someone . . . different. So different that I felt a shiver run down my spine.

His head twisted sharply to one side, as if the mask's ears had caught a sound beyond our hearing and its eyes had followed, staring out into the far distance.

'Lucius, love, no,' Acte said quietly; but his arm was already up in the traditional gesture of an actor commanding silence. My scalp crawled.

'"What's that?"' The voice that hissed between the parted wooden lips was much higher and stronger than Lucius's light tenor. The words themselves were Greek. '"Forces from Mycenae?"'

Acte drew in her breath sharply.

'Oh, no!' she whispered. 'Not that scene, please! Not now!'

The mask's eyes never wavered. Lucius's whole body was motionless and rigid as an iron bar. For a long time no one spoke.

Then Acte made an odd sound in her throat, part sigh, part sob. '"No,"' she said in Greek, her voice as deep as Lucius's was high. '"It is my mother, who gave me birth. Look how fine her dress is, how splendid the coach in which she rides."'

I recognised the scene myself now; and knowing the scene and its ending I knew why Acte hadn't wanted us, especially, to see it played. The mask swung towards her and tossed its hair backwards. At the same time Lucius's right foot came stamping down to emphasise his first word. As a mime of savage, violent joy it was beautifully performed; Paris himself couldn't have done better.

'"Good!"' The eyes burned. '"She is stepping straight into our trap."'

I risked a sideways look at Silia. Her gaze was fixed, like a rabbit's confronted by a snake. I leaned over and gripped her hand, hard; Lucius, I knew, would not notice. Serapis knows what god had him, but he held him fast.

'"What shall we do, then?"' Acte's face was completely drained of colour. '"Shall we . . ."' She stopped. 'Lucius, love, don't make me say it! Finish this now! Please!'

'No.' It was not Electra's voice, nor Lucius's, but something between the two. I felt the hairs on the back of my neck lift. '"Shall we . . ." what?'

Acte's head drooped like a cut flower. The gesture of defeat, I knew, was not part of the play.

'"Shall we kill her?"' she whispered. '"Shall we kill our own mother?"'

I felt Silia's fingers stiffen under mine. Her hand was trembling. I squeezed it gently.

The mask came up, tossing the horsehair ringlets.

'"Has pity seized you, then?"' The words came in a low, venomous hiss.

'Lucius, please!' Acte cried. Lucius's body stiffened into its waiting pose.

Again, after the silence, came Acte's strange half-sob.

'"But how can I kill her?"' I could barely hear the words. '"How can I kill the one who gave me birth, the mother who reared me?"'

'"Kill her as she killed our father!"' I could see a thread of spittle on the wooden lips. '"Kill her as she killed . . ."'

'*No!* That's enough!' Acte leaped to her feet, tore the mask from the emperor's face and threw it across the room. The light wood shattered as it struck the wall.

Lucius stood blinking and staring like an owl caught by the sunlight. In the corner of his mouth, a muscle twitched. He raised his hand blindly to his lips and wiped them. For a long moment he and Acte faced each other. Then he walked over to the ruined mask, picked it up and hung it as best he could from its nail. His hands were shaking.

'It's only a play,' he whispered. 'Only a play.' His eyes, still glazed, turned towards us. 'Titus. Silia. You tell her, darlings. I didn't mean it. Not really.'

We said nothing. I knew that Silia, like me, was too shocked to speak. Our hands were still locked together as if we were children afraid of the dark.

'Come with me, love.' Acte held out her hand. Her voice was low and strained. 'You're overtired. Petronius and Silia will excuse us, I'm sure.'

I nodded. Something seemed to have got hold of my throat, and it was squeezing the breath out of me. Lucius shook himself, gave a sudden sharp laugh, and then smiled one of his brilliant smiles.

'You see how much she loves me, poor girl?' he said, and staggered towards the door. Acte gave us a quick frightened glance over her shoulder and followed.

A moment later, the young slave Chryse appeared. Silently – and nervously – she escorted us down the staircase and back to the palace gates.

'He's mad, of course. Quite mad,' Silia said calmly as I dismissed the litters and helped her past the bowing door slave.

'Of course.' I tried to keep my own voice under control; not by any means an easy task under the circumstances. 'But quietly mad or dangerously mad? That's the question.'

'My dear Titus.' Silia looked at me gravely. 'There's no such animal as a quietly mad emperor. And after today's performance I am very glad I'm not Agrippina.'

We went home and made love; but neither of our hearts were really in it.

The Winter Festival came and went, and by halfway through February we'd still seen nothing of Acte. Then towards the end of the month a letter arrived from the palace; not a dinner invitation this time but a summons to an evening interview with Lucius, subject unspecified.

I showed it to Silia while she was being made up for her morning visits.

'What do you think this is?' I said.

Silia read the letter and laid it on the dressing-table in front of her. 'Goodness knows, dear. Maybe he just wants to see you again. You did seem to make quite an impression.'

'Nonsense. We've only met twice, and neither occasion was particularly felicitous.'

'That, my dear, is putting it mildly.' She held her cheek out to Lalage for the final powdering. 'None the less, darling, don't laugh but I suspect that for some reason the poor lamb looks up to you.'

I laughed.

'It's true, Titus. Isis knows why. Maybe he simply likes your beautiful eyelashes.'

'Silia, I have no desire to get involved with Lucius. For one thing it's too dangerous.' Absolutely true. If one believed the rumours current in the Market Square (and I did), since Agrippina's hold over him had slackened Lucius's private behaviour had become increasingly erratic, and his friends and advisers were finding it more and more difficult to control him. Cut loose from the maternal apron strings the young man had discovered the joys of sowing his wild oats; and that, with the power that Lucius wielded, was no light matter.

Silia, the powdering and general titillation over, removed the dust-sheet and read through the letter again.

'It seems an innocent enough request, anyway,' she said.

'Oh, my dear! So, no doubt, did Caligula's.' I took the scroll from her, rolled it up firmly and tucked it into the fold in my mantle. 'And like them it may well be the prelude to a throat-cutting.'

'Don't overdramatise, Titus! Why on earth should Lucius want to cut your throat? It's not as if you're anyone important.'

'Thank you. That makes me feel much better.'

'Well, you know what I mean, darling.' She hesitated. 'Will you go?'

'Do I have any choice?'

She bent over and kissed me quickly on the chin.

'Not really,' she said softly. 'But behave yourself, won't you? And don't say anything silly.'

The interview wasn't at all what I expected. Whatever that might have been.

The slave showed me, not into the formal audience chamber, but into a room of the imperial suite which bore all the signs of being a private sanctum. Scattered around was a magpie's collection of bits and pieces from every branch of the arts: tools, brushes, half-completed projects abandoned and buried under later efforts. There was even a mosaic-layer's frame, with half the pieces missing. Lucius was standing at the central table talking to a fat Syrian; I recognised Argyrio, the Saepta jeweller. The emperor looked up and saw me, and his face broke into a broad smile.

'Titus!' He hurried towards me with arms outstretched. 'So good of you to come, my dear!'

'Sir.' I allowed myself to be enfolded. He was wearing a long-sleeved Greek tunic even more ornate, if anything, than the one I'd seen him in before, and he reeked of expensive perfume.

'You know Argyrio, don't you?' The Syrian bowed, his curled ringlets spilling over his eyes. 'Of course you do, who doesn't? Argyrio, show Titus the necklaces!'

The fat jeweller stepped aside. On the table lay three huge

necklaces of gold and precious stones, any one of which would've cost me half my year's income.

'Titus, I want your advice.' The emperor was still hugging my shoulders. His breath smelt of cassia. 'Tell me which one's the best.'

'Sir, I . . .'

'Oh, come on, darling! Don't be silly! Which one would you choose?'

I pointed at random. 'That one.'

He beamed and turned to Argyrio.

'There you are, you see!' he said. 'I told you he'd pick the emeralds, didn't I?' Argyrio smiled and bowed, but said nothing. 'Titus has marvellous taste, simply marvellous! Now that's enough! Pack the other two up, dear, and off you trot!'

We watched as Argyrio casually swept the rejected necklaces into a lambswool bag and with yet another bow followed the slave from the room. The door closed behind him. Lucius picked up the necklace I'd chosen and held it up between his hands.

'It's for Acte, of course,' he said. 'A surprise. Do you think she'll like it?'

'I'm sure she will.' The emeralds sparkled in the lamplight. 'Any woman would. It's beautiful.'

'Then it'll suit the dear girl perfectly.' He tossed the necklace aside. 'I'd half decided myself, but I wanted to ask you first, just to make sure.'

'You flatter me.'

'Nonsense, darling. Acte's often told me your judgment's impeccable. The best in Rome.'

I found this difficult to believe, but one doesn't contradict an emperor.

'No better than your own, sir, I'm sure,' I said.

Lucius beamed at me. Then with a sudden sweep of his hand he cleared the two nearest chairs of their clutter.

'Sit down, my dear. Would you like some wine?'

I nodded. I was feeling more than a little bemused. There was a jug on a side table. He poured and handed me the cup, then pulled the other chair over, sat down himself and stared at me. Our knees were almost touching. I felt most uncomfortable.

'Well?' he said at last. 'What do you think?'

I frowned. 'Pardon?'

He giggled. 'The wine, you idiot! Go on, taste it!'

I wondered if he intended to poison me as he had Britannicus; but it would've been the height of bad manners (and probably equally fatal) to refuse. I took a sip.

'Good?'

I held the wine in my mouth for a moment before swallowing. Greek, of course – I should've expected as much – but not by any means remarkable.

'I'm afraid I'm not too fond of Rhodian,' I said diplomatically.

'Oh, stop farting about, Titus! Let's have your honest opinion! I won't bite you, my dear!'

I took a deep breath. 'Very well. My honest opinion, is you could do better for Rhodian. Who's your shipper?'

'Memnon.'

I nodded. 'I've had trouble with him before. He's overrated, in my view. Personally I favour Euelpides. Not so fashionable, but a far better judge of how well a wine will travel.'

His face clouded, and I mentally cursed my own stupidity. When asked for my opinion on another man's wine, my invariable rule is to say that it's excellent, even if it's absolute rotgut. If the other man also happens to be an emperor, the rule is even less open to modification.

'I'm sorry, sir,' I said. 'But you did ask.'

He was still scowling. 'No, no. Quite right. Quite right. I'd doubts myself.' He got to his feet, strode to the door, opened it and yelled: 'Straton!'

An elderly Greek slave appeared and bowed nervously. Lucius glanced at me.

'Straton,' he said. 'Cancel that order we placed with Memnon. Transfer it to Euelpides. In fact – another glance in my direction – 'double it, there's a good fellow. A thousand jars.'

The slave left, closing the door behind him. Lucius smiled at me.

'There you are, darling. Satisfied?'

My head was spinning. 'Sir, I really wouldn't like to . . .'

'Nonsense!' He threw himself into his chair again. 'You've done me a favour. You're right, it's terrible stuff. I've said so myself, many times, but you know servants, they just won't listen!'

'Yes, sir.' Serapis!

He pulled the chair even closer. Involuntarily, I drew back; but fortunately he didn't seem to notice.

'You see, other people haven't got our sensibilities, my dear,' he said. 'Rome's a terrible place, it's so full of boors you can't imagine. Sometimes I feel so dispirited I could just give up altogether and leave them to it. If it wasn't for civilised friends like you and Acte I would. Even Mother . . .' He paused and frowned.

'The empress . . .?' I prompted. I had the strangest feeling that I had strayed into one of these boring little tête-à-têtes so beloved of middle-aged matrons, all scandal and back-biting.

Lucius giggled suddenly. 'Well, we'll leave Mother out of it. She's a lovely girl, but so unworldly you just wouldn't believe!' I bit my tongue. 'What the poor darling would say if she knew how I . . .' He hesitated. 'Titus, my dear, we are friends, aren't we? Good friends?'

'Of course.' I was beginning to sweat. This 'interview' was turning into something unpleasantly like a seduction, and I was not wholly sure how I was going to handle it. I could see that Lucius's own forehead, under the crisped curls, was beaded with perspiration.

'It's nothing very terrible,' he said. 'Not really. It's only a bit of fun, and I get so bored being good all the time. You understand that, don't you.'

'Yes, sir.' I wondered if I should simply plead a sudden griping of the bowels and cut and run. 'Of course I do.'

'I knew you would. You really are terribly understanding. Like dear Acte. So you'll come with me tonight? Just to see?'

'Sir, I don't quite know . . .' Our knees touched. I flinched.

'Please, Titus! You'd enjoy it, I'm sure. It's great fun, honestly.'

Personally I reserved judgment on that. Lucius's idea of fun and mine, I felt, were unlikely to coincide to any marked degree. I said nothing.

'Oh, come on, darling! Say you will! Don't be such a spoil-sport!'

I took my courage in both hands.

'What exactly is it,' I said, 'that you want me to do?'

He smirked like a schoolboy. 'Oh, nothing very dreadful. Just take a little walk with me.'

I breathed again. It seemed that I had misjudged the lad.

'What kind of a walk?'

'Just a walk around Rome. With me and Otho and Paris and Senecio. We've been doing it every night for a month now. You'll love it, I'm sure.' He stood up suddenly, and I surreptitiously wiped my sweaty hands on my mantle. 'Just a little walk through the streets.'

'What, now?' No one in his senses walks in Rome for pleasure at night. Nor, for that matter, in the daytime.

'Yes, dear, now. It'll be quite exciting, I promise. Only . . .' He paused.

'Only what?'

His smile was dazzling.

'Only don't tell Mother. It's our little secret.'

15

The others were waiting for us by the gatehouse, wrapped in thick cloaks: against the chill, I thought, although I was only partly right. Lucius, too, had put on a thick travelling cloak – he was sensitive to cold – and had found another for me.

I knew Otho and Paris reasonably well, but not Senecio. Nor, on first glance, did I particularly wish to. He was the son of one of Claudius's freedmen; a big, brawny Spaniard with an accent thick as boiled corn-meal and breath stinking of raw onions.

'Who's this?' He scowled at me; evidently the instant dislike was mutual. 'We don't want company, Nero.'

'Oh, don't be silly, darling!' Lucius was fitting on a hat with an extra-large brim, which concealed his features even in the brightly lit forecourt. 'Titus is my guest. Behave yourself, there's a good boy. I won't have fighting.'

'Not yet, anyway.' Paris sniggered. Even covered by a woollen cloak he looked like what he was, the best ballet-dancer and mime artist in Rome. 'Hi, Petronius. Looking forward to your evening out?'

'Of course, my dear.' I was already beginning to have my suspicions about what they had in mind, but I wasn't such a fool as to voice them.

'So what's it to be?' Otho was grinning. 'The Eighth Region?'

'Naw. It's boring, and there's too much extra muscle around the Square.' Senecio had produced a vicious-looking club from the folds of his cloak and was tapping it gently against his palm. 'I vote for the Cattlemarket. Lots of punters round there, and we could finish up at Mammaea's.'

Lucius turned to me.

'Titus, dear, you decide,' he said. 'Guest's privilege.'

I may have been cabbage-looking, but I wasn't altogether green, and I didn't like the sound of this at all. Cattlemarket Square is definitely the wrong part of town, and Mammaea's is the roughest brothel on the Aventine: dangerous enough in daylight, sheer murder after dark.

'Don't ask him!' Senecio spat into the shadows. 'He's pissing himself already. I say the Cattlemarket.'

'Oh, let Senecio have his fun, Nero.' That was Paris. 'Petronius doesn't care, do you, Petronius?'

'Very well, then.' Lucius gave me a brilliant smile from beneath the shadow of his hat. 'Cattlemarket Square it is. All right, Titus?'

It was very much not all right; but again I was not fool enough to say so. Lucius had the guard unbar the gate and we were on our way.

It was starting to rain, and the streets were dark and deserted: of pedestrians at least, although there were plenty of heavy waggons around making their night-time deliveries. Most were slow as arthritic snails and made enough noise to wake the dead – city-centre residents need cloth ears after sunset – but we'd just turned into Tuscan Street when an empty cart nearly spared us the rest of Lucius's principate. Paris hefted a rotten cabbage. It bounced against the tailgate.

'Bastard!' Lucius yelled after the disappearing cart. 'Mother-fucking bastard!'

Paris muttered something I didn't catch – nor, I suspect fortunately for him, did Lucius – and Senecio laughed. Not a pleasant sound.

By the time we'd reached the first of the streets round the Cattlemarket Otho and I were trailing the others: I suspected that for all his blade-about-town manners he was as lacking in enthusiasm as I was. Prowling the streets looking for trouble and swearing at carters is a young man's game, and Otho could give Lucius and Senecio a good four years. Paris, of course, was older than any of us; but then Paris was the eternal adolescent, and a mad and bad one at that.

'You do this often?' I asked Otho. I kept my voice low.

Otho shrugged. 'When he gets the urge.' I didn't need to ask who 'he' was. 'Which seems to be most nights recently.'

'Why?'

Another shrug. 'Someone has to keep him out of trouble. He is the emperor, after all. As well as being a friend.'

'I meant why does he do it? I grew out of this sort of thing when I was seventeen.'

Otho grinned. 'Didn't we all, dear?'

Ahead of us the others had disappeared into a shop doorway above which I could just make out a crude wooden sign with a painted wine jar. We caught them up just in time to see Paris produce a crowbar from inside his cloak. He stuck its point between the door itself and the locking bar and heaved. There was a splintering crack and the bar hung loose.

Lucius giggled.

'Drinkies, gentlemen,' he said, stepping past them over the threshold. 'Titus, where are you? I need your advice.'

I hesitated.

'Better go, Petronius,' Otho whispered.

I followed Lucius inside. The place was pitch-dark, of course, and we collided.

'Where the hell's the torch?' he complained petulantly. 'Why does no one ever have a torch?'

There was no answer to that, or at least none that needed voicing. We weren't carrying torches because torches make one conspicuous. I felt other bodies squeeze into the narrow space behind us, and I could smell Senecio's oniony breath and Paris's perfume even above the scent of stale wine.

'Never mind, never mind! I've found a shelf-ful of jars up here.' Lucius had moved away. I could hear him fumbling about behind the stone counter. Earthenware scraped and bumped, then shattered. 'Oh, fuck! Never mind, there are plenty more. Try this one, Titus. See what you think.'

The jug caught me in the chest and I grunted with pain. Paris sniggered.

'Pass it back, dearie,' he said. 'Don't hog.'

'No, no!' Lucius's voice came out of the darkness. 'Titus gets first swig. He's our wine expert. Go ahead, Titus! Blind tasting.'

Paris sniggered again. I broke the wax seal on the jug, removed the bung and took a sip.

'Oh, do come on, darling! I'm waiting!'

There was nothing I could do but give a mental shrug and commend myself to Bacchus.

'Sorrentine,' I said. 'Not much body, I'm afraid.'

'Shit! Give it back here.' That was Senecio. The jug was pulled from my hands and I heard a slow glugging, followed by a hawk and spit. 'The pansy's right. Flat and sour as a Vestal's knockers.' Earthenware shattered on the stone floor and the smell of spilled wine intensified. 'Let's have another one, Nero.'

The emperor obliged. This one was Massic, and rough as only bad Massic can be. It, too, was consigned to oblivion.

Lucius chose a third – bad Massic again – and then a fourth, which contained a vicious aberration from Fundi. I'd been served it (or its close relative) once at a dinner party and despite drinking sparingly had had gutrot and a splitting headache for days afterwards. I broke the jar myself this time, out of pure kindness to humanity.

I must admit, crass though the admission is, that by this point I was beginning to perk up. Also either my eyes had become used to the darkness or the clouds had cleared away, because I could see grey shapes where before everything had been black. I even managed to field the fifth jar when it was thrust at me. I couldn't place this one exactly, but it was Etruscan, and the poorest of the lot.

As the flask hit the floor Lucius made a tutting noise.

'This is dreadful,' he said. 'Simply appalling. Whoever owns this place is an absolute boor.'

Mentally I agreed. Five separate wines, and none of them drinkable. The vintner would have been better employed selling lamp oil.

'Move on?' Paris suggested.

'Yes, darling. But first' – Lucius giggled – 'a little quality control. Pass me the crowbar.'

Paris reached past me and set the heavy metal bar down on the counter. Lucius picked it up and hefted it.

'By the power vested in me by the Senate and people of Rome

I hereby revoke this wineshop's licence to trade. The stock, such as it is, is forfeit. Mind your heads, darlings!'

I ducked; just in time. The iron bar came back and swept along the shelf of jars. In the narrow confines of the shop the noise was terrific. There was suddenly wine everywhere, the air was full of wine, drenching us and filling our noses with its stench. We began laughing like maniacs, stamping in the puddles and generally making adolescent fools of ourselves. How long that would have gone on for I don't know, because someone suddenly shouted: 'The Watch!'

I'd forgotten about Otho. He had stayed outside, either because he couldn't get in or because he'd wisely decided we needed a look-out. Whatever the reason, I blessed him. Without him we would've been caught like rats in the cellarage; and that would have been too embarrassing for words.

We poured out of the shop and ran, dodging down an alleyway and then several more at random and in quick succession, until we had lost them. Then Lucius slipped on a pile of dogshit and the rest of us piled on top. We picked ourselves up and dusted each other down. I was not feeling proud of myself, and besides I had twisted an ankle. Otho was cursing and holding a bruised shoulder, but the others were giggling uncontrollably.

Then Senecio saw the drunk.

He'd propped himself against a tenement wall by one arm and was being violently sick on to the pavement: a middle-aged man, greying at the temples, no purple-striper but reasonably well-to-do by the quality of his mantle. He had a pair of party slippers tucked under his other arm, and a wilted garland of flowers over one ear. God knows what he was doing alone and torchless in this maze of alleyways. Whatever the reason it was his pure bad luck.

As we walked (or in my case hobbled) towards him he gave one final retch, raised his streaming eyes from the ground, and saw us. He tried to run, but his mantle caught round his legs: not enough to trip him, but enough to prevent escape.

Senecio gripped the sleeve of his tunic. Paris grabbed him from the other side.

'Hey, pal!' Senecio was grinning. 'What's the hurry?'

The man stared at us, his vomit-flecked mouth slack with fear.

He tried to pull away, but Senecio and Paris held him fast. Paris was already feeling for his purse.

'Been to a party, eh? Must've been a good one.' Senecio shifted his grip and thrust the man hard against the wall. Between the drunk's feet urine trickled on to the pavement. Paris leapt aside to avoid the spreading pool of piss, and Senecio swore.

'You're a filthy little bugger, aren't you, pal?' he said.

''leathe,' the man said. ''leathe.' Half his front teeth were missing, and his mouth was badly bruised; obviously he'd been rolled already that evening.

Paris's hand came out from the tangled folds of his mantle. It was empty.

'The larder's bare, darlings,' he said. 'We just haven't been lucky at all tonight, have we?'

'Come on, Senecio.' Otho stepped forward and took hold of the Spaniard's free arm. 'Leave the poor bastard alone. He's plastered.'

Senecio sniggered but didn't let go. 'Poor's right. Poor and plastered and pissed. All the p's. Hasn't much going for him, has he?'

'Leave him,' Otho said again. 'Let's get on to Mammaea's. The first one's on me.'

Senecio shook his hand off. 'You go ahead. I'll catch you up once I'm done.'

So far Lucius had stayed in the background. Now he came forward. The hat he'd been wearing when we set out had come adrift in our dash through the alleyways, and he was bareheaded.

The drunk looked up and saw him. His bleary eyes widened. 'But you're the . . .' he said.

He never finished. Senecio's hand reached under his cloak, his arm came back and thrust forwards once, twice. The man gave a gasp, his eyes opened even wider and fixed themselves on something behind Senecio's shoulder. Then his mouth opened and he vomited blood.

Senecio stepped to one side and the dead man slid to the pavement.

'Look at that,' he said. 'All over my cloak.' He kicked the corpse. 'Bastard!'

The rest of us stood frozen, too shocked to move. Paris was the first to recover.

'It serves him right,' he said. 'He should've kept something back for us. A few silver pieces wouldn't've killed him.'

Senecio laughed as he bent down and wiped the blade of his dagger on the dead man's mantle.

'Filthy bastard,' he said again, this time almost lovingly.

'You didn't have to stab him.' I noticed, even in the half-light of the moon, that Otho's face was grey. 'A beating's one thing, but murder . . .' He made a curious gesture with his hand, like the sign to ward off bad luck. 'Murder's different.'

'I'd no choice.' Senecio straightened and put the dagger away. 'He recognised the emperor. That's right, isn't it, Nero?'

I glanced at Lucius. He was staring at the corpse, his eyes bright and fixed, and he was breathing heavily.

'Nero?' Senecio said again. His voice had lost its certainty.

There was no response. We might not have existed, as far as Lucius was concerned.

'That's enough excitement for the night, Senecio,' Otho said quietly. 'Sod Mammaea's. Let's go back.'

Paris was looking at the emperor.

'Perhaps we should,' he said.

We were already turning when Lucius let out a yell. He raised his foot and began kicking the dead man – ribs, face, head, back and groin. Even Senecio, I think, was appalled by the sudden violence of the attack. It was as if Lucius intended to kick the corpse into a lump of anonymous flesh.

Paris and Otho grabbed him and wrenched him away. By this time Lucius was screaming obscenities at the top of his voice, and any moment I expected – half wished for – heads to appear at the tenement windows, or the Watch to come charging round the corner; but tenement-dwellers mind their own business after dark, and the Watch has more sense than to patrol the alleys.

'Get that cloak round his face!' Paris hissed. Otho wound Lucius's cloak round his mouth and nose and pulled it tight. The muffled curses gradually died away, and Lucius slumped against the other man's chest. Otho slackened his grip and made sure Lucius could breathe normally again.

It took us an hour to get him back to the Palatine. He said

nothing all the way, not one word; made no sound at all, in fact. His face looked as slack and empty of life as the dead man's had, and he stumbled from foot to foot as if he had been drugged.

16

You can't, as the saying goes, hide good scandal or bad tunnyfish. Before the month was out Lucius's nocturnal escapades were public knowledge. I didn't go with him again myself: after that one disastrous occasion I kept my head down despite frequent invitations.

Scandal wasn't the worst of it. Under cover of the emperor's name, other youngsters began roaming the streets beating up and robbing innocent citizens. A lone pedestrian – or even someone in a litter – was asking for trouble if he went out even in the better districts after dark without a hefty bodyguard. The Watch were overstretched and martial law seemed inevitable. With Lucius himself one of the worst offenders, however, that was out of the question.

Early in March Acte sent me word from the palace that she wanted to see me urgently; and not only Acte, as I discovered when I arrived. I recognised Seneca's dry tones even before the slave bowed me into the room.

Acte glanced up quickly. She looked frightened.

'Petronius!' she said. 'Thank the gods it's you!'

'Who else would it be, darling?'

She reddened. 'I thought it might be Lucius.'

Seneca, who was sitting with his back to the door, turned round and stared. He, at least, didn't seem too pleased to see me.

'You know Annaeus Seneca?' Acte asked.

'We've met.' An overstatement: philosophers don't patronise my kind of parties and vice versa. The only time I'd seen the old fraud socially was at Lucius's abortive dinner.

'Young man.' Seneca inclined his head gravely.

'Sit down, Titus.' Acte was looking even more haggard than she had the last time I'd seen her. She'd never been beautiful. Now she looked a positive sight. 'We need your help.'

It was the first time she'd used my given name, but I didn't mind. We were, I supposed, old enough friends to make no difference, and I suspected that Acte needed all the friends she could get.

I pulled up an ornate gold and wickerwork chair: we weren't in the sanctum but one of the palace's public rooms, and the furnishings were eccentric. 'Help with what, dear?'

'With Lucius, of course. The poor love's causing himself no end of trouble.'

'Causing *himself* trouble?' Love may be blind, but Acte seemed afflicted with a moral astigmatism which was positively heroic.

'Philosophically speaking our friend here is quite correct,' Seneca put in smoothly. 'By his misguided actions the dear boy is tarnishing his soul; hence he can truly be said to be doing himself a disservice.'

I could have kicked his smug ankles. In any case I'd no intention of being diverted by dubious platitudes.

'From what I hear,' I said, 'any problems there are with the emperor's behaviour seem to be other people's. To speak plainly, the Emperor Nero is turning into a proper little thug.'

Seneca frowned but said nothing.

'So you don't know what happened last night?' Acte was chewing on a fingernail; the other nine, I noticed, were bitten to the quick. 'With Julius Montanus?'

I shook my head. The name was familiar: I remembered a thick-set middle-aged man with the build of a wrestler, not known for his equable temper.

'Lucius . . . came across him outside Marcellus's Theatre. Montanus punched him.'

I laughed. 'Oh, how marvellous! Good for Montanus!' A punch on the nose was just what the brat needed, in my view. 'Was he badly hurt?'

'You don't understand. When Montanus saw who it was he apologised. Lucius told him to go home and slit his wrists.'

Oh, Jupiter! Oh, good sweet Jupiter!

'He did *what*?'

'He told him to kill himself, Titus.' Acte stood up and walked over to the window; the room was on the first floor, overlooking the courtyard garden. She kept her back turned towards me as she spoke. 'It just isn't like him. Lucius isn't a monster, he even hates signing official death warrants. How could he do a thing like that? Kill someone for nothing?'

'Not for nothing.' I was remembering the dead man in the alleyway. He had recognised the emperor too. 'Did Lucius tell you this himself?'

'He didn't even mention it. I only found out this morning.'

'So what do you expect me to do?'

She turned round again to face me. 'Help. I don't know how. Just help. Lucius needs help. He has to be stopped now, before . . .' She bit her lip.

'Before he gets a taste for capricious killing.'

A nod, with lowered eyes. Seneca wasn't looking at me either.

'Acte, be realistic! I hardly know the man. Why should he listen to anything I have to say?'

'Because he seems to have a curious respect for your . . . ah . . . powers of judgment, Petronius,' Seneca said stiffly. 'Although a respect based on what evidence I'm not exactly sure.'

Again my foot itched to hack at his shins. 'Even more respect, my dear, than for the sterling advice that you give him so freely? Oh, Seneca, darling! Surely not!'

The large bland face coloured and the fat lips drooped.

'Petronius,' he said. 'You are a young man. I am not. The young will listen to the young where an older man's words, even if they are wiser, will go unheeded. I have talked to Nero. He refuses to admit that he encountered Montanus last night at all. More, he denies being engaged on any nocturnal . . . expeditions at any time.'

'But that's . . .' I was going to use the word 'insane' and thought better of it. 'That makes no sense at all. He's made no secret of what he gets up to at nights. I've been with him myself.'

Seneca pursed his lips with distaste. 'Exactly. He couldn't deny it to you. With me the case is different. I would have to start by calling the dear boy a liar.'

I saw his point, of course, and it was a good one. Seneca had no official standing at court, not even (now Lucius had reached adulthood) that of tutor. To provoke a quarrel would be extremely stupid, almost certainly futile and possibly disastrous for Rome.

'The nub of the matter' – Seneca was fingering a fold of his expensive mantle – 'is that the lad is emperor and can do what he likes. As yet he hasn't fully realised this. The longer we can delay realisation the better, for his sake and for ours.'

'And how does this involve me?'

Instead of replying Seneca looked at Acte.

'We thought we – you – might divert him, Titus,' she said. 'It's only boredom after all. Lucius doesn't really want to be emperor, he never has.'

'Divert him?'

'Into safer channels,' Seneca said. 'As Acte says, the lad needs an interest. Something to take his mind off mundane pursuits like . . . like . . .'

'Governing? Beating people up? Handing out arbitrary death sentences?'

He glared at me. I stared back impassively.

'Quite. At least until he develops a more responsible attitude.'

'And did you have anything particular in mind?' I tried to keep the sarcasm out of my voice.

'Titus, don't be difficult, please!' Acte crossed the room and put a hand on my arm. 'This is too important.'

'I'm sorry.' I was. She was quite right, it was important. 'It's just that I'm genuinely at a loss as to what you expect me to do.'

'Lucius is an artist. We felt' – she glanced at Seneca, who frowned – 'at least *I* felt, that if he had someone to encourage him, someone whose opinion he valued, an older man . . .' She stopped in confusion.

'What Acte is trying to say' – Seneca's lips were pursed again – 'is that the emperor is, or would like to be seen as, that rare bird, an aesthete. A *philhellene*.' He used the Greek word, pronouncing it carefully and with distaste.

Acte was nodding with relief.

'He likes Greeks,' she translated.

'Thank you, darling,' I said. 'I do understand the term. Only I still don't see what —'

'My dear Petronius, that is precisely the point,' Seneca interrupted me. 'Rightly or wrongly, Nero considers you ... unRoman, if I may coin the word. In his mind you are indeed '– he smiled smugly as he delivered the *mot* – 'rare birds of a feather. If you can use your influence to divert the emperor's attention from his other pursuits down that innocuous path then you will have our eternal gratitude.'

'I doubt if Rome would take kindly to a Greekling wearing the purple,' I said.

'It may be that or suffer another Caligula.' That came out flat. Acte drew in her breath, and Seneca turned briefly in her direction. 'I'm sorry, my dear, but it had to be said. I like it no more than you do, but the lad already expresses an admiration for his late unlamented uncle. You understand now, Petronius?'

'I understand.' I felt unutterably weary. 'Very well, I'll help if I can. What exactly do you want me to do?'

'Come back this evening,' Acte said. 'Lucius is staying in for once. I'll arrange a private chat.'

Oh, Serapis! If this was keeping my head down then I was a blue-arsed Briton.

17

He was in his private sanctum. I'd expected Acte, but we were alone.

'Titus! Oh, how nice!' He stood up, scattering papers from his lap. 'Acte said you might drop by. Come in and sit down, my dear!'

'Thank you, sir.'

'Oh, tosh! Tosh!' He had me by the arm. 'Call me Nero. Or better still Lucius, as Acte does. It makes you special. I feel we've known each other for years. Don't you feel that?'

'Yes, sir. Lucius.' I sat while he fussed around straightening things and pouring us each a cup of wine.

'I'm sorry the place is such a mess, but I won't allow the slaves in here.' He beamed. 'You know slaves. All sticky fingers and huge great feet. They do more damage to a room in five minutes than a marauding army. Here.' He handed me the wine. 'First of the new batch from Euelpides. I didn't forget, you see. You were quite right, it's miles better than Memnon's. Cheers.'

'Cheers.' I sipped the wine while he watched me closely.

'Good?'

'Good.'

'That *is* good.' He giggled and covered his mouth with his hand. 'I'm sorry.'

'Not at all.' I had been looking down at the papers he had let fall when I came in. Now I picked the top one up. 'Do you mind?'

'No. No, please.' He was blushing with pleasure. 'Go ahead. Only don't tell anyone else. Not just yet.'

It was an architect's elevation of an amphitheatre, and from the scale marked at the bottom a big one at that. I was a little taken aback: Lucius didn't like or approve of gladiatorial games, or wild beast hunts either. So what was he doing, I wondered, planning to give Rome another amphitheatre?

'It's not what you think, Titus.' He was grinning at me, and I felt again that curious sensation that he had looked into my mind. 'Oh, yes, it looks like something you fight in, but it isn't, not at all. That's the surprise.'

'Then what is it for? There isn't a great deal else you can do in an amphitheatre.'

'Oh but there is! Guess, my dear! Three guesses!'

'Sir, I really don't . . .'

'Lucius.'

'Lucius, then. I really don't have the slightest idea.'

His grin widened. 'I'll give you a clue. Olive, parsley . . .?'

The penny dropped. 'Greek games? Athletic contests?'

'Why not?'

'In Rome?' Serapis! There would be an outcry! He might as well have the Guild of Gladiators arrange a game of kiss-in-the-ring to take the place of the midday bout.

The emperor's smile faded. 'You don't think it's a good idea?'

'I think it's . . .!' I stopped, remembering why I was there. 'I think it's simply splendid.'

The smile was back, and he blossomed like a flower unfolding. 'Really?'

'Really. It's brilliant. So long as you don't tell anyone.' The amphitheatre would take two years to build, and it would be best to allow people during these two years to assume it was intended for the usual purpose. There was no point in raising hackles until the time came; by which time the lad might possibly have learned more sense. 'Of course you'll have to keep an eye on the work personally.'

'Will I?'

'Naturally. You know what contractors are, and this amphitheatre will become a showpiece. Where is it to be, by the way?'

'I thought Mars Field.'

'Good idea. Plenty of space. You must show me the site tomorrow and explain where all the various bits will be.'

'We'll go first thing.' He was almost jigging about with excitement. 'Oh, Titus, I'm so glad I told you first! Not even Acte knows!'

'I'm flattered.'

'Nonsense. But it is a secret. Don't forget, now, dear.'

'Of course I won't.'

'Wouldn't it be lovely if they caught on? Greek games, I mean. No more sword-fights or rioting on the terraces, just good healthy fun. We might even persuade people to join in, the way they do in Greece.'

Oh, sweet Serapis! I shuddered. The thought of how the majority of Romans would react if asked to jump a hurdle or pitch a discus in public like a prissy Greek made me feel distinctly queasy. Good healthy fun or not.

'I wouldn't mention that either for the moment,' I said carefully.

'No? You really think not?' He frowned. 'Perhaps you're right.'

I was looking round the room for an excuse to change the subject. My eyes fell on a beautiful Greek cithara with a mother-of-pearl-fronted sound box and gold and ivory pegs.

'Do you play?' I asked.

He blushed again. 'A little. Would you like to hear something?'

'Very much,' I lied.

'You're sure?' Eagerly, he took the cithara down from its peg and cradled it in his arms like a child. 'You don't have to. Honestly. Not if you don't want to.'

'I'd be honoured.' That was enough. Lucius beamed. While he was finding a plectrum and settling himself in a suitable chair I sat back and prepared to be bored, if not deafened, in the cause of duty.

I was neither.

I'd expected something large and self-important, a Euripides choral song, perhaps, or – considering what we'd been talking about – one of Pindar's odes. What I got was a simple little lament, beautifully played and beautifully sung. When the last note sounded I confess I had tears in my eyes.

Lucius laid the cithara aside diffidently, and with reluctance.

'I could've played that a lot better,' he said. 'Menecrates

is giving me lessons, but I still haven't got the hang of the vibrato.'

'It was marvellous,' I said. 'Marvellous.' I meant it.

'Really? You really, truly liked it?' His face was alight.

'I really, truly liked it. Whose was it? Bacchylides?'

He reddened. 'No, it was mine, actually. Although Menecrates helped with the setting. You didn't think my voice was too weak?'

'No, not at all.' It had been a medium-strength baritone, with more body than his usual tenor, and I knew from experience that it would have carried to the back of a fair-sized concert hall.

'Only I've been doing exercises, you see.' Lucius sat down and put his hands together. 'Breathing exercises with weights on the chest. As well as following a strict diet. I'm glad it seems to be working.'

'I've heard professionals who wouldn't have done as well. It's a pity . . .' I stopped. The silence lengthened between us.

'It's a pity I happen to be Emperor of Rome,' Lucius said quietly. 'That's what you were going to say, wasn't it, Titus? Oh, but I agree, darling. I agree completely.'

I said nothing.

'You know what I'd like to do? If I were ever good enough?'

'No.'

'I'd like to make the musician's tour of Greece. The big festivals. As a contestant.'

Jupiter! The establishment would burst a corporate blood vessel! 'You could.'

He shook his head. 'No, I couldn't. The ever-so-proper Roman Senate wouldn't let me. And anyway, I'd only end up winning everything I went in for. Do you think I want that?'

'No.' I looked at him directly; for, I think, the first time ever. 'No, Lucius. I don't think you do.'

'Thank you.' He smiled and ducked his head. 'Oh, I'd like to win, of course, but I'd want to do it fair and square. And you see as emperor I'd never know.'

'Being emperor does have its advantages.' I shouldn't be saying this, but I suddenly felt a strange affection, very close to pity, for the young man. 'You can be a force for good.'

'I knew you'd understand!' He was on his feet. 'Titus, that is so right! That's exactly what I want, more than anything else! To drag this rotten, barbaric city out of the mud and give it a soul!'

I felt myself agreeing. Lucius had put his finger on the problem. That, I'd always felt, was precisely the trouble with Rome: she was rednecked and crass, she had power without subtlety. If she had a soul at all it was weighed down with rods and axes and moneyboxes. For a moment I found myself totally on Lucius's side.

It was a pity he was mad.

There was a knock on the door, and Acte came in.

'I'm sorry,' she said. 'I thought I heard shouting.' She looked at me, anxious, one eyebrow slightly raised. 'Is everything all right?'

'The emperor's been treating me to a private recital.' I kept my face straight.

Lucius laughed. 'You utter pig! You said you liked it!'

'I did.'

'He is good, isn't he?' Acte said proudly. Lucius hugged her and kissed the top of her head. 'Admit it, Titus!'

'Oh, he's excellent. Too good for an emperor.'

'Haven't I always said so?' Acte reached over for the cithara and put it in Lucius's hands. 'Again, dear, for me. Please.'

It was late when I got back home. I had half a dozen slaves with me, plus three torch-boys, so if there were any of the pseudo-Neros around they wisely decided to leave me alone.

I dreamed that night that Lucius was sawing me in half, from crown to toe. The dreadful thing was, that in the dream I didn't know whether to be glad or sorry.

18

I got to know Lucius well, and certainly much better than I wanted to, over the next eighteen months. I also saw far too much of Seneca, who clearly considered it his moral duty to save my soul while I was helping him save Lucius's. Neither of us succeeded: mine had a rooted aversion to being taken to task by a sententious old bore who saw everyone's failings but his own, and Lucius's had as many sides to it as a Parthian envoy has faces.

That particular fact was indisputable. Seen from close up the poor lad was a bigger mess than I would have believed possible. Keeping him on the right side of sanity, for his own sake and for Rome's, was an uphill struggle. Nevertheless we could have done it, I think, if it hadn't been for the monumental stupidity of Otho.

Well, well, that's unfair. No doubt Poppaea Sabina would have got what she wanted in the end without Otho's kiss-and-tell bragging; but we really should've seen what was coming. As it was by the time even Acte knew Lucius was smitten with darling Poppy and had summoned us to the palace, it was too late to mend matters.

Acte herself, of course, was furious.

Her room was a shambles: chairs overturned, crockery smashed, the dressmaker's dummy tipped over against the wall. The girl Chryse who had shown us in had already fled white-faced.

'She's a bitch!' I'd never seen Acte angry, and it was frightening. 'A total, fucking, shit-faced *bitch*!'

Crash went another vase as it smashed against the door a foot from my head. I ducked in reflex.

'Do calm down, dear.' Silia hadn't moved. She brushed the single chair that had remained upright clear of debris and sat down. 'It's not the end of the world.'

'Oh, yeah?' Acte stared at her, then clenched her fist and banged it hard against the wall. 'I should've known she was after Lucius when she married Otho! Who the fuck would let that knock-kneed balding effeminate prat into them unless they had other plans for their maggoty cunt?'

I winced. She was quite right in her description of Otho, of course, but still . . .

Moving very deliberately, Silia stood up again, stepped towards her and slapped her hard on the side of the head. The two women stood glaring at each other for a long time. Then, all at once, Acte collapsed sobbing against the workbench.

'Find us a flask of wine, Titus,' Silia said. 'And take your time about bringing it, please.'

I left, hurriedly.

When I opened the door again later with the tray they were sitting side by side on the bench. Acte was still sobbing, with Silia's arm round her shoulders, but at least the air was clear of flying flowerpots. Silently I poured and handed Silia the cup. Acte drank the neat wine down in two swallows.

'You're all right now?' I asked.

She nodded. 'I'm sorry, Titus.'

'Don't be, darling. It was an education.'

'I meant every word. Poppaea's a bitch.'

'So I gathered.' I righted an overturned chair and sat down. 'Apart from that obvious fact, what exactly has happened? All your messenger said was that you wanted us to come immediately.'

'Lucius has invited Otho's wife to be his guest here at the palace,' Silia said. 'Indefinitely.'

'Jupiter!' I suppose I'd guessed as much already, reading between the extremely pungent lines which had greeted us as we came in, but the raw statement still came as a shock. Lucius had talked about Poppaea, of course, and Otho was for ever boasting of his new wife's beauty and sexual talents, but I hadn't expected things to go this far. 'What about Otho?'

'Lucius is sending him to Lusitania.' Acte took the wine jug from me and poured herself another cup. 'As governor.'

'I grieve for the Lusitanians. So Poppaea's to be an official mistress?'

'Not yet. But it's not for want of trying on her side.'

I frowned. I knew Poppaea, by reputation at least, and she was another Agrippina in embryo. If she had her claws into Lucius then we were in very deep trouble.

'The man's a fool,' I said. 'We've helped him get rid of one predatory female and he goes and saddles himself with another. I mean, honestly, darling!'

'It's not his fault.' Edged to the sidelines or not, Acte still rushed to Lucius's defence automatically. 'It's her. Poor Lucius can't help himself. She's a stunner, a real stunner and' – she blushed and lowered her eyes – 'she's good in bed. Very good. He likes that.'

True enough. We'd had many interesting and informative chats over the past few months, Lucius and I: his sexual tastes were refreshingly eclectic, albeit gross even by my generous standards. And from what Otho told us Poppaea Sabina was both energetic and inventive.

'Does Seneca know?' Not that the old man could do much directly, even if he wanted to.

'Otho told him. He's very upset. Otho, I mean.'

'So I would imagine. It can't be easy, being told to trot off to Lusitania just so the emperor can screw your wife.'

'Titus, this isn't funny!' Silia snapped.

'I'm sorry, dear. You're quite right.' I poured a cup of wine and added water from a jug on the table that had miraculously escaped destruction. 'So what does Seneca advise?'

Acte picked up a scrap of material from the bench – it looked to me like Coan silk – and blew her nose loudly. The wine seemed to be doing its work, and she was almost her usual feisty self.

'I don't know. He looked in earlier but' – she indicated the room – 'he didn't stay.'

I laughed. I could imagine Seneca's jowly, horrified face peeping round the door while Acte vented her feelings. A pity she hadn't slugged the old goat with a wine jug.

'Perhaps you should talk to him, Titus,' Silia said. 'Work out some mutual plan.'

'Me? Why the hell me?'

'Why not, dear?'

I felt a stand had to be made somewhere, and the sooner the better. Some things were being taken far too much for granted.

'Because, darling, unfortunate though the situation is it's really not my concern. I contracted to keep Lucius's mind off politics, yes, but not to interfere in his sex life.'

'Titus, that is pure flannel, and you know it. Besides, you owe it to Acte.'

'Hey, that's okay.' Acte's sad eyes looked at me over her wine-cup. 'Don't mind me. You're quite right, Titus, it isn't your business. We'll work it out somehow.'

Silia ignored her.

'Best go now, dear,' she said.

When I reached Seneca's mansion on the Caelian – only slightly less palatial than the palace – Burrus was already there, perched on a very uncomfortable-looking chair in the great man's study, about two feet from a charcoal brazier. He looked ill, and I wondered if it was the poor ventilation, or the heat, or simply his proximity to Seneca, who lay on the only reading couch with his best profile to the door and greeted me with a silent, regal wave of the hand.

'Petronius.' Burrus nodded. 'Good to see you. You've heard the news?'

'I've just come from the palace.' I took a seat as far from the brazier as possible. 'Acte sent for us.'

'How is the dear girl?' The Man Himself smiled. 'Still . . . upset?'

'She was when we arrived. She's better now.'

Burrus grunted. 'Highly strung, these Greeks. But I'm sorry about Acte. She was a good woman, ex-slave or not. And at least we knew where we were with her.'

'Burrus, you're talking as if the poor soul were dead.' Seneca frowned. 'She's not out of favour, my dear fellow. Far from it, whatever she may think herself. The emperor has simply . . . taken on an extra interest.'

'A bit on the side, you mean?' I said.

The fishy eyes turned in my direction.

'Poppaea Sabina is not Nero's mistress, Petronius. Not officially, anyway. And she has many good qualities. She is intelligent, witty, well read . . .'

'Strong-minded.' Burrus was leaning back with his eyes closed: he really did not look well. 'Ambitious. Unscrupulous . . .'

'All I am saying,' Seneca snapped, 'is that this is not the disaster you three – I include Claudia Acte – seem to think it is. Poppaea is no real threat. I would be far more worried had the Empress Agrippina been back in favour.'

Burrus's eyes opened. 'Agrippina learned her lesson with Britannicus. She's keeping her head well down these days, and very wisely, too.'

'That may be so.' Seneca's tone sharpened: the poor dear really did not like to be contradicted, especially on his own ground. 'But I would not count on the situation being permanent. She is still a considerable force, and the emperor, whether he will or nill, remains very much . . . attracted to her. Acte may be a sterling lady in her way, but she cannot satisfy the emperor's more unusual, er' – he looked down – 'physical yearnings.'

'Nero does very well on that score already, darling,' I said calmly. 'You take it from me.'

Burrus chuckled. Seneca eyed me with distaste.

'I am not talking about temporary liaisons. You must know by now that the poor boy has a need to be dominated – sexually dominated – by older women. Acte, as I say, is temperamentally incapable of satisfying that need, but satisfied it must be if the emperor is to remain tractable.'

That was fair, so far as it went. Also remarkably perceptive.

'And you think Poppaea fits the bill?'

'I do.'

'I disagree.' Burrus's brows were down. 'Oh, not with what you say about Nero's character, Seneca. You're quite right, the lad's always been tied up in apron strings and he won't grow out of it now. But I don't think Poppaea Sabina's quite the innocent you evidently believe her to be. The woman has ambitions.'

Seneca sighed. 'My dear fellow, please give me credit for a little intelligence! Of course she has ambitions, but she is not a fool, and unlike Agrippina she has neither great political acumen nor the empress's single-minded drive for political power. I am not particularly happy with having her as an additional factor, but comparing her with Agrippina she is by far the lesser evil.'

'You're making her sound almost like Messalina,' I said. 'She wasn't political either.'

As I'd intended, the name produced a sudden silence. We had all lived through the reign of Claudius's beautiful and viciously amoral wife; and we'd also all known people who hadn't been so lucky.

'That is nonsense,' Seneca said flatly. 'Messalina was a totally different case. In the first place she was a fool, in the second so was Claudius, and for all his . . . eccentricities Nero is not. In the third place the emperor is married already.'

'To Octavia,' I pointed out, 'whom he can't stand and who hasn't lived with him for years, never mind shared a bed. And there is such a thing as divorce.'

Seneca reddened: with anger, not embarrassment. For someone to have the temerity to contradict him was bad enough, but argument set one beyond the pale.

'Poppaea's mother may have come of reasonable stock,' he said, 'but she was certainly not noble. And her father was a complete nonentity. You're not suggesting that the lady is contemplating marriage, surely?'

I blinked. I hadn't considered that, like many provincials, Seneca might be a snob, especially when his attitude to class distinctions was otherwise so relaxed. Normally I would have found this unexpected blind spot amusing. In this case it was worrying.

'I'd've thought it was obvious that's what she's after,' I said mildly.

'I agree.' Burrus sat up. 'Of course she is. She'd be wasting her time otherwise.'

Seneca looked from one of us to the other like a baffled rhino. 'You're both wrong. Completely wrong. A mistress is one thing, a wife another. The emperor would never divorce his predecessor's daughter to marry Poppaea Sabina. Never.'

Ah, well. There was no point in arguing further, especially with the old bore in this bone-headed mood. I'd done my best, but in any case there was very little we could do in the meantime. To look ahead a little, though, it's only fair to add that Seneca wasn't completely unjustified in his opinion: it was to take darling Poppy four years to make an honest man of Lucius, and that wasn't, as Acte put it, for want of trying.

I called in on Otho on my way home. He was busy packing, and uncommunicative. I was sorry for Otho; he may have had his faults but he was an honourable enough man at bottom. Before we said goodbye to each other he took me aside. He was fingering the small silver figurine of Isis that he always wore round his neck.

'Tell Nero I'll be back,' he said; just that. But his eyes added: 'And I'll spit on the bastard's grave.'

I shivered as I climbed back into my litter. The day had turned grey and cold.

19

It didn't take Poppaea long to prove me right. I was kept abreast
of her plans by Lucius himself, who was completely disingenuous
where his sexual partners were concerned.

'Poppy wants me to marry her, Titus,' he said, setting down a
plate (we were in one of the palace dining-rooms; I was advising
him on the choice of a new dinner service). 'She asked me
again last night, and that's the fifth time this month. I mean,
honestly, darling, I'd love to indulge the girl but how can I? It's
so unreasonable!'

'Don't ask me about marriage.' I picked up a mushroom dish
from the selection on the table and held it to the light. 'It's the
one subject on which I'm not an expert. Not from the inside,
at least.'

He laughed. 'Oh, come on, don't be modest! What do you
think? I can't divorce Octavia. Mother would be furious, she's
always saying how much she likes the little wimp.'

I put the salver down – it would never have done, the
decoration was repetitive and hopelessly old-fashioned – and
tried to keep my voice light.

'You see the empress often these days?'

'Oh, no! Just now and again. She's a lot less frosty than she
was, but Poppy can't stand her any more than Acte can.' He
frowned, presumably at the juxtaposition of the two names: Acte
still lived at the palace, but he hardly ever visited her now and
never mentioned her. 'Titus, I really can't divorce Octavia, can
I? I mean, we don't live together and so on, and I've never liked
the woman. But she is old Claudius's daughter, and she hasn't
actually done anything, has she?'

'No,' I said. 'She hasn't. And,' I added carefully, 'I doubt if she would, either. Forget about her. Octavia's quite content as she is.'

He nodded. 'That's right! That's just what I'm always telling Poppy!'

He picked up a delicately fluted spoon. 'How about these? They'd go very nicely with the soup bowls, wouldn't they?'

'Yes, very nicely.' I moved on to more sensitive ground. 'You say your mother's becoming "less frosty".'

'Mmm.' He laid the spoon to one side and reached for a fruit dish with a raised boss in the shape of a satyr's head. 'She can be terribly critical, you know, and she's no time for art. But we had quite a cosy little chat the other day about modern painting. She's obviously taking an interest at long last.' He held up the fruit dish. 'He's an ugly-looking devil, isn't he?'

'What?' I was momentarily distracted. 'Oh, the satyr. Yes, he is.'

Lucius giggled. 'He looks a bit like Seneca. Don't tell the old bore I said so.'

'Oh, my dear!' I examined the dish more closely. The satyr glared at me with blank, toad-like eyes. He looked constipated. 'Oh, you're quite right! Especially the expression.'

'Shall we take it? Just for fun. I'll present it to him at the next dinner party as a going-home gift.'

'Good idea.' I took the dish from him and put it by the spoons. 'But to get back to Agrippina . . .'

He laid his hand on my arm. 'Now, Titus, darling, don't you be silly! I know perfectly well what Mother's trying to do, and it won't work. The poor thing hasn't an artistic bone in her body, however much she pretends otherwise. But it is rather flattering. To think she's taken the trouble.'

'Yes, I suppose it is. The empress' – I was dry – 'is most condescending.'

He giggled again. 'As well as having the finest pair of breasts in Rome. Excepting Poppaea's, of course. And your Silia's.'

'But naturally they are the finest! They have suckled an emperor!' I spoke in my pompous Seneca voice; and then I could have bitten my tongue off, because he paled.

'That's right, darling,' he said softly. 'So they have.'

Fortunately at that precise moment Seneca himself arrived. I doubt if I've ever been more relieved.

'Ah, my dear Nero!' The old man was affable and smiling, but I could detect signs of agitation. There was a trace of sweat on his forehead, and the drape of his mantle wasn't quite as impeccable as usual. One was never totally sure of one's welcome when visiting Lucius. 'You sent for me?'

Lucius's face clouded.

'Did I?'

'You did. Less than an hour ago. I came as quickly as I could.' He nodded to me. 'Good morning, Petronius. Choosing silverware?'

'Yes.' Lucius was smiling again. 'Isn't it lovely? Especially this fruit dish with the head.'

Seneca picked it up and examined it carefully. I could see he hadn't noticed any resemblance. 'Oh, yes. Very nice. Most unusual.'

'Oh, I remember!' Lucius snapped his fingers. 'It was about my tax idea!'

Seneca stiffened. I could understand why: hitherto Lucius had taken very little interest in the minutiae of government, and fiscal matters especially bored him solid. Our whole plan of campaign was directed to keep him out of public affairs.

'Your "tax idea",' he said. His voice was expressionless.

'Yes. It's simply marvellous.' Lucius waved us both on to couches. 'Sit down, please. Both of you. I can't possibly explain this to you standing up.'

I sat. Seneca lowered himself gingerly, as if he were afraid his couch would bite him. Lucius remained on his feet.

'Comfy?' he asked.

'Perfectly.' Seneca's face was a study. 'Now. What tax idea is this?'

'You know the problem we have with tax farming?'

'Yes.' Tax farming was the bane of the Treasury officer's existence. In the interests of economy, the collection of indirect taxes was farmed out to private concerns. The result was a system administratively cumbrous, riddled with corruption, totally arbitrary and the cause of constant complaints from provincials.

'Well, I just thought, why not scrap the whole thing?'

I was watching Seneca carefully. The poor darling went three distinct shades of green. There was a terrible silence.

'I beg your pardon?' he said at last.

Lucius was pacing the floor. 'It's simple. Ditch the lot. Import-export duties, port dues, everything. We don't need them, silly fiddling things.'

'But where,' Seneca said carefully, 'is the money going to come from, Nero? The shortfall to the Treasury would be crippling.'

'But don't you see, there wouldn't be a problem!' Lucius beamed. 'Make trade free and you'll double the market overnight. Not to mention the administrative savings. It's brilliant!' He turned to me. 'What do you think, Titus?'

'Alas, I'm no economist, my dear. Not in your exalted class.'

'Don't smarm, you pig. Seneca?'

'It's . . . an interesting idea.' The old fraud looked glazed, and I didn't blame him. 'Certainly . . . radical. Whether it would work in practice is another matter.'

'But you'll put it to the Senate?'

'I will' – Seneca swallowed painfully – 'put it to the Senate. If you insist. All the same, my dear fellow . . .'

'Oh, I do insist!' Lucius was still beaming. 'And it is brilliant, whatever you think. Scrap indirect taxes and everybody wins, everybody's happy, except the tax monopolies, and these crooks can take a running jump to themselves.'

'I hope you don't mind me asking, dear boy, but did you . . .' Seneca shifted uncomfortably on the edge of his couch. 'Was this your own idea, or was it . . . ah . . . suggested to you?'

'Oh, it's all mine.'

'The Lady Poppaea didn't . . . I mean no disrespect, you understand, but I was just wondering whether she or someone else might just have . . .'

Lucius was watching him squirm with a most intelligent smile on his lips.

'No, she didn't,' he said abruptly. 'Although she did remind me that I'm the emperor, and that perhaps I should be doing a little more . . . emperoring.' He turned away. 'Now I'm not pushing, Seneca, but I really do think it's a splendid idea, and I'd be very grateful if you'd pass it on to the Senate.' He paused:

another dazzling smile. 'Tell them it's your own suggestion, if you like.'

I thought Seneca's sudden fit of coughing would finish the old devil.

He cornered me later outside, as we were waiting for the litters.

'I don't like it, Petronius. I don't like it one bit!'

'The emperor's tax plan?'

'Oh, no. I thought he was quite good over that. It's totally unworkable, of course, but you have to give the lad credit for good intentions. And the present system does need drastic revision. No. I meant this new . . . independence of mind.' His litter arrived and he climbed in with difficulty. 'That worries me. Oh, and you may have been right about Poppaea. I suspect I've rather misjudged her.'

I was so surprised that I almost forgot to hand him the fruit dish I was carrying for him. Seneca never admitted he was wrong. Never. I also forgot to mention the bit about Agrippina's breasts. They, to my mind, were even more significant. But by the time I remembered Seneca had gone.

A month or so later I happened to be in Naples when Terpnus gave a performance at the concert hall, and Lucius (who'd travelled down specially) invited me to join him in the imperial box. Not alone, naturally: he never went anywhere these days without a following of elegant young men, artists and musicians. There would be a good dozen of us squeezed cheek by jowl into a space meant for half as many.

I was late, unavoidably so. Terpnus was tuning up when I arrived and Lucius was already seated.

'Titus! What kept you?'

'I'm sorry. Domestic crisis.'

'Never mind, we saved you a place.' He grinned. 'Come and sit beside Poppy.'

I hadn't noticed Poppaea on his other side, possibly because I hadn't expected her to be there. And Poppaea Sabina was not the sort of woman one failed to notice.

Seated, she was taller than Lucius, with the perfect regularity of features which ought to have produced an ordinary prettiness but went beyond it into beauty. At the same time she radiated a coldness which was unique in my experience: as if her beauty and softness were overlaid with a frozen coating. As I climbed over protesting bodies towards her she turned and looked at me. It was like being run through with an icicle.

'I'm sorry,' I said again, to Lucius. 'The friend I'm staying with tripped over his mistress's cat and broke a leg.'

Lucius laughed.

'His own leg or the cat's?' he said. 'Or was it his mistress's?'

'Don't be a fool, dear.' Poppaea frowned. 'Petronius is making it up.'

'It's the truth! I swear!' It was. By the time I'd finished laughing and got the poor man's slaves to summon a doctor I had been abominably delayed.

'Oh, never mind, darling, you're here anyway.' Lucius waved a hand to Terpnus who along with the rest of the audience had been waiting for the disturbance caused by my arrival to subside. 'Now do sit down and shut up, there's a good fellow.'

I squeezed past Poppaea, incidentally (and accidentally) confirming what Lucius had said about her breasts. From what I could see of them from above – which was quite a lot – they were flawless, white as Parian marble. She caught my eye and glared at me. We were not, obviously, destined to be friends.

The whole auditorium fell silent as, with another glance towards Lucius, Terpnus began to play. Naples is a Greek city, and so civilised. In Rome we'd've been lucky to hear anything above the cracking of nuts and roasted melonseeds. Here the audience treated the performing artist with the courtesy he deserved.

Terpnus sang, of course, in Greek – mostly his own compositions with some older works. Both the singing and the lyre-playing were excellent, but one song I completely failed to place. When it was over, and while Terpnus was refreshing his throat with a cup of water, I leaned towards Poppaea (there was no point in antagonising the lady by ignoring her) and whispered: 'Whose was that last one? It was very good, wasn't it?'

Poppaea's lips set firmly into a line. Lucius, who must have heard, grinned at me and looked smug.

'There you are, Poppy!' he said. 'Didn't I tell you Titus had a good ear?'

The pressed lips were exchanged for a definite scowl. I didn't attempt further conversation with her until the concert was over.

We went backstage, of course, after the performance. Terpnus was in the star's dressing-room, changed out of his finery and sipping from a cup of Numentian wine mixed with barley water. Lucius embraced him.

'Splendid, my dear!' he said in Greek. 'Simply splendid!'

'It was your own composition that was splendid, sir.' Offstage Terpnus was a little puffed-up pigeon of a man with a few grey hairs plastered over his bald pate. 'I only hope I didn't spoil it too badly.'

'It was rather good, wasn't it?' Lucius turned towards me, beaming, his arm still round the little man's shoulders. 'Titus spotted it right away.'

Poppaea was still scowling. 'Petronius knew all the time. He only asked about it to please you.'

'Oh, nonsense! Nonsense!' Lucius pulled her towards him with his free arm and hugged her. 'What a horribly devious mind you have, darling! Titus didn't know it was mine. No one did except you and Terpnus. Isn't that right, Titus?'

'Of course it is.'

'Genius,' Terpnus murmured sententiously, 'cannot be hidden. The rest of my performance was a mere shadow.'

'Tosh!' Lucius coloured up with pleasure and gave him another squeeze. Terpnus winced. 'Mind you, I am coming along nicely. In a year or so I'll give you a proper run for your money. Eh, Poppy?'

He smiled at her. Standing, their eyes were on a level.

'I think Terpnus is quite right, darling,' she said. 'You're much the better already.'

'There's my lovely girl!' Lucius kissed her. 'Well, maybe I am. We'll see.'

'The Lord Nero's musical genius is surpassed only by his skill on the tragic stage,' someone behind me said in a slow, bored voice. I turned. Lounging against the doorpost was a tall dark-haired man with heavy Semitic features.

'Alityrus!' Lucius cried, and let go of both Poppaea and Terpnus. 'Oh, how marvellous! Where did you spring from, darling?'

I'd never met the man properly, but I knew who he was: a Jewish comic actor and a friend of both Poppaea's and Lucius's. Whether the word was a euphemism or not I didn't know. Nor did I particularly want to.

'I'm on at the local theatre.' Whatever the man's relationship with Lucius, he was undressing Poppaea with his eyes.

She stared back at him without expression. 'Or will be from tomorrow.'

'Really? What play?'

'Cratinos's *Flood*.'

'Oh, my dear!' Lucius grinned. 'Not Cratinos! Oh, you poor thing!'

Alityrus shrugged and took his shoulder from the wood. He hadn't, I think, moved his gaze once from Poppaea even while he was talking to Lucius; and he certainly hadn't acknowledged Terpnus's presence, let alone my own. I doubt if I'd ever encountered anyone quite so self-centred.

'It's a play,' he said. 'And the gent who's paying likes them old and wrinkled. Me, I'm different.' He half-winked at Poppaea; her breasts rose and fell. 'But then I've got to eat, haven't I?'

'Alityrus, you haven't congratulated our host yet,' Poppaea said quickly. 'That is *not* polite, dear.'

The heavy-lidded eyes swung towards Terpnus. The puffy little Greek was scowling, and clearly resented no longer being the centre of attention.

'Congratulations,' he said.

That was all. Terpnus merely nodded – neither the single word nor the tone called for anything more – excused himself and stormed out as noisily as he dared.

I wondered what the man thought he was doing, and how he could be so stupid as to insult the emperor's favourite so blatantly; and then I looked at Lucius and understood. Alityrus was perfectly safe, from Terpnus at least. The emperor was fussing like an ugly spinster in the presence of a suitor half her age, biting his lips to redden them and touching the tightly curled fringes of his hair. Older men have never interested me. I was faintly amused and, I confess to my shame, faintly repelled.

'I don't think I know the *Flood*,' I said.

Alityrus favoured me with a slow stare. Having got rid of one irrelevancy to the company he was obviously preparing to remove the second.

'There's no reason why you should,' he said. 'It hasn't been performed in years and the jokes have beards longer than a rabbi's.'

'This is Titus Petronius, dear.' Lucius's arm was over Poppaea's shoulders again. His fingertips brushed the top of her left breast, but his eyes never left the other man's face. I was treated to the barest of nods before the lazy eyes swung away from me.

'Of course we've got Helorus for set design,' he said, addressing Lucius, 'so the effects are good. That always pulls the crowd.'

'Do tell!' I could almost see Lucius's ears prick up. He had a child's love of gadgetry, and the palace was full of the odd, clever machines which the Greeks delight in.

'Oh, they're brilliant. The boat stops the show.'

'Boat?'

'For the flood scene. It's the length of the stage, with hinges all along the deck. Lovely work. You'd think it was real.' For the first time Alityrus's voice held a trace of colour. 'When it opens up the punters go wild.'

'A hinged boat! Oh, how very clever!' Lucius nodded, his eyes still fixed on Alityrus while the fingers of his left hand stroked Poppaea's breast. I suddenly had the most curious sensation of being invisible. 'You're quite right, my dear, we must see this boat of yours. Tomorrow, you say? The first night's tomorrow?'

'As ever is.' Alityrus was staring at Poppaea, who stared coolly back.

All at once Lucius shivered, like a dog shaking water from its coat.

'Then we'll go,' he said. 'We'll all go just to see the marvellous hinged boat. A little theatrical outing. But tonight' – he gave a sudden brilliant smile that embraced them both and excluded me – 'tonight, my darlings, we'll have some supper together, to whet our appetites. After that . . . well, after that we'll see, shall we?'

I made my excuses, and left quickly.

If we'd thought Poppaea was the only cloud on the horizon, however, we were wrong. At the end of February Seneca suddenly called Silia and myself to what proved to be an emergency council of war in his house on the Caelian. Burrus and Acte had already arrived. They were seated in the study when the slave led us through.

I hadn't seen Burrus for months. He looked old and tired and ill.

'Ah, Petronius!' He smiled thinly. 'I hope the emperor's Arbiter of Elegance has brought a miracle along with him. Jupiter knows we need one.'

I glanced enquiringly at Seneca. His pudgy face was lined and grey.

'I'm terribly afraid, my dear fellow,' he said, 'that we're losing him. We may indeed have lost him already. It's just a matter of who to.'

'"Who to"?' I pulled up a chair for Silia and sat next to her. 'What do you mean, who to?'

Seneca looked at Acte.

'Poppaea or the empress, Titus,' she said dully. 'One or the other. Me, I can't see that it matters.'

'Agrippina?' A cold finger touched my spine.

'They're sleeping together. They have been for days.'

'You're sure?' Silia frowned.

'Oh, yes, lady. I'm sure. Chryse told me. It's common knowledge at the palace, among the slaves, anyway, and they always know what's going on.'

'Chryse is only a girl. Perhaps she made a mistake. Misinterpreted.'

'No mistake. And Chryse's sharp as a needle.'

'Tell us, then,' I said.

Acte shrugged. 'Not much to tell. Agrippina came round after dinner, when Lucius was three parts drunk, dressed up like a third-rate Damascus whore. She seduced him. Had him right there on the dining-room couch. She's been having him ever since.'

There was silence.

'So that's it, Petronius,' Burrus said at last. 'What do we do?'

I shook my head. 'I'm sorry, but I don't believe it. The emperor's no fool, drunk or sober, and he knows his mother's only interested in power. Chryse's mistaken.'

'I'm afraid not, my dear boy.' Seneca, as if to disassociate himself from his words, was staring at the bookshelves which lined the walls. 'There were others present. Not at the final . . . joining' – his mouth pursed – 'but during the, ah, preliminary stages. It was, as Acte says, a deliberate act of seduction, with the emperor's full co-operation.'

'Then he's mad!'

Burrus gave me another thin smile.

'Of course he is,' he said. 'We've known that for years.'

'I mean mad to let her get a hold over him again. I thought we were rid of Agrippina for good.'

'Didn't we all?'

'He loves her,' Acte said calmly. 'He's always loved her. Or lusted after her, anyway. He can't help it.'

'In any case her reasons are plain enough.' Seneca was dry. 'You know, of course, that Poppaea has almost persuaded the emperor to divorce Octavia?'

'That's nonsense! Nero has no intentions of . . .'

'Petronius, please!' Seneca held up a hand. 'You warned me yourself right at the start that that was what she wanted and I wouldn't listen. Don't make the same mistake I did. That isn't opinion, my dear fellow, it's fact. With Octavia gone Nero would be free to marry, and his new wife would be Poppaea, in which case I very much doubt if Agrippina would long survive the wedding.'

'He's right, Titus,' Silia said. 'She has to act now. Before she loses him altogether.'

Burrus nodded. 'I agree. Agrippina or Poppaea, one of them will have the boy soon. The question is which side do we choose? Which is best for Rome?'

'How about Lucius's side?' I said.

Seneca's eyebrows lifted, and he turned towards me. 'I beg your pardon?'

'How about choosing the emperor's side? He is, after all, my dears' – I spread my hands – 'the emperor.'

'Don't be idiotic, Titus!' Silia sniffed. 'The poor lamb hasn't got a side.'

'Are you sure?' I was getting just a little angry with all of them; with myself, too, if truth be told, because their assumptions were my own. And some demon seemed to have got hold of my tongue. 'Silia, the emperor is not a "child" or a "boy" or a "lamb". He's twenty-one years old and a man in his own right. Perhaps we should try to remember that occasionally.'

They stared at me. All of them.

'Must be his time of the month,' Burrus murmured. It was the only crude remark I ever heard him make.

'My dear fellow,' Seneca said smoothly. 'but of course Nero is an adult, physically at least. But you must admit that in the field of judgment —'

'His only real fault,' I interrupted him, 'is that he was born to the wrong mother and pushed into a job he was never fitted for. The poor devil would be perfectly content as third actor with a second-rate touring company or playing for money on street corners, and instead he's the most powerful individual in the world. That is worth bearing in mind too.'

I noticed that Acte was nodding. Burrus, however, was not.

'But, Petronius,' he said wearily, 'that's exactly the point. Nero's emperor whether he likes it or not. Whether we like it or not. The boy's . . .' He caught himself. 'I'm sorry, the *man*'s well meaning enough, I grant you, but still . . .'

'And that's another thing.' I was properly angry now. Goodness knows where all this was coming from, but I must have been bottling it up for months unknown even to myself because I meant every word. 'Yes, he is well meaning. Now I'm no altruist like you and I don't take pleasure in manipulating people like Seneca or even darling Silia here . . .'

'Oh, my dear fellow!'

'*Titus!*'

'. . . but as a person who regards himself as reasonably cultured I have a lot of sympathy with what Lucius is trying to do.'

'Which is?' Burrus seemed genuinely interested.

'To take Rome by the scruff of the neck and civilise her, whether she likes the experience or not. Although I doubt if it's possible this late in the day, and I'm not wholly taken with the young man's methods, I still applaud his attempt.'

'Hey, Titus!' Acte said quietly amid a growing pool of silence.

'Titus, have you quite finished?' Silia's voice could have come straight off a glacier.

'I think so, dear,' I said. 'More or less.'

'Good.' She turned to Seneca. 'Now we were discussing what could be done. Perhaps . . .'

'Wait a moment. I agree with Petronius.' That was Burrus. I stared at him. 'Oh, no, not that rot about Nero's mission or whatever you like to call it. We've had that conversation before and he knows my opinion. Greece is a moral swamp and any sensible person will leave it alone. But he's right about not taking sides. Personally I don't want to support either Poppaea or the empress, and I don't think anyone else in this room does either.' He paused and looked round the faces. 'Well? Am I right?'

There was no answer.

'Fair enough. Not that I suspect we could do anything constructive in any case. So what's wrong with doing what Petronius suggests and leaving the lad – I'm sorry, Titus, but he *is* a lad, adult or not – to solve his own problems?'

Seneca cleared his throat. 'You think, then, that the poor . . . ah, that the emperor is capable of that?'

'Certainly not.' Burrus held his gaze. 'I'm not the idiot that Petronius seems to have become. But I think it might be safer and more . . . *politic*' – he let the word hang, and I swear the old hack blushed – 'to let him try.'

We left it at that. In the event I think we were right; although none of us imagined that Lucius's solution to the problem would be as drastic – and as final – as it turned out to be.

Silia was uncharacteristically quiet on the way home. We'd

almost reached the Palatine when she said: 'I don't really manipulate people, Titus, do I?'

I smiled.

'All the time, darling. It's one of your most endearing qualities.'

'Like Seneca?'

'Not like Seneca.' I leaned over (we were in a double litter) and kissed her cheek. 'Besides, dear, you only do it for their own good. And the poor lost souls need someone to organise their lives for them.'

'That' – she sat back with a contented sigh – 'is what I thought.'

We finished the journey in politic silence.

22

What Lucius's solution was we discovered before March was half over. He usually celebrated the five-day Festival of Minerva at Baiae, not far from Naples. The celebrations were by all accounts impressive. I'd never been invited myself, but that, unfortunately, was about to be remedied.

My invitation came early in the month, together with a request that I visit Lucius at the palace as soon as possible. The slave took me to a small gymnasium furnished with a single chair. Lucius lay on the floor, dressed in a short tunic. He had a slab of lead on his chest, and he was wheezing like an old pair of bellows. I waited politely until he nodded to the slaves standing on either side. The slab was removed.

'A breathing exercise, Titus,' he said. 'You should try it. It does absolute wonders for the voice.'

'Oh, no, my dear, not me! I've too much respect for my ribs. And' – I indicated his face – 'I've never been all that fond of purple.'

He laughed and threw himself into the chair. Slaves mopped the sweat from his forehead and dabbed on perfume. There was very little left now of his fragile, boyish prettiness. His throat and lower jaw were beginning to swell, giving his whole face a coarse appearance.

He was also, I noticed, getting fat.

When the slaves had finished he waved them out and we were left alone.

'You got the invitation?' he asked. 'For the festival?'

'Of course. That's why I'm here.'

'Good. Now, dear, I'd like you to organise a party for me and

Mother. We'll have it at the villa in Bauli.' It took me all the powers of dissimulation I possessed to keep the look of shock from my face. Even so Lucius looked concerned. 'There's no problem, is there? You can do it in the time?'

'No. I mean yes, of course I can do it, if you want me to.'

He beamed. 'That's lovely. Don't spare any expense, mind, I can afford it, and Mother's worth every penny. Besides, she gets out so seldom these days, poor dear.'

There was a peculiar breathless catch to his voice that I couldn't quite place. It was both disturbing and tantalisingly familiar.

'Will Poppaea be there?' I tried to keep my own voice neutral.

'Oh, no. Poppy can't manage it, unfortunately. A migraine headache. She can feel them coming on months in advance sometimes. It'll just be me and Mother.' There it was again. Perhaps it was an after-effect of the lead slab. 'What's wrong, Titus? You seem a little hesitant.'

'No. Not at all. What kind of party were you thinking of?'

'Oh, that's up to you, darling! You're *so* good at parties I wouldn't even dare suggest. Cater for fifty.' He lay back and closed his eyes. As if by prearrangement (which it probably was) a pretty slave-boy no older than five or six slipped into the room. Completely ignoring me, he began to massage Lucius's feet and ankles. 'But remember. Whatever you decide on Mummy must enjoy it. Despite all the terrible things that Poppy tells me she's been saying about me recently she is my own darling mummy, and she deserves her treat.'

'Terrible things?' I was watching fascinated. The boy's hands had moved above the hem of Lucius's tunic and were caressing his bare privates.

'Terrible, Titus.' Lucius spread his legs. 'I couldn't possibly repeat them.' His voice dropped to a murmur. 'But she is my own dear mummy, and she shall have her party. Whatever Poppy says.'

Just then the boy ducked his head beneath the tunic, and I left quickly. Neither of them, I'm sure, saw me go.

I wasn't happy. Despite what I'd said, ten days is far too short a time to organise a proper party, especially when it's an imperial commission. However, what Seneca had called Lucius's new independence of mind was getting stronger by the day. He was quite simply beginning to realise the basic truth that everyone had been taking pains to hide from him: that an emperor can do what he likes, in reason or out of it. So far our relations had been excellent, but I was very well aware that the relationship was changing. I wasn't alone, of course; Seneca and Burrus were the same. Presumably Poppaea and Agrippina also. We were all in our different ways walking on glass; softly, and with bated breath. I shuddered to think what the response would be, now, if anyone made the mistake of seriously crossing Lucius.

He'd told me that the party had to be a good one. I knew that for my own safety it had to be better than good.

It was. Because Lucius and Agrippina would come by sea from Baiae I began by mooring six rafts offshore on which sat two dozen 'Sirens', girls chosen for their beauty and their singing voices. Around these islands swam other beautiful boys and girls dressed as Tritons and Nereids. Their job was to escort the imperial boat through the shallows to the landing stage. In the gardens leading up from the beach (lit, like the islands, by coloured lamps and torches) were more nymphs and satyrs, and a group of hidden musicians with flutes and lyres. The effect, although I do say so myself, was magnificent.

But not more magnificent than Lucius, when he finally arrived at the villa where I was waiting to welcome him. His mantle, covered in gold leaf and spangles which glittered in the lamplight, belonged on a stage rather than at a dinner party, and his eyelids were dusted with powdered pearls.

'Titus, it's beautiful! You've excelled yourself!' He hugged me. 'Hasn't he, Mother?'

'Very nice indeed, dear.' Agrippina looked frankly royal in stiff cloth of gold with a ruby tiara. She held out a hand, palm downwards. I kissed it. 'A lovely surprise.'

'I'm glad you're pleased, darling.' Lucius kissed her on the cheek. He looked back down towards the landing stage where the boats of the other guests were mooring and shouted: 'Anicetus! Are you all right?'

A figure disentangled itself from two hamadryads – recruited, like most of the nymphs and satyrs, from the Naples Prostitutes' Guild – and waved.

'The poor dear was terribly sick coming across.' Lucius grinned at me; at such close quarters the smell of his perfume almost had me rocking on my heels. 'For a Commander of the Fleet he's really the most dreadful sailor. And in a flat calm, too. Disgusting.' He giggled. 'I must see he gets more practice. Now, what else have you got for us?'

I led the way inside. I was rather proud of how I'd decorated the villa. Bushes and small trees in pots, interspersed with leafy branches and more coloured lights, broke up the stiff formality of the rooms into a series of grottoes with couches and tables strewn with flowers. The air was delicately scented with expensive perfumes; not that one could smell them in the emperor's presence, of course. By prearrangement as we entered, the most beautiful boy the Naples Guild could provide stepped forward and held out a wine tray with two golden cups.

Lucius took one of them. His eyes undressed the boy: not difficult, since he wore only a *cache-sexe* and a wreath of flowers.

'Titus!' he said. 'What a perfect little Ganymede! Wherever did you find him?'

The boy offered the other cup to Agrippina. She took it, frowning. Lucius turned to her.

'Oh, don't be silly, Mother!' he said. 'The child's an absolute pet!' He stretched out his hand and, his eyes never leaving her face, delicately fingered the lad's gilded nipples. 'Or don't you think so?'

'Yes, dear.' Agrippina, I could see, was not amused. 'He's very pretty.'

'Isn't he? Off you go, little one.' Lucius turned the boy round and patted his behind. He was still looking at Agrippina. 'Bring us some more wine later.' The child trotted off. 'Now, Titus, what's for dinner? I am starving, simply starving!'

'I thought you and the empress would like to dine in private,' I said.

That brought the first smile I'd seen so far from Agrippina. She reached down and squeezed Lucius's hand.

'Oh, how very thoughtful!' she murmured. 'Isn't it, dear?'

Instead of replying Lucius brushed the powdery whiteness of her forehead with his lips. Agrippina may still have been a very beautiful woman, but she was – I saw now in the brighter light from the oil lamps – very heavily made up. Under the white lead I could see the clear signs of crow's feet at the corners of her eyes and the edges of her mouth.

The villa's major-domo was waiting in the background. I called him over.

'The emperor and empress will eat immediately,' I said.

He bowed and waited for them to follow.

Lucius took my arm. 'Well done, Titus! Marvellous! Simply splendid!' he whispered, then winked. 'See you later, eh?'

I watched them go, then went back to the party.

It was an enormous success, especially the food: the Bay of Naples is famous for its fish. I'd carried the grotto theme to the gardens and the seashore, and we ate al fresco before turning to other more strenuous pursuits. I was sorry Silia had missed the festivities – she'd conjugal duties to perform – but I managed to enjoy myself well enough in her absence. Ganymede may have been otherwise engaged, but he had a friend, and I found two of the most delightful nymphs to make up a foursome.

I didn't see Lucius or Agrippina until much later, when the major-domo came to tell me that the imperial couple were leaving. Lucius's mood was strange. He had his arm around Agrippina's shoulders, hugging her close; and she smiled up at him with a curiously self-satisfied smile of her own, like a contented cat.

'Mother's a bit tired, Titus,' he said: there was that strange breathless quality to his voice which I'd noticed in the gymnasium. 'She wants to get straight back.'

'The empress's boat is waiting, sir.' The major-domo bowed. I could see the man was nervous, and wondered why.

'Ready, darling?' Lucius kissed Agrippina on the mouth. She responded, and I caught the flick of a tongue before he drew his head away. 'Off we go, then.'

'I'll see you to the landing stage,' I said.

We walked together through the now dimly lit gardens, trying not to step on the couples (or sometimes threesomes) who impinged here and there on the path. Agrippina, snuggled deep into Lucius's embrace, said nothing all the way.

The boat alongside the jetty was different to the one in which they'd arrived. It was lower in the water, and it had a large canopy covering the entire stern. Agrippina paused.

'What's this?' she said.

Lucius giggled and hugged her.

'A last little surprise. Isn't it beautiful? Go on. It's got such a lovely couch. You can sleep on the way back.'

'You're not coming?'

'My stomach's a little upset, darling. I'll go by road and meet you there.'

The crew were already on board, together with Agrippina's personal maid. The empress, I could see, was hesitating.

'You're sure you won't come, Nero?' she said.

'I said I'll go by road!' Lucius's face had suddenly darkened. 'Now don't be silly, Mother! It's perfectly safe! Off you go!'

They stood looking at each other for a long time, not touching. Then without another word Agrippina walked across the gangplank and stepped down into the covered cabin. Slaves undid the hawsers and the ship moved off.

'If your stomach's upset,' I said, turning to Lucius, 'why not . . .'

I stopped. He was watching the disappearing boat with empty eyes from which ran black, mascara'd tears.

'Don't leave me tonight, Titus,' he whispered. 'Come back with me to Baiae.'

Memory is a strange thing. As soon as he spoke I remembered where I'd heard that curiously breathless, excited voice before. It had been at our first dinner party at the palace, the night Britannicus died.

I felt, despite the warmth of the evening, suddenly cold.

23

I wasn't such a fool, of course, as to show him I'd noticed anything strange in his behaviour, far less guessed what lay behind it.

'There's no reason for us to go back to Baiae, surely,' I said. 'Why not stay here tonight?'

'Oh, I couldn't do that.' Lucius's eyes were still glazed. He was smiling, or his mouth was, and he suddenly jerked his head sideways in a curious spastic motion. The effect was ghastly. 'Not after promising Mother. The poor darling would be terribly disappointed if I didn't turn up.'

'Let me see if the carriage is ready, then,' I said; and gratefully escaped.

The hallway was empty – most of the remaining guests were occupied in the bedrooms upstairs, or out in the garden – but as I dashed through I collided with Anicetus. The little Greek might be Lucius's Commander of the Fleet but he'd never look anything other than the inky-fingered schoolmaster he'd once been.

'Has she gone?' he said. 'The empress?'

'Yes, she's gone.' His eyes shifted, much as Lucius's had. 'Anicetus, what's going on?'

'For Apollo's sake, don't ask!' He was pale as a ghost. 'How's the emperor?'

'I left him on the jetty. He wants me to go back with him to Baiae.' A slave came up and I sent him to see to the carriage. 'Anicetus, for the last time, what the hell's happening?'

He looked over my shoulder. His eyes widened and he put a skinny finger to his lips. I turned. Lucius was coming from the direction of the garden.

'Titus, where's that bloody carriage?' he said. His voice was more controlled now, and the suppressed excitement was back. 'I want to get home.'

'It's just coming.'

'Well, I wish it would hurry up. I'm completely knackered.' He grinned. 'Anicetus, you'll join us, of course.' It was an order. The little man bowed.

We went out of the front door to wait in the drive.

'Mother should be well on her way now.' Lucius gazed up at the sky. 'Isn't it a glorious night for a sail?'

Neither Anicetus nor I replied. The carriage arrived and we climbed in.

The journey to Baiae was uneventful. Lucius said nothing, simply stared out of the window into the blackness. In the corner next to me Anicetus snored gently.

We were a scant mile from the town when I realised that Lucius was looking straight at me, or rather through me. His eyes were empty as they had been on the jetty, and he was crying.

'You only wanted power, darling,' he said softly. 'You didn't love me, not really, not for myself. I couldn't do anything else.'

I closed my eyes and pretended to be asleep.

It wasn't until the next morning when the messenger arrived from Bauli that we discovered that Agrippina was still alive.

The boat had collapsed, as it was meant to, halfway between Bauli and Baiae. Agrippina ought to have been crushed at once by the heavy iron weight which was concealed under the stern canopy, but the sides of her couch supported it long enough for her to roll clear and into the water. Despite a deep gash in her shoulder she swam quietly away and was picked up by some fishermen, who took her back to the villa.

Her maid wasn't so lucky. To give Agrippina time to escape she'd cried out from the water that she was the empress, and ordered the crew to help her. They had split the girl's skull with a boathook.

I didn't know all this until much later, of course. Agrippina's freedman carried quite a different story.

He came sidling in while we were having breakfast – Lucius,

Anicetus and I – in the imperial villa at Baiae. Lucius lay back on his couch and smiled at him with an air of expectancy.

'Well?' he said.

'I've a message, sir, from your mother. From the Lady Agrippina.'

The smile became a frozen mask.

'*From* my mother?'

'Yes, sir. She says that by divine mercy, sir, and your own lucky star she's escaped a dreadful accident.' The over-formal words came stiffly, and the last was carefully stressed. 'She says to tell you she's only slightly hurt, and she doesn't want you to visit her until she's better.'

Lucius was on his feet. He had caught the small table beside his couch with his knees as he stood up and tipped the contents out over the floor. A silver plate rolled across the marble and clattered to a stop against the far wall.

'Then she's not dead!' he whispered.

The man swallowed. 'No, lord. Only hurt. And she says . . .'

'*Guard!*'

The double doors burst open and the two soldiers on duty outside threw themselves into the room, their swords drawn. They stopped, confused.

Lucius held his hand out to the nearest.

'You!' he snapped. 'Give me that thing!'

The man glanced at his colleague, then handed the sword over hilt first.

Lucius dropped it at the messenger's feet.

'He tried to kill me,' he said calmly. 'This man tried to kill me. You all saw it. Titus. Anicetus. He's an assassin, sent by my mother to kill me.'

The messenger was gazing down at the sword in horror.

'Sir, I never!' he whispered. 'Jupiter strike me, I never!'

'*Arrest him!*' Lucius screamed.

Amid total silence the second soldier stepped forward. He took the man's arm and led him out without a word. Anicetus and I looked at each other.

The unarmed soldier bent to pick up the fallen sword and prepared to follow his colleague.

'Wait a moment.' Lucius laid a hand on his arm. 'Where's

your own weapon, darling?' The man simply stared, slack-jawed. 'Don't you know it's death for a soldier on guard duty to be without his sword?'

The soldier said nothing, but I could see the whites of his eyes. His left hand – half hidden behind his back – made the sign of the horns: the peasant's protection against madness and ill-wishing.

Lucius gave the man a violent shove towards the door.

'Oh, go away!' he snapped. 'I'll let you off this time. But don't let it happen again.'

The doors closed behind him. Lucius stood rigid for a moment. Then he started to shake, and his eyes bulged like a terrified bullock's.

'Help me, Titus,' he whispered. 'Help me. She wants to kill me. She's sent one man. She can send others.'

I was too shocked to speak. Anicetus was deathly pale and trembling like a leaf himself. Suddenly Lucius rounded on him, his forefinger stabbing the air.

'You! You're my fucking Commander of the Fleet! You do something! Take a warship over to Bauli and kill her!'

'Sir, I c-c-c- . . .' Anicetus stammered.

Lucius covered the space between them in two strides and grabbed the man by the neck of his tunic. The cloth tore.

'*Finish her, you bastard!*' he screamed. '*Fucking finish her!*'

Anicetus staggered out. I watched Lucius as I would have done a savage animal that had escaped from its cage, but he paid me no attention. Stumbling back to his breakfast couch, he lay down on his side and hugged his knees tight against his chest. One thumb stole into his mouth.

I left him as quietly as I could, still in his foetal crouch, sucking.

Anicetus and his men found Agrippina alone in her bedroom at the Baulan villa. When she knew that death was inevitable she tore her nightshirt to the groin and bared her stomach.

'Strike me here,' she said, pointing.

Her body was burned that evening, on one of my flower-decked party couches.

24

The next two days were dreadful: Lucius was in a dangerously unstable mood, at the same time remorseful and exultant and absolutely terrified of the consequences of Agrippina's death. If I'd dared I'd've gone back to Rome, but in his present state he would have viewed that as desertion and black treachery, and reacted accordingly. Worse, I had him all to myself: Anicetus was gone. When after the murder he had reported back to the emperor looking green as an unripe apple ('I was sick three times at the villa, Petronius. It wasn't the blood, though, it was the smell.') Lucius had thanked him coldly and packed him off to Misenum.

Seneca arrived post-haste from Rome. His carriage wheels had scarcely stopped before he was out and closeted with Lucius. I stayed up late, and alone, in the hope that he'd come and talk.

He did, eventually, at two in the morning. I motioned him towards the guest couch, but first he poured and drank a full cup of wine.

'I needed that,' he said simply. He sounded almost human.

'How's Nero?' I asked.

'Asleep. I persuaded him to let the doctor give him some poppy juice.' He leaned back wearily on the couch. His jowly cheeks were pouchy and grey as wash-leather, and he looked old. 'We'll weather it. It's not the end of the world.'

It irked me a little that he was taking the situation so calmly.

'Personally,' I said, 'I'd've thought you'd be delighted to be rid of Agrippina.'

'No one delights in murder, my dear fellow.' He pursed his

lips. 'I applaud the result, I deplore the method. It only remains to minimise the damage.'

'What a very moral attitude.'

'Don't judge me, Petronius. You called me a politician and you were right. It's the politician's task – and the philosopher's – to make the best of a bad job. Sometimes morality must give way to pragmatism. I'm only doing the best I can for Rome.'

It was late, and I'd no wish to quarrel. Besides, the man was clearly exhausted. I shrugged.

'I'm sorry. You're right, of course. So what does Rome think?'

He closed his eyes. The effect was horribly corpse-like.

'The Senate's glad to be rid of her, at any price, but the ordinary people are not happy. Not happy at all, in fact.' He frowned and then recited: '"Alcmaeon, Orestes and Nero are brothers/They all drew their penknives and did in their mothers."'

I laughed. 'What the hell's that?'

'A piece of doggerel I saw scrawled on a wall near the Appian Gate. Not by any means a unique graffito, I may say.'

'How sweet. At least it's literate.'

'Alcmaeon was misspelled.' He paused, and the eyes opened again. 'The army's a potential problem, too, of course. But then they always have been where the empress was concerned.'

I nodded, understanding. Hulking great legionaries can be soft as butter over the silliest things, and Agrippina had been the daughter of their hero Germanicus.

'Do you think there'll be trouble?'

'I hope not. There are no obvious contenders for the throne, Burrus is keeping his eyes open, and the officers at least are on our side. As I said, we'll weather it.' He reached over and poured himself another cup of wine. 'Do you mind?' I shook my head. 'My main worry – and this is confidential, Petronius – is the emperor himself. You will no doubt have noticed a certain deterioration in his condition.'

'He has seemed a little . . . distraught these last two days.'

Seneca gave a mirthless smile. 'Distraught. Yes. An understatement, of course. When I saw the lad he was raving. He claims Agrippina committed suicide after sending her freedman to murder him.'

'That's not true.'

'Oh, I know that perfectly well! The point is that Nero quite genuinely believes it.'

'He can't possibly. I was there.' I described the scene in the breakfast room. 'The poor man was executed for nothing.'

'Quite.' Seneca hesitated. 'If you take my advice you'll forget that little drama. And it was a drama, you know, pure theatre, despite its unpleasantly real conclusion. I wonder at times if the emperor is altogether sure of the difference between play-acting and reality any longer. You're very fortunate, my dear fellow, not to be packed off like our friend Anicetus. I doubt if Nero will want to see *him* again in a hurry.'

'I agree. So what do we do?'

He spread his hands. 'We do nothing, of course. What else can we do? Nero's in a state of panic at the moment, but that will pass when he sees that he's quite safe. And for the future all we can do is act as we have been acting these five years. Keep the poor boy's mind, such as it is, off the realities of power and occupied with his . . . other pursuits.' He tried a thin smile. 'Incidentally, your help there is invaluable and greatly appreciated.'

'Thank you. But I still feel that . . .'

There was a crash as the door of the room was thrown open. We both turned, startled. Lucius stood on the threshold supporting himself against the jamb, his eyes wide and staring.

'She was there!' he whispered. 'She was there, in the corner! Looking at me!'

He stumbled across the room towards us. Behind him a frightened slave held up a cloak as if it were a birdcatcher's net. We were both on our feet by now. Seneca was the first to move. He grabbed the cloak from the slave and wrapped it round Lucius's shoulders. Meanwhile I filled a cup with wine and held it ready.

'It's all right,' I said quietly, as I would have done to a terrified child. 'It's all right, Lucius. You've been dreaming. It was just a dream.'

Lucius turned his blank gaze in my direction. 'But I saw her! Standing in the corner! Her hair was loose and blowing in the draught from the window, and her belly . . .'

He made a horrible cutting and sagging movement with his

hand across his own stomach, and I felt the hairs rise on the back of my neck. Then he turned his head away and was violently sick on the floor. The room suddenly stank of vomit and stale poppy juice mixed with wine.

'My dear boy.' Seneca spoke firmly. 'The empress is dead.'

'You think I don't know?' Lucius's head swung towards him, his mouth flecked with sick. 'She said I'd killed her! How could she lie to me like that?'

'It was a bad dream.' Seneca's hand was on his shoulder. 'Nothing but a bad dream. Now go back to bed, my dear fellow, and . . .'

'No!' He lurched over to the nearest couch and collapsed on to it, his face buried in his hands. 'It wasn't a dream! I saw her! I saw her and she lied and lied and her eyes burned me, they burned! How could she say those things? I'd never hurt Mummy, never, no matter how bad she was!' Suddenly he sat up. 'Maybe she isn't dead after all. Maybe it's all a mistake. Seneca!' He grabbed the old man's wrist. I could see his fingers whiten and I wondered that the bone didn't snap. 'Make her dead! Please! Make her dead!'

'Nero,' Seneca said quietly, but with great firmness, 'listen to me, my boy. She's dead already. You've had a nightmare, that's all. It's very late. Go back to bed and sleep.'

I motioned to the slaves – there were three of them now, wide-eyed as owls. Gently, as Seneca prised the emperor's fingers from his wrist, they eased him to his feet and half-carried, half-walked him towards the door.

When he had gone we looked at each other. Then Seneca shook his head, and left without another word.

I didn't sleep much myself that night. Yes, it was a dream. Of course it was. It couldn't have been anything else.

The strange thing was that I'd been present when Anicetus had made his report, and he hadn't given any details of the murder to Lucius. Certainly he had not told him that he had stabbed the empress in the belly.

25

Seneca was right, although the ease with which the affair blew over was sickening. Lucius stayed in Naples until September. The Senate and provinces sent message after message congratulating him on his narrow escape from assassination. Agrippina's statues went to the lime-kilns, her name was chiselled from the public monuments, and her birthday was included in the calendar of unlucky days. All no more than the dreadful woman deserved, of course, but still distasteful.

To celebrate his return, Burrus organised a show of gladiators in the Taurian Amphitheatre on Mars Field.

'Seneca's not happy about it, and the emperor won't be either,' he told me privately when the arrangements were made. 'Neither of them are what you'd call fans.' That was putting it mildly: one thing Lucius did share with Seneca was his irrational hatred of blood sports. 'But it's for the best, Petronius. The mob need a bit of blood to get them back on our side. And there's nothing wrong with a good clean sword-fight. The lad'll just have to grit his teeth and play the Roman.'

When I saw him in the tunnel leading to the imperial box Lucius already looked a little green, even beneath the carefully applied make-up. He was with Poppaea and Burrus, who were pointedly ignoring each other, talking to a man with thick curly black hair bound at the back in a horseman's queue. Seneca was not present.

The emperor looked up and saw me.

'Ah, here's my arbiter! Titus, come over here and let me introduce you to Tiggy!'

The other man turned. Even with hindsight I believe our mutual dislike was immediate. He had the coarse features and large teeth of a southern Italian peasant, and he was trying not to scowl as he held out his hand.

'Ofonius Tigellinus,' he said.

'Titus Petronius.' I took the hand. It was as big as a shovel-blade, and almost as hard. His grip nearly cost me my four fingers. 'Delighted to meet you.'

Lucius was eyeing us with amusement.

'Tiggy breeds the finest racehorses you've ever seen,' he said. 'And he's marvellous fun. I'm sure you'll be great friends.'

'I don't doubt it,' I said. Tigellinus gave my hand a final painful squeeze before releasing it.

'If you're ready now, sir, we'll go up.' The harassed official who was orchestrating the day's arrangements stepped aside.

'Oh, all right!' Lucius frowned. 'If we must I suppose we'd better. Let's get it over with, darlings.'

Trumpets blared as we entered the box. For a moment I was dazzled by the sun shining straight into my eyes, and then the roar of the crowd hit me like a fist. The amphitheatre was packed to capacity. Even on this relatively cool day I could smell its distinctive odour of human sweat and animal dung, faintly overlaid with a miasma of stale blood. I noticed that both Lucius and Poppaea were holding scented handkerchiefs to their noses.

The emperor waved to the crowd while we sat. I was between Burrus and Tigellinus. Burrus and I exchanged nods. He was looking iller and older than ever. Lucius took his place in the ornate president's chair, with Poppaea beside him. The trumpets blared again, the gates to the side of the arena swung open and the cheering swelled to an ear-hurting howl as the fighters emerged.

Burrus had done us proud. There were fifty of them, top-grade specimens, muscle-heavy or sleek as leopards. They lined up facing the box in their matched pairs and gave the traditional formal salute.

Tigellinus was grinning. His elbow caught me a painful blow in the ribs.

'Some nice stuff here.' he whispered. 'Better than the broken-winded hacks we get down south.'

The gladiators filed out, leaving the first two pairs – heavily armed Fish-men against Skirmishers – alone on the sand. As the gates closed the four men gave another salute and then crouched facing each other.

'This should be good,' Burrus grunted. 'Two sets of brothers. According to the trainer their families hate each other's guts.'

The taller of the Skirmishers lunged, his light spear darting towards an opponent's chest. The Fish-man leaped back, pulling his oblong shield round to protect his ribs, then chopped viciously sideways with his short sword; but the Skirmisher was already away, moving like a dancer to the edge of the arena. The crowd yelled.

Meanwhile the second of the Fish-men had drawn blood. As his brother had moved back he had rushed forward past his opponent's guard and thrust at the man's stomach. The edge of his sword slid across the outside of the retreating Skirmisher's thigh, laying it open to the bone. The man stumbled and almost fell.

'Got the bastard!' Tigellinus muttered.

'Wait!' That was Burrus.

The wounded Skirmisher brought his shield round hard, catching his opponent's sword-arm a sickening blow on the wrist just where the protective armour ended. The Fish-man's sword thudded on to the sand and a spear drove into his throat beneath the rim of the visored helmet. Blood jetted. The Fish-man crumpled to his knees in a clatter of ironware.

'Good stuff!' Tigellinus's hand pounded the rail. 'Didn't I tell you, Petronius? Straight in and no messing!'

I agreed; the fight was shaping up very nicely indeed.

Half the crowd were on their feet, screaming. The victorious Skirmisher drew out his spear and raised it high above his head; just as the first Fish-man turned and buried his sword to the hilt full in his unprotected back.

'Oh, well done!' Burrus said. 'Jupiter, what a fight, eh? Two clean deaths in five minutes!'

Tigellinus's eyes were alight. 'The stupid bastard never knew what hit him!'

I looked past him to the imperial couple. Poppaea was sitting stiff as a statue, her hand clenched in her lap. Lucius had turned away. He was looking greener than ever.

It was one against one now. The remaining Fish-man's helmeted head swung slowly round towards his remaining opponent, who stood waiting several yards off. They stared at each other while the crowd yelled above them. Then the Fish-man dropped his own sword, stooped and picked up his brother's. He moved forward at a lumbering run.

The Skirmisher danced away, keeping a ten yards' distance. There were some boos, but most of the crowd shouted encouragement, knowing it was in the lighter-armed man's interest to tire his opponent out. Clearly the Fish-man realised what was happening, because he stopped and waited.

'That fellow's no fool,' Burrus grunted. 'Nor's the other one. This is going to be a long hard slog after all.'

I settled back to watch as the two fighters circled each other. The Skirmisher darted forward, but his spearpoint scraped against the iron facing of the Fish-man's shield and the heavy short sword hacked at the shaft. The Skirmisher spun away, moving towards the other man's blind side.

'Time for drinkies.' Tigellinus produced a leather flask of wine, unstoppered it and drank. He passed it to me without wiping the top. 'You want some?'

I shook my head. Tigellinus shrugged and took a second, longer swig. Below us, the two fighters were still circling each other. The crowd was getting restless. Someone to my left, in the strong tones of an Ostian bargeman, yelled: 'Get on with it!' Whether he was shouting at the Fish-man or the Skirmisher, I didn't know. Perhaps he didn't know himself.

Suddenly the Skirmisher made his move. He had slowly been retreating backwards, enticing his opponent towards him and gradually increasing his speed. Now he darted left and lunged at the gap between the Fish-man's mailed sword-arm and the edge of his shield. The Fish-man's sword flashed up and down, catching the spearshaft a foot above the head and severing it cleanly. Then, as his opponent tried to regain his balance, he swung his shield round and with all his force smashed its massive iron boss into the man's side. The Skirmisher screamed and fell, dropping both spear and shield and clutching his shattered ribcage.

I expected – everyone expected – the Fish-man to wait for the life or death verdict from the emperor, but he didn't. Throwing aside his own shield, he dragged the screaming man by the hair across to where his brother lay. There he pulled his head back as far as it would go and slit his throat above the corpse. The crowd yelled its approval.

Lucius was on his feet, white-faced and swaying like a drunkard.

'*Bastard! Fucking barbarian bastard!*' he screamed.

Poppaea and Burrus gripped him by the arms and pulled him down; although I doubt if anyone noticed that. Not the Fish-man, who had his helmet off and was waving his bloody sword aloft in triumph. Not the crowd: they were shouting themselves hoarse and throwing fruit, coins, nuts – anything that came to hand – into the arena. Tigellinus was laughing quietly to himself and sipping from his wine flask.

Between them, Poppaea and Burrus got the emperor settled as the Fish-man made his triumphal tour of the arena and raised his sword a last time in salute to the imperial box. Slaves with hooks dragged off the dead fighters while others scattered fresh sand over the pools of blood. The second set of gladiators marched through the gates.

Instead of returning their salute, Lucius turned to Burrus. He was pale-faced and shaking. His finger stabbed towards the spot where the three corpses had lain, and the baying crowd beyond.

'That's your Rome!' he hissed. 'That's the peak of your fucking so-called civilised Roman society! Well, you can stay and watch the other murders if you like. I'm going home!'

We stared at him in silence. Burrus's expression was unreadable. As slaves sprang to open the door of the imperial box, Lucius paused. He was still trembling, his face now purple with fury. 'Oh, and once this shambles is over I want to see you at the palace! All of you! Seneca as well!'

26

Burrus sent an urgent message to Seneca to meet us on the Palatine. If he was surprised to see Tigellinus with us when he arrived he didn't show it, but I noticed he was even more formal and reserved than usual. The warning was well taken. While we kicked our heels in the palace waiting-room we kept our mouths firmly shut.

Lucius received us in his private sanctum. He was on his feet, pacing the room, and he still looked angry.

'Well? Did you enjoy your little blood-bath, darlings?' he demanded. 'Do you feel suitably purged, all of you?'

'Speaking personally, yes,' Burrus said equably. 'And the mob was happy, which is the main thing. They cheered you at the end, Nero, even if you did choose to deprive them of your presence.'

I winced. It was dangerous to oppose the emperor in his present mood, but Burrus was right and Lucius knew it. No ruler can afford to ignore the mob; and Lucius wanted, more than most, to feel loved.

'My dear fellow, I sympathise with your feelings, believe me.' Seneca was more conciliatory. 'I've no time for legalised butchery myself, as you well know. But Burrus has a point. Unlike us the mob are crude souls. We can't expect them to be capable of true catharsis, they simply haven't the intelligence.'

Lucius threw himself on to a bench and picked up a small bronze statuette from the floor. He was scowling. 'Oh, sit down! Sit down, all of you!' He waved irritably towards the chairs. 'You're quite right. It's just it's such a terrible waste! Perhaps I was wrong to be upset. It's not the people's fault, not really, poor dears. As Seneca says, they don't know any better. And they absolutely adore me.'

'Who wouldn't, when they knew you?' Tigellinus's flattery was so outrageous it took my breath away.

'Exactly.' Lucius was nodding, and absently stroking the bronze; it was Corinthian, a boy athlete, and beautiful. 'The personal touch, that's what's missing. I've been thinking about it a lot lately. All the people need – all Rome needs – is to be shown how a truly civilised man behaves, to be educated by example, and all this silliness will vanish. You agree?'

Beside me, I felt Seneca hesitate.

'In principle, yes,' he said cautiously. 'Mind you, one cannot change human nature overnight. Philosophers have been trying for centuries. It's a long-drawn-out process, and uncertain at the best of times.'

'Oh, I know that, darling.' Lucius set the statuette aside. 'I'm not a fool. But I am the emperor, and if anyone can do it I can. Yes?'

'Of course.' I swear Tigellinus winked at me; but I wasn't about to fall for that nonsense. I kept my face straight, all studious attention. 'You're quite right. If anyone can civilise us it's you.'

Seneca cleared his throat. 'What exactly, Nero, did you have in mind?'

The emperor was becoming excited. 'Well, you see, for a start there're all these silly barriers. Us and them. And then this stupid anti-Greek prejudice. We've got to get rid of all that. Open people's eyes to the wider world, for their own good.' He turned to me. 'Titus, dear, you know what I'm getting at, don't you? You're on my side?'

'Oh, yes.' I wondered where this was taking us.

'My dear boy,' Seneca said calmly. 'It's not a question of sides. Perhaps if you could tell us a little more about your plans we might understand better.'

'But it's so simple!' Lucius was on his feet now, and beaming at us. 'I've been training for this all my life! Think of it as a divine mission!'

Burrus stiffened. He was the oldest of us, and had the clearest memories of the mad godlet Caligula.

'Divine mission?' he said.

Lucius smiled at him.

'To civilise Rome. To bring her a little basic culture.'

There was a silence.

'For example?' Burrus's face was wooden.

'Athletics. Ballet. Theatre. Musical performances. All the usual stuff.' I thought of the plans he'd shown me two years before, for a 'Greek' amphitheatre in Mars Field. They had come to nothing in the end, but the idea, it seemed, had persisted. 'Darlings, it would be brilliant! A total renaissance!'

'And your part in this would be . . .?' Burrus said.

'Oh, an active one, of course! I mean, I may be emperor, but I've got to have some fun, haven't I? And we'd offer prizes, naturally, to encourage people to get involved.'

'"People"?' I wondered how Nero's Commander of Praetorians could get the word out between his clenched teeth.

'Anyone who likes! Anyone at all! Naturally I'd expect the top families to set an example. They're not all stuffy old faggots like you, my dear. They'd be thrilled to be asked, I'm sure.'

Burrus had gone beetroot red. He half rose from his chair.

'That's . . .' he began.

'. . . an interesting idea, my dear fellow,' Seneca finished smoothly, his hand gripping Burrus's wrist. 'But perhaps one that needs some discussion before we put it into practice.'

Lucius ignored him. He was striding the room. 'I thought we could start with the new Vatican Racetrack. I might give a little demonstration of chariot-driving.'

I thought Burrus would have a stroke there and then.

'You mean,' he whispered, 'you would drive a chariot yourself? In public?'

'Of course, darling. Why not?' Lucius turned his smile on Tigellinus. 'I'm good enough, aren't I, Tiggy?'

Tigellinus was smiling too. He was the only one of us completely at his ease, and I wondered if Lucius had discussed this with him already.

'You're very good, sir,' he said. 'Better than Hermippus any day.' Hermippus was the leading charioteer of the Greens, Lucius's favourite team.

'There you are.' Lucius's smile broadened. 'And Tiggy knows what he's talking about. He'll be supplying the horses.'

Ah. So he had known. And it also explained why Tigellinus had been invited to this little confab.

'Nero, I'm sorry,' Burrus said, 'but you cannot possibly do this.'

Lucius went very still, as did we all.

'But I'm the emperor, my dear,' he said quietly. 'And I can do anything I fucking well like.'

'Burrus, please!' Seneca's face was impassive, but I could see sweat on his forehead. 'Our young friend is perfectly correct. We can only advise. If he chooses not to take our advice, then there is an end of it.' He turned to Lucius. 'Perhaps at first . . . a few invited guests . . . to give people a little time to get used to the idea? You said yourself it would be a mistake to force things along too quickly.'

'Did I?' Lucius frowned. 'Perhaps I did. It doesn't matter much. And if it'll keep old poker-arse here happy then we'll do it that way. But in principle you're not opposed, are you?'

'How could I possibly be? As you say, my dear fellow, you are the emperor.'

'And there's an end of it.' Lucius was beaming at us again. 'Oh, good. I'm glad we're all friends again. Don't worry, you'll see I'm right.'

'Might I ask' – Seneca was delicate – 'what else you have in mind?'

Lucius sat down on the bench. 'I told you. Lots of things. A theatrical festival, for a start. Ballet, tragic recitals. I've got some wonderful songs lined up.' He giggled. 'Poppy's been on at me to shave my beard, she says it tickles. That would be the excuse. I mean, a first shave's awfully important to you old Romans, isn't it, Burrus darling? Terribly traditional! I thought we might call them the Youth Games.'

Burrus's lips set in a line. Lucius, noticing, scowled and turned away from him.

'Oh, please yourself, you old fart!' he snapped. 'That's enough for tonight anyway, you're all giving me a headache. Now go away and sulk.'

We left.

* * *

Seneca had a dinner engagement elsewhere on the Palatine. I shared my litter with Burrus, who was still fuming.

'The fool's lost what little sense he had!' he burst out as soon as the curtains closed. 'If he goes through with this idiotic scheme he'll have the whole establishment up in arms!'

'Things could be worse,' I said. 'At least he hasn't gone paranoid like Tiberius, or wants us all to burn incense to him like Caligula.'

But Burrus was not to be pacified.

'Perhaps if he had the decency to go properly mad I'd have more sympathy for him,' he growled. 'At least then we'd know where we stood.'

I liked Burrus, and felt I owed him a little bit of honesty.

'Personally I'm quite looking forward to it,' I said. 'Rome could do with a good sharp breath of fresh air.'

He stared at me as if I'd gone mad myself.

'You're not serious!'

'Of course I'm serious. Compared with Greece Rome's a bore, and only two steps this side of barbarism. I've always thought so.'

He sighed as if giving me up as a bad job. 'Petronius, we've had this conversation before. The Greeks are fine in their way, but they're water to Rome's oil. An emperor who tries to mix the two will have his work cut out, and he'll fail in the end.'

'We'll see. But I think Nero's got a valid point, and I wish him luck.'

'Then you're as big a fool as he is.'

We subsided into silence, until I thought he'd fallen asleep. I pulled the litter's curtain aside and stared out into the darkness. Then he suddenly said: 'By the way, what did you think of Tigellinus?'

I turned back.

'Not a lot, my dear.'

He chuckled. 'Me neither. The man's a complete chancer, and rotten as a maggoty apple.'

'Who is he exactly?'

'An ex-slave of Agrippina's. Caligula exiled him for having it off with his mistress and her sister and he went over to Greece. He made a small fortune in the luxury fish business and then oiled his way back to Italy. These days he breeds horses for the racetrack near Tarentum.'

'A colourful character. Nero seems quite fond of him.'

He grunted and nodded. 'Yes, doesn't he? And that's worrying. Like I said, the man's a chancer. We'll have to keep our eyes on darling Tiggy.'

But it was two years before Tigellinus began to make his presence properly felt; and by that time Burrus was dead.

27

Lucius's demonstration of chariot-driving raised even more metaphorical dust than literal. Dressed in gorgeous robes of Coan silk, made up to the eyebrows and with his hair bound back with a golden charioteer's cord, the ruling Emperor of Rome galloped his four horses round the Vatican Racetrack beneath a blue canopy studded with gold stars. Did it well, too: Tigellinus had exaggerated when he compared him to Hermippus, but not by much.

Rome was delighted. She was horrified. She was scandalised. The drive cocked a glorious snook at convention, and it split the city. The mob was wildly enthusiastic, of course, but then the Roman mob will cheer anything. The upper classes were another matter. Some were laughing in their sleeves. Some, mostly the younger element and those who appreciated what Lucius was trying to do, applauded, while the diehard traditionalists watched with frozen faces and tight lips, and privately consigned him to ten kinds of hell.

I'd arranged to watch the up-and-coming Youth Games with Silia, but in the event we were a group of four.

'I've asked Acte up to stay, Titus,' she said when we were finalising arrangements; Acte had moved out of the palace several months before and was living in the villa Lucius had bought her at Puteoli. 'She's had such a lonely time of it, poor dear. Oh, and Gnaeus as well. I wouldn't usually inflict him on you but he's terribly upset just now over some little Corinthian flute-player and the poor lamb needs comforting. You don't mind too much, do you?'

'Of course not, darling! Not at all!' What could one say? All the same it had all the makings of a disastrous outing. Arruntius was five steps to the right of Cato and he wouldn't normally be seen dead at a concert.

The games began with a religious ceremony that was almost pure theatre. After a bull-burning that left the whole city smelling like a cookshop Lucius climbed the steps of Jupiter's temple holding aloft a beautiful pearl-studded gold casket. This box contained his beard-shavings, which in accordance with tradition he deposited with the god. ('The old dear'll like a bit of camp, Titus,' he'd confided to me earlier. 'He's quite a show-off himself, and he'd've made a simply marvellous actor.')

That was just the start. Our major task over the next few days was to keep Arruntius from apoplexy. There was the female ballet-dancer, for example, who gave us a tolerable Cassandra ('Her brother was City Judge, Petronius!') and, worst of all, the scene where Pasiphae, shut up in the hollow wooden cow, is made love to by her husband's bull – the latter danced superbly by Paris. ('Jupiter! He's screwing her! The fellow's actually screwing her!')

Paris was, too, but very tastefully. Not even Acte blushed. Under the circumstances I thought it better not to tell Arruntius that 'Pasiphae' was the wife of a noted senator and had volunteered her services. That information, I suspect, would've finished the poor darling off totally.

On the last day Lucius took the stage himself.

It was meant as a surprise, of course, but I doubt very much if there was anyone in the packed theatre who didn't know beforehand. Even so, the silence as he stepped on to the platform in his spangled harpist's gown was absolute. Silia and I had to hold Arruntius down.

The applause came wave upon wave. It was led by a specially recruited clique of youngsters whom the emperor had trained himself in great secrecy: Lucius was taking no chances. There were three groups, scattered throughout the theatre. The first kept up a low buzzing, the second applauded with cupped hands and the third with their hands stiff. The result was impressive. It went on for what seemed hours before he held up his hand for silence, and struck his first note.

He gave us one of Terpnus's best, the lament of Niobe over

her slaughtered children. Each note was pure as a bell, and the total had me almost in tears.

'Isn't he good?' Acte whispered proudly.

I nodded, quite speechless. He was better than good. Emperor or not, madman or not, and flattery aside, Lucius was a superb performer. Composition, performance and phrasing were all excellent. Even a Roman audience, I felt, must appreciate quality when they heard it.

Some of them all too evidently didn't. Arruntius, wedged between me and Silia, had a face like an ancestral death-mask. He was swearing under his breath.

The song ended and the applause began. It was deafening as before, but the lad deserved it, every bit. I was only sorry that it meant nothing at all. As Emperor of Rome, Lucius would've got as much if he'd sung like a crow.

As an encore he played a piece of his own: the death-song of Attis. I doubt if Terpnus himself could've faulted it. I looked around the audience. There were some rapt faces, to be sure, but there were more closed ones, and when the song ended these were often the people who applauded loudest. I spotted Seneca, sitting in the front row, and Burrus off to the left with the honour guard of Praetorians. I couldn't see their expressions, but I noticed that they'd the decency to keep their applause within reason.

Arruntius, too, was barely clapping.

'It's a disgrace,' he muttered. 'A disgrace.'

'I thought he did very well, dear,' Silia said. 'Who would have thought he'd have such a lovely voice?'

'In the past any citizen who appeared on stage lost his citizenship automatically.' Arruntius may have been angry but he wasn't a fool; he kept his voice down. 'That's still the law, so far as I know. And for an emperor to do it is nothing short of blasphemy.'

'Nonsense.' Silia sniffed. 'Besides, how can it be blasphemy, dear?'

'You know what I mean! Nero's . . .'

I laid a warning hand on his arm. Lucius had raised his hand for silence, and the covering noise of the applause was dying away.

He gave us another song, and then another. Finally, after the fifth encore – and a good hour after the concert had been scheduled to end – he made his bow and left the stage. The applause continued, but the emperor did not reappear.

I let the rest of our row – a frozen-faced senior finance officer and his party – clear itself and then stood up.

'Let's go backstage and offer our congratulations,' I said. 'He'll expect it.'

Arruntius looked at me as if I'd made an indecent proposal.

'You can do as you like, Petronius,' he said slowly, 'but I'm going home.'

'Oh, Gnaeus, don't be such a sourpuss!' Silia took his arm. 'Come on, dear! You too, Acte.'

'Not me.' She was shaking her head. 'Lucius – the emperor, I mean – won't want to see me.'

'Rubbish! You're not in disgrace, dear! You chose to leave Rome, he didn't send you away. Now come along, both of you!'

'Silia, I've told you.' Arruntius pulled his arm roughly from her grasp. 'I'm going home. I'll see you later.'

And without another word he walked away from us towards the exit. Silia looked after him fondly.

'He is an old grouch, isn't he?' she said. 'Never mind, we're better off without him.'

Lucius was in his dressing-room, together with some fifty other people. The result was a full-scale party.

'Titus!' He beamed. 'Silia, dear! Lovely! Come over here and give us a kiss! Paris, get them a drink, darling! The good stuff, not that rotgut you've been palming off on me, you stingy bugger!'

I fought my way through the crowd, dragging Silia by the hand behind me. They were all, I noticed, theatrical types or their hangers-on. Grey or bald pates and broad purple stripes were not much in evidence, and there was no sign of either Burrus or Seneca.

'Who's that you've got with you?' Lucius had kissed first me and then Silia and was peering over our shoulders. 'Not Acte?' He pushed past us and enveloped her in a hug. 'Acte! How marvellous! I thought you were sulking in Campania!'

'I wasn't sulking.' Acte's broad ugly face was alight and wet with tears. 'You know I wasn't. Lucius, love, you were wonderful!'

'I was, wasn't I?' Lucius grinned and kissed her. 'Paris, make that three wines, darling! And if you spill them I'll have your wollocks docked!'

'Here, gracious lord.' Paris spun through the crowd with a silver tray held high, then fell at Lucius's feet in a single fluid motion, arms raised and eyes rolling. On the tray were three cups of wine, filled to the brim. The silver was unmarked. As an exercise in movement, it was breathtaking.

Lucius laughed and prodded him with his toe.

'Don't be sarcastic, you old poof!' he said. 'And get up, you look like a manic chimpanzee.'

Paris mimed huff, and went back to join his own group of admirers.

'Now.' Lucius turned to us. 'Tell me again how marvellous I was. And don't spare my blushes.'

'You were superb,' I said. 'Really superb.'

He looked at me closely, then nodded as if satisfied.

'I was nervous as a cat all the time, of course. And my breath simply *stank* of onions. Gods, how I hate onions!'

'Then why eat them?' Silia was for ever practical.

'The best thing for the voice, darling. That and chives in oil, which are even more loathsome. Still, it was worth it, wasn't it? I could've gone on for hours, they absolutely lapped me up. Except for old Seneca and Burrus, of course. Did you see them, the old farts, with their bum-faces, trying to pretend they were enjoying it? I thought I'd burst, honestly!'

'I liked the support group,' I said, sipping my wine. 'Very impressive.'

'He didn't need them.' Acte was still radiant. I'd never seen her look so proud.

Lucius bent and kissed the top of her head.

'Perhaps not,' he said, 'but they did well, didn't they? Some of them were sailors I got off a boat from Alexandria, lovely boys. I may keep them, just for fun.' There was a movement by the door. Lucius glanced up and frowned. 'Oh, hell, here come the bum-faces! Stand by your beds, darlings!'

I turned round. Seneca was pushing his way through the crowd as quickly as his dignity would allow.

'Oh, my dear fellow!' He reached us and embraced Lucius. 'Well done! My heartiest congratulations!'

'Thank you. Where's the other . . . where's Burrus?'

'He sends his congratulations too.' Seneca's smile enveloped us all. 'Petronius. Silia. Acte, my dear, delighted to see you again.'

'You enjoyed the performance, then?' Lucius was smiling back.

'Certainly.'

'How much? Tell me.'

Seneca's smile froze. 'Do forgive me, Nero,' he said. 'I don't quite understand you.'

'It's an easy question, darling. Just how much did you enjoy my singing?'

'Very much.' He hesitated. 'Very much indeed.'

'Very much isn't enough.' Lucius hadn't raised his voice, but the room was suddenly still. 'Not enough by far.'

Seneca wasn't smiling now. He looked at me for support.

'What Annaeus Seneca is saying, sir' – I put on my best pompous voice – 'is that he enjoyed your singing as much as a bum-faced old fart with no ear for music can enjoy such a sterling performance.'

It was as if a string that had been wound too tight had suddenly snapped. The emperor blinked, and hugged me.

'Oh, Titus!' he said, grinning. 'Isn't he terrible, Seneca? Imagine calling my chief adviser a tone-deaf bum-faced old fart! Whatever next?'

'Not at all, my boy.' I could see that the old man was desperately trying to regain his composure. For a moment he'd been frightened, and I didn't blame him. 'He's quite right. I never have appreciated music properly. But I do enjoy it, as far as lies within my power.'

'Then that's all we can expect, isn't it? It's not your fault you've got a tin ear. Or that you and Burrus are a pair of bum-faced old farts. So long as you try.' People were sniggering around us. As if he were onstage, he held up a hand for silence. 'We really will have to educate them, won't we, Titus? Seneca and Burrus both.'

Seneca thanked me, later, as we were leaving the building. I laughed it off as nothing, but we both knew that the emperor had given his two advisers a clear and final warning.

28

I was afraid that Lucius would go too far too quickly after his victory over the Roman philistines. In fact he acted very sensibly.

'Some people were terribly upset about the games, Titus.' We were in the Greens' stable at the racetrack ten days later: Hermippus had a new team to show off. 'I mean, I know it's silly but there you are. The next day in the Senate House it was like talking to a row of mummies. Apronianus was biting his cheek so hard I thought he'd draw blood.'

We moved down the row.

'At least it was his own cheek,' I said. 'And presumably the facial variety.'

'Oh, come on, darling!' Lucius sniggered. 'I'm serious! They were terribly complimentary to my face, of course, but they don't like what I'm trying to do one bit. Do they?'

'No,' I said. 'They don't. They don't like it because they don't understand it.'

He stroked the nearest horse's nose; it was a gelding of pure Spanish blood and must've cost the Greens a fortune.

'Exactly. Bloody Romans. Well, I'm afraid they'll just have to lump it. I've decided to put on another festival next year. A proper Greek one this time.'

I wasn't unduly surprised. The Youth Games had been tremendously popular with everyone but the hard-liners. We'd come a long way since Cincinnatus at his plough, and it was about time we acknowledged the fact.

'You'll be taking part, naturally?' I was politic.

The horse in the stall next door whickered and nuzzled

Lucius's arm. He took an apple from the basket by the wall and held it out for the pink lips to grasp.

'No. No, I don't think so,' he said. 'I've scratched that particular itch for the time being, and it causes too much bad feeling. There'll be no ballet-dancing, either, for obvious reasons.'

I nodded. Greek festivals were solemn religious occasions, and ballet-dancers an insalubrious lot: Mysticus, one of Paris's colleagues, for example, had recently caused a scandal by his part in the deaths of two purple-stripers at a party. One heart failure *in coitu* I could have understood – the gentlemen concerned were septuagenarians, after all, and Mysticus was an energetic soul – but two in one evening was careless.

Lucius had taken more apples and was moving along the line of horses. They were from Sicily, black as midnight with not a white hair among them. I thought of Tigellinus.

'Aren't they lovely?' he said. He patted the last black head. 'This one's the best. Brontes. A real hundred-racer, you can see. I wouldn't mind driving him myself.'

'Why don't you?'

'The farts again. I can't afford to offend them too much, Titus, and I have made my point.' He called the groom over and wiped his hands on the towel which the man held out. 'Actually I was meaning to ask you about another idea of mine.'

'Oh, yes?' I said guardedly.

'Don't look so worried. It's nothing special. What do you think of having regular poetry evenings?'

'You mean recitations?'

'Gods, no! Something on the Greek model. Where people can come to supper and give whatever they're working on an airing, so everyone can chip in with comments and suggestions.'

'I think it's an excellent idea. Who would you invite?'

'Anyone. Everyone. Even Seneca, if he'll promise to behave.'

'Burrus?'

'That old goat wouldn't recognise an anapaest if it reared up and kicked him, darling.' I laughed. 'I'm serious. He has his talents but literary criticism isn't among them. What do you think of the idea, though? Really?'

'I've told you. It's excellent.'

'Good.' He patted Brontes's neck. 'I thought you'd like it. We'll start at once.'

I enjoyed Lucius's literary evenings, but they led to my first little tiff with Seneca. The prime cause was Lucillius, a podgy Greek who wrote epigrams. He was giving us a few of these after supper one evening, and the last went something like this:

> Thyestes ate his own child: poor old fellow,
> He has my sympathies. Still –
> Wouldn't it be nice if Seneca had done the same?

Naughty and not very tactful, especially since the great man was sharing his couch at the time. Everyone roared: I was eating a grape and choked on it, and my own couch-partner had to pound me on the back.

Seneca swelled up like an outraged rooster.

'If that,' he said, 'is a hit at my recent tragedy then it is not particularly funny.'

Lucillius shrugged and raised a beautifully curved eyebrow. While Seneca puffed himself up even more, he turned towards the emperor and held up a languid hand in the classic pose of a gladiator appealing for the verdict. The room erupted, and Seneca looked angrier than ever.

'Oh, come on, Seneca!' Lucius said. 'Don't be such an old killjoy! It was just a joke.'

'So's his *Thyestes*,' Lucillius muttered, but loud enough for everyone to hear. There was fresh laughter, in which Lucius joined.

By this time Seneca was coldly furious.

'Perhaps, my dear Lucillius,' he said, turning to the Greek, 'you would be so good as to tell me what precisely is wrong with the play.'

Oh my. A less conceited man would've seen the dangers of such an invitation, but modesty and a true assessment of his own literary abilities had never been Seneca's strong points. Gleefully, Lucillius took the thing apart, and others chipped in. I doubt very much if the old ham had ever had so much valid criticism given him in his life, and if much of it was malicious he'd only himself to blame.

Finally his temper snapped.

'The emperor liked it, at least!' He turned to Lucius, who hadn't taken part in the baiting. 'You told me so when I gave my recital, did you not, dear boy?'

'But of course I did, darling!' Lucius beamed at him. 'Your *Thyestes* is splendid theatre! Blood and guts by the bucketful! A glorious rant from beginning to end, and so deliciously evil!' He gave a shiver. 'Lovely stuff!'

This wasn't quite what Seneca had been looking for. His face was puce.

'But as poetry, my dear?' Lucillius prompted. 'As literature?'

Lucius's smile widened. 'Oh, as literature the thing's a monstrosity.'

Seneca's mouth fell open. The room dissolved.

He said very little for the rest of the evening.

He was still smarting when we shared a litter home.

'I cannot imagine what the emperor sees in some of these so-called writers!' he said. 'Tonight was dreadful, absolutely dreadful!'

'I quite enjoyed it myself,' I said.

Even in the darkness I could feel him glaring.

'I mean no disrespect, Petronius, but you would. There's too much of the anarchist in you for your own good. And for everyone else's.'

'Really?' I said mildly. 'And for everyone else's, eh?'

'Certainly.' He straightened a cushion. 'Don't forget you have responsibilities. The way you pander to the emperor at times is quite appalling. It sets the poor fellow totally the wrong example.'

I was too taken aback to be angry. 'Seneca, don't be ridiculous! As far as pandering to Lucius goes, you could give me lessons any day of the month.'

'That is completely different!' he said stiffly. 'A wayward ruler must be indulged in small things to safeguard the greater. If Nero wants parties and dancing girls . . .'

'How about dancing boys, dear?'

'. . . then I am willing to give him parties and dancing girls. But that does not mean I approve, and I certainly wouldn't encourage him, let alone suggest any . . . refinements. You seem to be doing both.'

'Perhaps that's because I quite like parties and dancing girls myself. And dancing boys.'

'Oh, don't be disgusting!'

'At least I'm not hypocritical.' Although I knew the reason for his foul mood he was getting under my skin, and I had to work to keep the irritation out of my voice. 'Personally I think Nero's done wonders with Rome these last few months. He's shaken some of the dust off and put a bit of colour back into life.'

Seneca snorted. 'Nero is nothing but a spoiled child. Spoiled children, especially if they happen to be rulers, need careful guidance. Like it or not, you are one of the guides, and I'm afraid to say at the moment you are not making a very good job of it.'

'I disagree.' I was getting angry myself now. 'For a start the emperor is not a child. I've said that before. But he *is* an artist. His priorities may be different from yours, but they're just as valid, and the fact that you can't appreciate them doesn't —'

'Oh, stop being a child yourself!' Seneca snapped. 'This is nonsense! Whatever his artistic pretensions Nero is first and foremost a ruler. He has many good qualities, but he is and always will be mentally unbalanced and oversusceptible to the influence of others, and that, in a ruler, is a recipe for disaster.'

'Accepted, but —'

'There is no but! We are like a chariot, Petronius, with a runaway horse and only a single rein. The last thing we need is some well-intentioned idiot urging the beast on to greater efforts.'

'Oh, what a lovely metaphor, my dear! And so flattering to the emperor and myself.'

'It's valid, damn you!'

'Perhaps it is,' I said carefully; I had never, ever heard Seneca swear before and it was an indication of just how upset he was. 'But what if the horse is going at a reasonable pace in the proper direction, and your idiot has his doubts about his co-driver's right to give orders?'

'Then the man's even more of a bloody fool than I give him credit for!'

There was no more to be said. We finished the journey in hostile silence, and I dropped him off at the Caelian like a hot brick.

29

Ah, well. I suppose it was inevitable we should fall out eventually. Seneca was all head, whereas I've never claimed to be an intellectual. Perhaps that was why I got on so well with Lucius. We were very alike in many ways. We still are.

Incidentally, I'm beginning to realise that telling this story has been a journey for me as much as (hopefully) it has been for you, my reader. I feel, for example, a little more sympathetic towards Seneca than I did when I started (Dion is smiling! Rot you, Dion!), and certainly more than I felt at the time. Perhaps it's the loss of blood, and my powers of judgment are going, or changing. Seneca slit his wrists too of course, in the end, and shared suicide does inevitably engender some sympathy, as if we were members of some exclusive club. If I'd been slower to condemn him as a hypocrite, and he'd been less convinced of his own perfection, we might still never've been friends but I think we could at least have reached a better understanding.

But that's enough of maudlin philosophy, my friends. It is not, as they say, my bag.

As it was, after that quarrel in the litter we treated each other with a certain wariness. The only time the barriers were lowered and we found ourselves on the same side was two years later, after the murder of City Prefect Pedanius.

Pedanius was a bastard: a thin, sour-faced Cato who weighed life by the scruple and never forgot an injury. He had a chef called Cycnus who'd saved enough from his tips to buy his freedom. After the deal was made Pedanius went back on it without returning the money. That night Cycnus took his best filleting knife along to his master's bedroom and cut the poor dear's throat. Then he gave himself up. As a self-confessed murderer he deserved all he got, but under Roman law where a slave kills his master every other slave in the household is executed with him. Which meant in this case four hundred innocent men, women and children.

When the news broke there was rioting in the streets and crowds surrounded the Senate House where the case was being debated. Thanks largely to the eloquence of another upper-class paragon named Cassius Longinus, the death sentence was confirmed; and to make sure there was no further trouble from the mob a company of Praetorians were detailed to line the route by which the condemned slaves were taken to execution.

Like every other decent person in Rome, I was stunned and shocked; so shocked that I actually set out for the palace hoping to persuade Lucius to override the Senate's decision. I was on my way there, via my banker's in the Market Square, when I bumped into Arruntius. He told me how delighted he'd been by the result of the debate.

'Cassius really stuck it to them,' he said. 'You should've heard him go, Petronius! Marvellous stuff, simply marvellous!'

'"Fortunate ears, to be so blessed,"' I quoted in Greek.

'What's that?' Arruntius frowned: I don't think he'd caught the meaning, let alone the reference. 'Oh. Indeed, yes, certainly. Anyway, he got a standing ovation, and it's not often that happens. It sent a clear message to these wishy-washy liberals that we've had enough, I can tell you.'

I'd had enough myself. Of Arruntius.

'Meaning the emperor, darling?' I said loudly. Several heads turned in our direction. 'And who might "we" be?'

Arruntius paled and glanced quickly to either side.

'Don't do that, you fool!' he hissed. 'You know bloody well who I mean! Anyway, Cassius was right. Someone's got to state the obvious sometimes, just to remind us it *is* obvious.'

'It's obvious that four hundred innocent people have to die because they happened to be under the same roof when a murder was committed? Oh, Arruntius, dear, how simply lovely!'

'Not people. Slaves. And not so innocent either.'

'How many does it take to cut one person's throat?'

He scowled. 'Don't be so bloody literal! Do you think one or two of them didn't know before the event? That that bastard of a chef kept it a total secret?'

'Even so . . .'

'Even so nothing!' Arruntius turned to go, having mentally, I suspect, washed his hands of me as a kindred spirit. 'Executing them all will make sure it never happens again. The next time some crack-brained sod takes it into his head to murder his master he won't get within a mile. I'll see you around, Petronius.'

When I finally got to the palace Seneca was already in the anteroom. He looked grey as death.

'Petronius.' He gave me a stiff nod.

'Seneca.' I was equally cool; we hadn't seen each other in months, and even then we'd hardly been on speaking terms. Luckily the secretary appeared at that moment and led us straight through to the emperor's private suite.

Lucius, too, looked haggard. Although it was late in the day he hadn't shaved and he was wearing a rumpled tunic. Even before the slave had closed the door behind us he was holding up a placating hand.

'I know!' he said. 'I know! Don't look at me like that. There's nothing I can do.'

Seneca lowered himself into a chair. His hands were shaking.

'You once said, my dear fellow, when you were asked to sign an order for execution that you wished you'd never learned to write.'

'This has nothing to do with me! It's the law!' Lucius turned towards me. 'Titus, you tell him!'

'You're the emperor.' I sat down too. 'You're above the law.'

'I am not!' Lucius's hand thudded on to the desk beside him. 'The Senate made the decision. The Senate's responsible, not me.'

'You have the power of veto.'

'Darling, I can't! Honestly! Don't you understand?' I stared at him. 'Don't blame me, blame the Senate and their fucking, twisted, Roman ideas of justice!' I thought of Arruntius. *Twisted* was a good word. 'You weren't there, either of you, when Cassius made his speech.'

'He was only one voice,' Seneca said quietly. 'There must have been others.'

'Oh, yes.' Lucius was pacing the room. He was almost in tears. 'Lots of them. Mostly agreeing, because Cassius's argument was a clincher with these hide-bound bastards: "It's the law as our fathers made it, gentlemen, it's how we've always done things. We've had enough changes these last few years. Make your stand now, before it's too late. Vote for the good old Roman ways!"' He stopped and faced us. 'Do you think I'm a fool? That I didn't see the implications?'

'Cassius made it a political issue.' I felt sick. That was what Arruntius had meant about sending a clear message to the liberals.

'Of course he did! And most of the Senate are with him. I can't fight them, I don't dare, not over this!' Suddenly, Lucius spat. 'Barbarians! Fucking barbarians! I hate them!'

'They're not barbarians.' Seneca had clasped his hands in front of him. His eyes were lowered. I thought perhaps he was praying. 'Just misguided.'

'As misguided as you think I am?' There was no answer. I held my breath, but Lucius didn't press the issue; he was almost gentle. 'My dear, what would your historians – your good, solid, patriotic, Roman historians – write about Cassius and me if we both died tomorrow? They'd say that Nero was a sport of nature, a degenerate who aped the Greeks and gave public performances in theatres. And Cassius? A good old-fashioned Roman who defied tyrants like his namesake. Whose side would you cheer for, Seneca, even when the corpses were counted?'

Seneca said nothing, only looked at his hands. Lucius threw himself on to a couch and slopped wine into a cup.

'They'll regret this, you know,' he said conversationally. 'All of them. I won't forget.'

Seneca and I exchanged glances. Lucius caught us, and smiled with his mouth, not his eyes.

'Oh, don't worry, my dears! I'm not my Uncle Gaius, I don't

mean that! But they will regret it, eventually. Now piss off, I'm feeling low. Interview over. Request denied.'

We left.

They died. All of them. All four hundred.

30

I think even Cassius would've hesitated if he'd known what the execution of those four hundred slaves would mean in the long run, and not only for the Senate. Eleven months later, a gentleman named Antistius Sosianus gave Lucius the opening he needed by reciting verses satirising him at a dinner party.

The verses were pure doggerel, and if they'd been written before the Pedanius incident I think Lucius would've ignored them as he'd already done others; like many artists he was so sure of his own talent that anyone who refused to recognise it was beneath contempt. However, he decided to use the situation to send a clear message to the Senate. Through a sympathetic intermediary, Sosianus was charged with treason.

The Senate were shocked. When Lucius had come to power he had promised to end the treason trials which had scarred Claudius's reign and were a notorious money-spinner for professional informers. A throwaway line or an ill-advised joke blown up out of all proportion could result in death or exile; and most of the victims were senators or their narrow-stripe relatives. The very thought that the emperor might reintroduce them sent a cold draught up more than one patrician back-passage. I was a bit worried myself.

'But, Titus, it's a lovely plan!' Lucius insisted when I called in at the palace accidentally-on-purpose to test the wind on behalf of some broad-striper friends. 'A bit of fear's good for them. It's what they understand. Besides, they don't appreciate how lucky they are having me in charge, they really don't.'

We were walking in the palace gardens. Lucius stopped

occasionally to pick a spray of evergreen for the garland he was plaiting.

'You lived through some of the trials yourself.' I tried to keep the tone light. 'Do you really want all that nonsense back again? Inoffensive old buffers put to death just because they wear a purple cloak to a party?'

'Of course not! Don't be silly.' He frowned at a peacock cut from the centre of a boxwood hedge. 'I just want them to see that things could be a lot worse if I were that way inclined. Besides, Sosianus is a smarmy little bugger. Rome would be better off without him.'

I felt cold. 'You'll let the Senate execute him?' Technically, the penalty for treason was death. 'Just for a bit of bad poetry?'

'Oh, no.' He giggled. 'I'm not a monster, darling, you should know that by now. They'll want to, of course, because I shall be terribly upset and angry, and the sycophantic bastards will assume I'm as callous as they are. I'll step in at the last moment and show them how a proper civilised person behaves.' He set the garland on his head and tilted it over one ear. 'It's a salutary reminder, Titus, that's all. And the poor hack can spend his exile polishing up his iambics.'

In the event Lucius didn't have to intervene, which I'm afraid was partly my fault, although I never told him: he never could resist the grand theatrical gesture. The case went exactly as he'd said it would. The consul-elect, a prime crawler named Marullus, demanded the death penalty, and he would've got it if I hadn't already told old Thrasea Paetus – one of the few decent members of the Senate – what Lucius's real feelings were. As a result, Sosianus escaped with exile.

Although Sosianus's trial frankly bordered on farce, six months later Lucius made a decision that had much more immediate – and far-reaching – consequences.

I found out about it on a routine visit to the palace to make the final arrangements for the Spring Festival party Lucius had asked me to organise. As usual his secretary showed me in to the private suite. On the guest couch to the emperor's right, chewing his way through a hothouse peach, was a man I'd been trying to avoid for over two years.

'Titus! Come in, my dear!' Lucius was beaming. 'Meet the new Commander of Praetorians!'

'Joint commander.' Tigellinus set the peach down and gave me a slow, not very pleasant smile. 'With Faenius Rufus.'

'What's happened to Burrus?' A silly question but I was shaken. Burrus commanded the Praetorians. Tigellinus had been in charge of the City Watch since Lucius had brought him to Rome the year before, but from that to Guards Commander was a huge step.

'He's dead. He died last night.' Lucius was still smiling. 'That lump in his throat finally did for him. So sad. Titus, sit down, dear, you look quite pale.'

It felt like someone had sandbagged me from behind. I reached for a chair. I'd known Burrus had been suffering for the past few months from a growth in his windpipe, but he'd seemed a permanent fixture. Now, suddenly, he was gone. It was like an amputation.

'Rufus is only a sop to the Senate,' Lucius was saying. 'He doesn't really count, he's a useless old buffer at the best of times. Tiggy'll be in charge, really. Won't that be nice?'

'Very,' I said. Tigellinus was watching me with dark, amused eyes. 'I'm sorry about Burrus. I didn't even know he was dying.'

'Nor did I, darling.' Lucius made a throwaway gesture. 'Still, it was quick at the end. One moment here, the next a bag of old bones. Comes to us all in time. I must write a poem for him.'

'Speaking of bags of old bones, Petronius' – Tigellinus pulled a grape from the bunch in the fruit bowl beside him – 'how's your pal Seneca these days?'

Something cold touched my spine. 'I don't know. I haven't seen him recently.'

'We'll have to have a talk soon, the pair of us. That's right, isn't it, Nero?' His eyes shifted momentarily from mine as he tossed the grape in the air and caught it neatly in his mouth. He chewed and spat the pips into his palm.

'If you must, love. Although why you should want to's a total mystery to me. Old Grizzleguts is hardly a barrel of laughs.' Lucius frowned. 'And speaking of that, Titus, you don't seem to be terribly taken with my new appointment.'

'I'm sorry?' I was still watching Tigellinus, who was selecting another grape.

'Thrilled. Delighted. Over the moon. Ravished.' Tigellinus chuckled. 'At the idea of Tiggy taking over the Guards, darling.'

'Of course I am.' I tried to smile, although it wasn't easy with those black eyes boring into me. 'I was just a little surprised to hear about Burrus. My heartiest congratulations, Tigellinus.'

'Thank you.'

The emperor watched our stiff exchange with amused interest. 'Ask me why,' he said.

'Why what?'

'Why Tigellinus.' He got up from his couch, moved over to the one Tigellinus was occupying and sat on its edge. 'You're dying to know, really. Aren't you?'

'I don't have to ask why. I think it's an excellent idea.'

'No you don't, my dear.' Lucius's fingers had embedded themselves to the knuckles in the other man's hair, and he was flexing them against the scalp as if Tigellinus were a monstrous cat. 'You disapprove, and you're curious. Be honest.'

The black eyes were still staring into mine. 'Very well,' I said. 'Why Tigellinus?'

'Because he's efficient. Because he's been an excellent Watch Commander and because he'll make an even better Commander of Praetorians. Does that satisfy you?'

'No.' I was watching the fingers. They had moved down to the nape of the neck. Tigellinus's smile widened, and he stretched. His joints cracked.

'It's true. All of it.'

'Perhaps. But these aren't the main reasons.'

'No, they aren't.' The index finger brushed the dark hairs gently upwards. 'All right. Try this, then. I like him. We get on well together. He has a sense of humour. He knows how to enjoy himself. His . . . carnality amuses and excites me. Right, my dear?'

Tigellinus arched his muscular back without answering. He was almost purring.

'I'm afraid that doesn't fit either,' I said; the dark eyes still hadn't wavered, and I was finding their effect hypnotic. 'Whoever commands the Guards holds one of the most important political military posts in the empire. You're careful over those. You wouldn't give one to someone because he happened to be a friend.'

Lucius smiled. 'Oh, well done! Quite right, I wouldn't. Or not just because of that, anyway.' His hand travelled the length of Tigellinus's spine and rested at its base. 'Shall we tell him, my dear?'

'Go ahead,' Tigellinus said. He hadn't moved or acknowledged the presence of the emperor's hand in any way.

Lucius went back to his own couch and lay down.

'Tiggy's an ex-slave, Titus,' he said. 'He's been a bad boy all his life, he's clawed his way to the top of the heap and he has no time for convention or morality. He's a natural survivor with only one interest. Gaius Ofonius Tigellinus. Am I right, Tiggy?'

Tiggellinus smiled. 'On the nail. But there's a but.'

'Of course, dear. I'm sorry.' Lucius turned back to me. 'He's also completely loyal to me, because I can give him everything he wants and without me he's nothing. Yes, Tiggy?'

Tigellinus nodded. 'Yes.'

He meant it, I could see. The man was no fool. My mouth felt dry.

'You still haven't quite answered the question,' I said. 'Why Tigellinus?'

'Haven't I?' Lucius frowned. 'Oh, but Titus, the answer's obvious! Tiggy's perfect because the Senate'll absolutely loathe him. What other reason would I have?'

I said nothing. He was right, of course. If Burrus had been a provincial at least his family were respectable and he was what Arruntius would call a 'sound fellow'. With Arruntius and his cronies – which meant a good two-thirds of the Senate – Tigellinus would be as popular as a rotten squid in a barrel of Baian oysters.

'They have asked for it, after all.' Lucius went on, his voice reasonable. 'They've been asking for it for years, the po-faced Roman bastards. And Tiggy's just what they deserve. Aren't you, Tiggy?'

Tigellinus smiled and lowered his eyelids.

'Don't be modest, darling, of course you are!' Lucius stretched out his hand in front of him, fingers spread as if they were gripping something. His voice was soft and razor-edged. 'So I'm going to take him like this, Titus, and I'm going to ram him up their bloody Roman arses as far as he'll go. Do you understand me now, dear?'

'Yes,' I said; I was shaking. 'I understand. Thank you.'

'Don't mention it, Petronius,' Tigellinus said with a smile. 'In fact, don't mention it at all. To anyone.'

'That's right.' Lucius settled back. 'It's our little secret. And now, what did you want to see me about, darling?'

Hesitantly, I started to explain my ideas for the up-and-coming Spring Festival; but my heart wasn't in it.

Somehow organising parties didn't seem quite so vital any more.

31

I'd received a clear warning not to mention Lucius's plans for the Senate, but he'd said nothing about keeping the actual appointment secret; and in any case it would be common knowledge in a day or so. I went straight round to Seneca's. He was sitting at his study desk. In front of him was a book-roll, the exposed part of which was half covered with his small, neat writing.

I needn't've bothered coming. He'd already heard the news. He also knew, of course, that Burrus was dead.

'Some people think the poor fellow was poisoned,' he said slowly. 'It isn't true. The doctor only gave him a month or two at the turn of the year. Besides, why should Nero bother?'

I'd never seen him look so weary. Even his cheek-pouches, purple bags of skin shot with broken veins, sagged empty and dull.

'He never told me he was dying,' I said. 'Burrus himself, I mean.'

'No. No, he wouldn't.' Seneca rolled the pen he was holding absently between his palms. 'But after all – and I intend no disrespect – why should he?'

I said nothing. It was a fair comment. I might have respected Burrus, but we'd had our differences.

Seneca seemed to realise that he was still holding the pen. He set it down carefully on the manuscript.

'And how was our friend Tigellinus?' he asked.

'Quietly content. Like a cat who's got the cream.' I shifted in my chair. 'Which he has. So what'll you do now? Carry on as the emperor's adviser?'

'No.' He shook his head. 'There wouldn't be any point to that. I'll resign. After a decent interval, naturally. Or ask Nero to allow me to go into retirement, rather, since my position's never been official.'

'Is that necessary?'

'No, not exactly. But I can't help the lad now, and I've been no more than . . .' He hesitated. 'No more than an inconvenience to him for some time. Besides – he indicated the book-roll – 'I have my writing to catch up on.'

'Philosophy? Or another play?'

'Philosophy. What else, at my time of life? The plays were never more than a spiritual emetic. I don't think you ever quite understood that, my dear fellow. Also if I'm not too much mistaken they would be rather too . . . too close to reality in future for everyone's comfort. I only hope the dear boy leaves me in peace. But what about you, Petronius? What will you do?'

I shrugged, feeling suddenly uncomfortable. 'Plan parties. Go to parties. Butter him up. What I've always done.'

'You may find it a little more difficult in future,' he said drily. 'Now you've been replaced, as Burrus and I have been.'

'I'll survive,' I said, getting up.

'Oh, you will, you will.' There was no friendliness in Seneca's smile, and he got to his feet with a shade too much alacrity. 'You will certainly survive. For a year or two yet, anyway. Meanwhile come along, my dear fellow, and I'll show you out.'

We walked through the hallway in silence, avoiding each other's eyes. At the door, he paused.

'You remember the conversation we had some time ago? About the chariot and the runaway horse?'

'Yes.' I'd been trying not to think of it all day, since I'd seen Tigellinus and Lucius together.

'Well, the chariot has another driver now. Or soon will have.' As the slave opened the door he turned to face me. 'Do you feel he's better than the last? And are you still sure that the horse is heading in the right direction?'

I didn't reply. The door closed softly behind me.

A month or so later, Seneca left Rome for his villa in Campania, and Lucius hardly noticed he'd gone. This indifference worried me, because it didn't only extend to Seneca. Although I was spending more and more time with him than before our relationship was changing, becoming more distant, and I felt now less like a friend than a hired social organiser. Matters came to a head one day when I went to the palace and found him as usual in conference with Tigellinus. For a moment, until he saw who I was, he had frowned. Then he turned to Tigellinus with a shrug and said: 'Never mind, dear. It's only my Adviser on Taste.'

Tigellinus sniggered.

Lucius's Adviser on Taste. Why the phrase should've rankled so much, even more than the shrug or the snigger, I don't know. I talked it over with Silia that evening as I watched her get ready for one of Lucius's frequent and increasingly interminable parties.

'Personally I think you're being silly, darling,' she said, fastening the pearl earrings Arruntius had given her at the Spring Festival. 'It's a tremendous compliment, really. And you do do it so well.'

I rubbed a speck of wax from the arm of my chair.

'Perhaps so. But I'm not some kind of major-domo earning a bonus by booking some flavour-of-the-month entertainer for his master's business dinner.'

'Aren't you?' Silia turned her exquisitely made-up eyes on me. I winced. 'Oh, I'm sorry, Titus, I didn't mean it that way. But what's wrong with helping the emperor bring a little civilised living to the city? You've always said you rather admired him for it.'

'I do. But there's a . . .' – I hesitated, feeling for the proper phrase – 'an angry hardness about him these days that wasn't there before. Then he was working for the good of Rome. Now I don't think he particularly cares. In fact I suspect he'd be just as glad if they fought him all the way.'

'"They"?'

'The Senate. Or the establishment, rather. The hard-line traditionalists. He's always disliked them, and it's quite mutual. Now with dear Tigellinus whispering sweet nothings in his ear he's beginning to wonder about taking them on properly.'

Silia had picked up the mirror to check the effect of the

earrings. Now she put it down and said gravely: 'You're worried about Tigellinus, aren't you?'

'Yes. He's an animal, completely amoral. He causes trouble just for the kick it gives him, without thinking of the consequences. And Lucius follows his lead because Tigellinus has the courage to do what he wants to do and Lucius doesn't. Oh, yes. I'm worried about Tigellinus.'

Silia took up the mirror again and made a play of examining her eyebrows.

'You may like to know,' she said slowly, 'that he's having an affair with Poppaea.' I sat forward in my chair. 'Oh, a very discreet one And they may not even be sleeping together.'

'That's nonsense! Tigellinus would never be such a fool.'

Silia shrugged. 'Take it or leave it, dear. But my informant tells me that Lucius's darling Poppy made the first approach.'

'Which informant?'

'You remember Acte's maid Chryse? She's in Puteoli, of course, but her sister still works at the palace, and she passes me the occasional bit of privileged information.'

'Gossip, you mean?'

'If you want to call it that,' Silia said with great dignity. 'We all have our little interests, and I happen to enjoy a bit of scandal.'

'Do you trust her?'

'Implicitly.'

I sat back. This was important. Lucius had his good qualities, but he was easily swayed by anyone strong-minded enough to make the effort and whom he found sympathetic. With Burrus and Seneca gone the only two real influences on him (I could hardly count myself any more) were Tigellinus and Poppaea. If they'd joined forces then we were in trouble. *I* was in trouble. Both were unscrupulous, and neither of them was too taken with Titus Petronius.

'They don't sleep together?' I said.

'They *may* not be sleeping together, dear. Chryse's sister's a very conscientious informer, even if the poor girl is the tiniest bit thick.'

'So it could be a . . . political affair?'

Silia smiled. 'My dear Titus, have you seen Poppaea recently?

She's stunning, absolutely stunning! And Tigellinus may be a dreadful shit, but he's an extremely attractive one. Political it may be, but if so the deal was signed between the sheets.'

'I bow to your superior knowledge of the world, darling.' I was thinking rapidly. Power as such – apart from the power to disrupt, which he already had – didn't interest Tigellinus. He'd bed Poppaea willingly enough if she made him the offer, but if he did it would be with no other motive than pleasure in the act itself. Poppaea was another matter. She was desperate to become empress; which meant, of course, getting rid of Lucius's virtually estranged wife Octavia. So far Lucius had refused, because Octavia was as popular as Poppaea was disliked, and a remarriage would serve no purpose. If she could persuade Tigellinus to help her, then . . .

'Titus, what do you think?'

'Mmm?'

Silia was holding two necklaces up for my inspection. 'Oh, come on, darling! Please! We really must be going, and this is important. The pearls or the rubies?'

'The pearls,' I said.

Her nose wrinkled. 'Not the rubies?'

'The pearls, darling. Quite definitely.'

'Very well.' She replaced the ruby necklace in her jewel-case. 'I wish I hadn't mentioned that dratted girl, you'll be dreadful all evening. Now do stop moping and tell Simon to fetch the litter.'

Both Tigellinus and Poppaea were at the party. They sat apart, and didn't seem especially interested in each other as far as I could see; but that proved nothing.

32

It came as no surprise to anyone when, a short time later, Tigellinus's co-Commander of Praetorians was relieved of his post. The excuse, that he'd been friendly with Agrippina, was farcical: Lucius's mother had been dead long before the appointment was made. There was no replacement.

Lucius was quite open about the affair, to me at least: 'Why should I bother to invent anything decent, Titus?' he said. 'Nobody'd believe the doddering old fool was, capable of any real wickedness. If he had been I might not've had to sack him. And anyway, darling, those bumsuckers in the Senate wouldn't dare say boo whatever reason I gave them.'

Both observations were true enough; what was chilling was that Lucius was able to make them. His third comment – almost thrown away – was even more ominous: 'Now Tiggy can *really* begin to enjoy himself.'

Tiggy did so, with two political assassinations. His first victim was Faustus Sulla, the aristocratic husband of Octavia's sister Claudia, exiled four years before. The murderers walked into Sulla's house in Marseilles, stabbed him and, in line with their instructions, brought the head back to Rome. ('Tiggy thought we'd be as well to kill him,' Lucius told me later. 'And it was a mercy, really. He was going *terribly* grey, poor dear.')

The second was Rubellius Plautus. Plautus was another relative who had been exiled following the appearance of a comet. Comets, notoriously, announce the deaths of rulers, and Lucius had sensibly suggested that his distant cousin make himself even more distant by withdrawing to his Asian estates before anyone got any bright ideas. His head, too, had been brought back, pickled this time in vinegar. ('Hasn't he got a long nose, Titus?' – pulling the head from its jar by the hair and showing me it – 'Tiggy said he was dangerous, but I'm not so sure. Not with a nose like that. Still, best to be safe than sorry, eh?' I had thrown up all over my best mantle. Lucius only laughed.)

What could I do? What could anyone do? After the incident of the pickle-jar I went home and wept. Yes, I was sorry for Sulla and Plautus, and I was sorry for Rome; but I was even more sorry for Lucius, because I honestly believed and still believe that to him the killings were no more than stage deaths and the heads only papier-mâché props. If anyone was to blame for them and for the others that followed it was Tigellinus, who'd shown the poor lad what marvellous, innocent fun it was to kill, and our upright band of venerable senators, who not only expelled the murdered men from their ranks but voted us a day of national thanksgiving into the bargain.

Do I sound bitter? Do you detect an unaccustomed seriousness here, my dear reader, that conflicts with Petronius's story so far? I am, and you do. I can't help myself.

Draw a line across the page here, Dion. No, don't ask why, boy. Just do it, please.

33

A month or so after the murders, Arruntius having to go off on one of his official tours, I'd arranged to take Silia away for a few days to Tibur, where an old friend had a villa. When I called to collect her she was sitting by the ornamental pool with her friend Junia Calvina.

'You're not ready, are you, darling?' I said. It hadn't needed genius to make that deduction. There'd been no sign in the hall of the huge quantities of luggage Silia found necessary for even a night away from home.

'Titus!' She looked up and put a hand to her mouth. 'Oh, goodness, is that the time? I'm sorry, dear, but Junia came round with the news and we got chatting. I am all packed, though, really. It's just that the slaves haven't carried the stuff through.'

'What news?'

'About the divorce, of course.' Junia's plump face was grave.

'Whose divorce?' I pulled a chair across. Whatever Silia said, I knew we wouldn't be leaving for some time.

'The emperor's. He's divorcing Octavia.'

I sat down heavily. 'No!'

Junia nodded. 'The announcement's being made this morning.'

'Why? What possible reason can he give?'

'The official reason's barrenness, but of course that's a non-sense. Nero's never . . .' She blushed and started again. 'Octavia's still . . .' The blush spread until the poor girl looked like a beetroot. 'I mean, well, it's *wrong*, Titus. Totally impossible. I know.'

I remembered what Acte had said years ago about the marriage

never having been consummated; and also that Junia Calvina
was one of Octavia's very few close friends.

'You two talk while I get ready,' Silia said. 'I won't be
long, dear.'

I watched her hurry off upstairs, frowning. Nothing to do with
her lateness, I'd planned for that and we weren't meeting the
carriage until noon. It was much more serious. I'd talked with
Lucius several times over the past few days and he hadn't so
much as hinted about a divorce.

'Octavia's horribly upset,' Junia was saying. 'She's dreaded
this for years, and she's been so terribly careful you wouldn't
believe!'

'You've seen her?'

'I was round early this morning. It's all Poppaea's doing, of
course. Her and that beast Tigellinus. You know they've been
. . . getting together recently?'

'So I've heard.'

'Do you think the emperor knows?'

I'd wondered about that one myself. Not that Lucius would
necessarily care, even if it were true.

'I doubt it.'

'But it's so unfair!' Junia's face twisted with anger. 'Poppaea
really is such a bitch, Titus! Goodness knows what Nero sees
in her!'

'He sees his mother, darling,' I said.

She gave me a startled look: Junia always had been naïve, very
much like Octavia herself, which was why they were so close.

'Do you think so? The empress? But that's dreadful!'

'Lucius has never really loved anyone else, dear. If there's one
thing the poor darling can't understand or abide it's innocence.'

'So he'll persecute Octavia for nothing while he'll let Poppaea
get away with murder! What kind of . . .' She stopped, her eyes
wide. 'Oh, Titus!'

I had a cold feeling in my own stomach. 'Octavia's quite safe,
believe me. She's one of the imperial family, and she's far too
popular for Lucius to risk harming.'

'You're sure?'

'Of course I am. Now sit down like a good girl.' She did, and
began chewing her fingernails. 'Besides, Lucius isn't . . .' It was

my turn to stop: I'd been about to say, *Lucius isn't a killer*. 'Lucius isn't interested in anything but marriage with Poppaea.'

'That's bad enough!'

'Oh, I agree. Only . . .'

There was a movement on the stairs. Silia reappeared carrying a light travelling cloak.

'Titus, I've had a lovely idea,' she said. 'Why doesn't Junia come with us?'

'I don't see why not.' It would certainly take the girl out of herself. 'Marsus won't mind, I'm sure.' Marsus was the friend with the villa.

'Junia, dear? You haven't any other commitments, have you?'

'No. Only Octavia might . . .'

'Darling, you are *not* staying behind just to mope!' I stood up and helped Silia on with the cloak.

'I quite agree, Titus,' Silia said. 'Octavia will be fine, dear. Besides, Tibur's beautiful at this time of year, and from what Titus has told me his friend is an absolute pussycat.'

I certainly hadn't said anything of the sort. Marsus was my ex-banker, a dry old stick of seventy, ugly as sin, and possessed of all the conversational skills of a block of marble. A pussycat he was anything but. However, I wasn't going to contradict Silia in such a good cause. Junia would find out for herself.

'All right.' A smile lit her broad face for the first time. 'If you're certain he won't throw me out, Titus. Just let me nip back home and put my little bag together.'

Ah, me. One learns by experience. I sent a slave off to cancel the original arrangement and order the biggest coach he could get, for mid-afternoon.

34

Lucius had the good sense to keep his remarriage low-key. Silia and I were invited to the private ceremony, of course. So was Junia, but she didn't go.

Lucius and Poppaea greeted the guests in the formal hallway before the reception room itself where the ceremony would take place. The bridegroom was more gorgeously dressed – and wore more make-up – than the bride.

I'd thought long and hard about a wedding present – what, after all, *can* you give the man who literally has everything? Finally the problem had solved itself when I was offered an interesting piece of historical erotica, an Egyptian papyrus dating back to before the first Ptolemy and detailing no fewer than ninety-seven coital positions for couples and trios of the same and mixed sexes. Lucius was delighted.

'We'll give it to Chaeremon to translate, Titus,' he said.

'Do you think he's up to it?' I didn't mean academically: Chaeremon was another of Lucius's ex-tutors, a former professor at the University of Alexandria and an expert in Old Egyptian esoteric lore. He was in his eighties, and paralysed down one side.

'But that's the whole point, dear!' He giggled. 'The shock'll finish the old satyr.'

I gave Poppaea a piece of jewellery from the same source: an ornamental headdress made up of hundreds of thin gold plates. It had come, my agent told me, from the tomb of a queen who'd ruled before the Greeks took Troy. I thought she'd like it, but she didn't. In fact she was unwilling to touch it.

'Oh, don't be silly, Poppy! It's lovely!' Lucius kissed her on the cheek, then turned to me. 'She's terribly superstitious, didn't you know? She thinks the thing might have a curse on it. Don't you, petal?'

'It came from a grave. An Egyptian grave.' Poppaea was scowling at me. 'The Egyptians know about curses.'

'I shouldn't worry, my dear,' I said lightly. 'The man I bought it from is seventy-five, has four mistresses and owns the biggest house in Alexandria next to the palace. If there ever was a curse it's worn off long since.'

'Curses don't wear off. Ever.' She motioned to a slave-girl, who took the thing away and put it with the growing pile of other presents. 'Thank you for the thought, Petronius. It was very much . . . in character.'

I inclined my head and joined Silia who was already in the reception room.

'Well, that went down like a fart at a funeral,' I said.

'What did, dear?' She handed me a cup of wine.

'Poppaea's present. She hated it.'

Silia sniffed. 'It serves you right for trying to ingratiate yourself. You know she doesn't like you. You ought to have given her a nice necklace and saved yourself the trouble.'

'What trouble's that, Petronius?' It was Tigellinus. He was standing with his back to us talking to Marius Celsus the consul. I noticed that Celsus moved away pretty sharply as soon as Tiggy transferred his attention elsewhere and joined a tight knot of whispering purple-stripers in the corner.

'Oh, nothing serious,' I said blandly.

'Good.' He glanced briefly over his shoulder at the group in the corner and smiled, drawing his lips back from perfect white teeth. 'Silia, lover! You're looking good enough to eat, as usual.'

'Thank you, Tigellinus.' Silia was cool. 'I didn't know you included cannibalism among your other accomplishments.'

'Ouch.' Tigellinus winced and smiled. 'Straight in the balls. That's what I admire about you upper-class bitches. You've got the put-down to a fine art.'

'It does take practice, naturally,' Silia said. 'And a certain amount of style.'

'You see what I mean, Titus?' Tigellinus grinned at me. He was quite unperturbed. 'So Poppy didn't like your little present?

What a shame. I could've told you if you'd asked me. The poor girl's even careful which sandal she puts on first when she gets out of bed in the mornings.' He mimed consternation. 'Oh, my, what have I said? And on this day of all days!'

'Perhaps the headdress was a bad choice.' I was more careful about antagonising the emperor's closest confidant than, obviously, Silia was. 'I knew the empress was superstitious, but not to that degree. The thing hasn't seen the inside of a tomb for a hundred years.'

'Oh, that wouldn't matter to Poppy. She's a sucker for the mysteries of the east. Not like Octavia. Now she is a strictly practical little madam.'

'Really?' Silia said frostily.

Tigellinus had raised his voice on Poppaea's predecessor's name; quite intentionally, because he looked round and smiled into the sudden hush. A heartbeat later the interrupted conversations around us resumed at a lower pitch, as if everyone were listening.

'Really,' he said.

'I wouldn't know anything about that.' I raised my own voice: it wouldn't do for Tigellinus to think I was frightened of the name. 'I've never met Octavia.'

He laughed. 'That makes sense. She wouldn't let you get within twenty yards. Me neither. Although' – he became ponderously confidential, and his arm went round Silia's shoulders – 'I could tell you some stories about that little ice-maiden you wouldn't believe!'

'I'm sure you could,' Silia said in her normal voice, removing the arm.

Tigellinus ignored her. His mouth was a bare inch from my ear. Behind him I could see at least four people watching us out of the corners of their eyes and not saying much themselves.

'The rumour is, all this virtuous Roman matron stuff's shit,' he murmured. 'Our sweet little Octavia's been dropping her pants in secret for months.'

'Really?' I raised my wine-cup so he couldn't see my expression. 'You're quite right, of course.'

He looked puzzled. 'What d'you mean, I'm quite right?'

'About my not believing your stories, my dear.'

Silia smiled. Tigellinus scowled.

'It's a fact,' he said. 'And guess who the lucky man is?'

'You, darling?'

I knew that baiting the oily-skinned bastard was stupid, but I couldn't help myself. He was trying to control his temper and not doing too well.

'I told you, Petronius, she's got no taste. She wouldn't let me near her honey-pot in a million years. This is the most unlikely candidate you could ever think of.'

'Amaze me.'

He grinned and glanced over his shoulder. The people around us – I could see at least a dozen whose names were prominent in politics and society – had given up the pretence and were frankly eavesdropping. 'No. No, I've said enough. You'll find out in time. And if you should want to try your luck, then you go ahead. Now the thaw's on and the pipe's cracked she may appreciate another plumber.'

Silia's knuckles were white around her wine-cup, and I suspect she was within a hair's-breadth of throwing the contents into Tigellinus's face; but just then, luckily, old Aelius Tubero the high priest of Jupiter arrived and the marriage ceremony began.

Silia and I went home right after we'd thrown the nuts and the happy couple had gone off to enjoy their first night of properly wedded bliss. In the safety of our litter we talked about what Tigellinus had said. Silia was upset: she knew Octavia through Junia Calvina, and although they weren't exactly friends they had a certain amount of respect for each other.

'I don't like it, Titus,' she said. 'I don't like it at all. That worm's up to something.'

'Do you mean Tigellinus or the emperor?'

'Does it matter? They're both the same anyway, nowadays.'

'You can add Poppaea, dear. She's pulling the strings. The whole thing's a total fabrication, obviously.'

'Obviously.' Silia sighed. 'Titus, that poor woman! They can't do this to her.'

'They can. They will.'

'But it's so unfair! She's never so much as looked at another man! Isn't divorce enough?'

'Not for Poppaea. She wants Octavia exiled or dead.' I stared out of the litter's uncovered window. The Palatine wasn't by any means the busiest part of Rome, but there were a few people – mostly party-goers – in the late-evening street. 'It may not work, even so. It isn't plausible enough, and Octavia's much too popular just to be got rid of. Especially by the likes of Poppaea.'

'Do you think that'll stop them? Really?'

I didn't answer, which was an answer in itself. Probably it wouldn't. Lucius might worry about his own popularity, but most Romans – high or low – were realists. Also with Poppaea and Tigellinus in league against him poor Lucius didn't stand a chance.

'Who's the man, do you think?' Silia said after a while.

Suddenly I felt tired, bone-tired.

'Jupiter knows. Who's unpopular currently? With Tigellinus and the emperor, I mean?'

'Most of the Senate, darling.'

'Even Tigellinus and Poppaea can't accuse Octavia of sleeping with most of the Senate. And Tigellinus mentioned one man.'

'Thrasea?' It was a good suggestion, and worrying enough. Thrasea Paetus had been a thorn in Lucius's side for years, largely because he gave the lie to the belief that all senators are hypocrites. Thrasea was his own man, and an honourable one at that; which was another thing about him Lucius disliked. Pretended goodness he understood and despised, the real article made him nervous. And when Lucius was nervous he was at his most dangerous.

'Possibly,' I said.

'I'm only glad Junia's brother and nephew are safe. They'd be prime candidates, and the shock would kill the poor girl.'

I nodded. Silia was right, I could see how Tigellinus could persuade Lucius to get rid of these two. Silanus and Torquatus, like Junia herself, had imperial blood in their veins, and they were the last of the family. However, Silanus was in Asia at present and Torquatus was only fourteen. Not even Lucius could cite them as the guilty parties, if he had any concern at all for credibility.

In fact it was none of these people. Tigellinus hadn't been joking; the man eventually accused of seducing Octavia was one of the most unlikely in Rome.

35

A few days later, however, having evidently reconsidered the wisdom of implicating a public figure, Lucius and his new advisers had Octavia accused of adultery with one of her own slaves. Even so, they had underestimated the Roman mob, who unlike our pusillanimous Senate had no hesitation at all in expressing their disapproval, and gleefully treated us to six days of street riots. Poppaea was terrified; not so much of the mob itself but that Lucius, being the complete coward he was, might give in and dismiss the charge.

There were problems, too, with proof. Even under torture most of Octavia's slaves refused to give the necessary evidence. In the end, Lucius suddenly announced that the real adulterer had confessed. The guilty party, he revealed to a bemused Senate and people, was Anicetus.

I was one of the few people who wasn't surprised. The notorious seducer had told me so himself when I'd bumped into him coming out of the palace the day before.

I hadn't seen Anicetus since Agrippina's murder. With his two-day stubble and general appearance (and odour) of having slept in his clothes for a month he looked even more ineffectual than ever.

'Petronius!' He grabbed my arm. 'Oh, thank the gods, for a friendly face! You've got to believe me! I never touched her!'

The guards on the gate were sniggering, and I caught the tail-end of a ribald comment.

'No, darling,' I said. 'Of course you didn't. Now who exactly are we talking about?'

He was hopping from one foot to the other as if he had a full bladder and was ten miles from a latrine.

'Octavia, of course! Nero . . .'

I'd heard enough. I put my hand over his mouth and frog-marched the little Greek out of the gates past the now-rigid guards. Even soldiers – not the brightest intellects in the empire – know when to play deaf.

We found a quiet bit of wall and I let him go.

'Now, Anicetus,' I said. 'What's all this about?'

'I had to promise, you see.' He was shivering. 'Otherwise he'd've had me executed anyway. And Sardinia isn't so bad.'

'That's a matter of opinion, darling. Now control yourself and start from the beginning.'

He took a deep breath and let it out, filling the air round us with the sharp smell of wine and anchovies.

'You know I'm still Commander of the Fleet at Misenum?' he said.

'Of course.' Lord Serapis knew why. The poor radish couldn't've commanded a rowing boat.

'Well, a message came three days ago ordering me to Rome. I was surprised because I've hardly seen the emperor for years, not since . . . not since . . .' He bit his lip.

'Not since you killed his mother. Yes, I know.'

'It wasn't my fault! I didn't have any choice! You were there, you heard . . .'

I sighed. 'Anicetus, will you *please* get a grip on yourself, dear, and tell me what happened.'

'I'm sorry. I'm just . . .' He took another deep breath. 'I came straight here. Nero was quite friendly, really, he gave me a cup of wine and we chatted about this and that. Old times, you know? Then suddenly Poppaea said . . .'

'Poppaea was there?'

He looked at me as if I were the one who was being stupid. 'Oh, yes, of course. And Tigellinus. He's a dreadful man, Petronius, simply dreadful!'

'I know, dear. Go on. So Poppy said . . .?'

'She said, 'Oh, get on with it!' and Nero said, 'I hear you've been making love to my ex-wife.' Only he didn't say "making love" he said . . .'

'Anicetus, please!' I was trying to keep my fingers from his throat.

'I'm sorry.' He swallowed. 'I'm sorry. It's just I can't ... Anyway, I just gaped at him, naturally, because I'd never even met Octavia. Tigellinus laughed, the way he does, and said, "I'd admit it if I were you, sunshine. It'll save a lot of trouble in the long run."'

'Yes, it probably would.' Two senators passed, walking in the direction of the gate. They looked away when they saw us, and increased their speed. 'So the emperor made a deal with you.'

'Hardly a deal. He gave me a straight choice. Either I admit that Octavia seduced me to get at the fleet or he'd tell the Senate that we were both plotting treason and have me executed. Petronius, what could I do?'

'Nothing.' I looked at him. As an adulterer the poor dear was already a joke; to charge him with treason would've been utterly farcical. Lucius must be desperate. 'And he promised you a comfortable exile in exchange? In, the gods help us, Sardinia?'

'Sardinia's a nice place. In summer, anyway. And at least it's quiet, so I can get on with my writing.'

'What about Octavia?'

He shrugged; I could have hit him. 'She's being exiled as well.'

'Where to?'

'Pandateria.'

'Serapis!' Pandateria is a tiny island off the Campanian coast, a favourite dumping-ground for unwanted members of the imperial family. The trip is usually one-way. 'He said that? Lucius?'

'No, Poppaea. The emperor looked surprised, but he didn't correct her.'

'So you go trotting off to retirement in Sardinia as the innocent party while Octavia's accused of treason and gets Pandateria.' I realised I was gripping the man's mantle hard at the neck. I relaxed my fingers. 'It sounds like a fair deal to me, darling.'

'Petronius, I'm not to blame!' Anicetus's voice was shrill. 'She'd've been sent there anyway, whether I agreed or not! It's not my fault Nero wants rid of her!'

I suddenly felt tired. I hadn't thought that Lucius was capable of a protracted cruelty like Pandateria even in one of his mad moods; and certainly not when he was rational. But then the emperor was no longer the man I knew.

'No,' I said. 'No, dear, it isn't your fault. But I mustn't keep you. I suppose you'll be going back now to Misenum to pack.'

'I only wanted someone to know that I was innocent.' For the first time Anicetus looked more indignant than frightened: a puffed-up little figure with inky fingers and a weak chin. 'They'll say I did it, but I didn't. You can tell everyone that for me, Petronius. Explain that I really never touched her.'

'Well, at least you can rest easy on that score, darling,' I said. 'No one would believe anything else.'

Then I left him for my overdue meeting with the emperor.

I didn't see Anicetus again. He spent a comfortable two years in Sardinia enjoying the delicacies that Lucius supplied him with and writing monographs on the lesser-known Greek lyricists, before dying peacefully (and perhaps conveniently) in his sleep. Octavia wasn't so lucky. Only a few days after her transfer to Pandateria she was followed by a picked group of Tigellinus's Praetorians. They bound her and slit her wrists; then, because terror made the blood flow too slowly, they carried her into the steam-room of the island's tiny baths where the heat and humidity were increased until she suffocated. Her head was brought back for Poppaea to see. She was not quite, I think, twenty years old.

I don't know whether Lucius knew these details or not. If he did, he never mentioned them.

36

Poor Octavia's exile and murder found its way through even the Senate's thick skin. Not that they actually got off their well-padded backsides to register a protest, naturally, but there was more than a little whiff of revolution in the air that autumn. I even caught a few rumbles of discontent from Arruntius when I invited him and Silia round one evening to split a boiled ostrich.

We'd almost finished the meal. Arruntius, who'd made severe inroads into my best Setinian, was more than a little drunk and eyeing up the young Persian boy I'd bought a few days before to train as a wine waiter.

'So you're not so struck on your pal the emperor these days, then, Petronius,' he said suddenly.

'Pardon?' We'd been talking about the price of bayside properties near Baiae: Arruntius was thinking of investing some of the bribes he'd squirrelled away from his Highways and Aqueducts post in the purchase of a small villa. This was a complete non-sequitur.

'I said' – he reached over and absent-mindedly stroked the Persian lad's bottom as he poured – 'you're less enamoured of our artistic overlord than you have been in the past. Or so rumour has it.'

'We get on well enough.' I cracked a nut. Arruntius was an acceptable dinner companion, but not one to swap cosy secrets with. 'He may not take me into his confidence as much as he used to, but then I've never been a politician like yourself, my dear, so it doesn't really signify.'

Silia was peeling an apple. She looked up.

'No politics, Gnaeus, they're boring. And,' she added carefully, 'bad for one's health.'

The Persian boy – I'd called him Xerxes, just for fun – smiled a hooded smile and padded off to top up the wine jug.

'Oh, don't misunderstand me, Petronius.' Arruntius had ignored her. He waved his newly filled cup, spilling a few drops on to the couch. 'You wouldn't be alone, old son. Lots of people having second thoughts about Nero this past year, what with that new wife of his and bastard Tigellinus running things. Too many deaths, my friend. Too much grief.'

'Gnaeus!' Silia spoke quietly, but her voice held a curious warning note. 'That is *quite* sufficient!'

'Oh, Petronius is safe, darling.' Arruntius shifted his weight round to look at her: he'd got a great deal heavier over the years I'd known him, and now he was quite gross. 'Like he said he hasn't the balls for politics. But the magic's gone for him as well as everyone else. Eh, Petronius? Am I right or not?'

I said nothing, and nor did Silia: she was looking daggers. Arruntius grinned and reached for an almond cake.

'Of course I'm right. And do you want me to tell you why so many people are pissed off with Nero these days, my dear? Because he isn't a winner. any longer. We're tolerant of winners, we'll forgive them a lot.' He paused and stared directly at me. 'You think we're hypocrites. The Senate, I mean. Well, we're not. We're realists. Us and the emperor, it's like a marriage. You've got to have respect both sides. Doesn't matter what each partner does so much, as long as each fulfils the terms of the contract.' He turned suddenly to Silia, spilling the rest of his wine on the table. 'You agree, dear?'

'Gnaeus, I'm terribly sorry but I'm afraid you're drunk, darling.' Silia's voice was frosty. 'We'd best be getting back.'

'No. Oh, yes, I know I'm drunk. But we're not going home. Not just yet.' He dabbed at the spilled wine with a napkin. 'Don't worry that I'll get personal. I didn't mean it that way; you and Petronius can do whatever the hell you please, I couldn't care less. But you see my point, don't you, Titus? Governing's a contract, and Nero isn't honouring it.'

'Really, my dear, I think Silia's right. It is getting rather late.' I shared her concern, and it had nothing to do with Arruntius's drunkenness. The servants were all reliable, but we were verging very closely on treason here.

Arruntius had heard me, but he paid no notice. Xerxes came back in and he beckoned him over.

'Here, boy. Come and sit by me. You don't want us to go home yet, now, do you?'

Oh, Serapis. We'd had this problem before. The only thing to do was to let the poor darling talk himself out and fall asleep where he lay. We could always throw a blanket over him and leave him there for the night. I raised my eyebrows at Silia, but she was looking the other way.

Arruntius draped his left arm round young Xerxes and held up his empty cup to be filled.

'He's ballsed up the Armenian war for a start,' he said. 'We could've held Armenia against the Parthians if he'd shown a bit more spunk. Then there was the business with the corn.'

'That wasn't his fault,' I said. Nor it was. Through an unlucky combination of events almost three hundred grain ships had been lost with their cargoes, and Lucius had ordered a barnload of corn which had gone mouldy dumped into the Tiber. As a result Rome's granaries had been left almost empty.

'Maybe not his fault, but his responsibility. It's the emperor's job to look after the city's corn supply. Otherwise the mob gets upset and we're all in trouble.' Arruntius's forefinger was stroking the lad's nipple through his tunic. 'And another thing. Three hundred ships wrecked, then that fancy new Greek gymnasium of his struck by lightning. Then the earthquake at Pompeii. Too many disasters all in one year. I may not be superstitious, Petronius, but even I get the feeling someone's trying to tell us something. It all adds up.'

'It all adds up to what?'

'I told you.' His voice was becoming slurred: that last cup of wine might have done it. Surreptitiously I signed to Xerxes to keep topping it up. 'To Nero being a loser. Even then we might be more sympathetic if he'd back up a bit where we're concerned, but he couldn't care less.'

'You being the Senate again?' All this was quite alarming. I was used to Arruntius shooting his mouth off when he was drunk, but usually it was only hot air. This sounded more serious.

'Us being the Senate. Nero may hate our guts but he's a fool to make it so obvious, because some of us may just decide we've had enough and do something about it.'

'Arruntius, I really feel that . . .'

'Piso for one. Ever since that slimy bastard Romanus tried to get Seneca indicted he's . . .'

'Gnaeus! That's enough!' Silia snapped. She'd been getting more and more restless, and I'd assumed it was because of Arruntius's bad manners – his left hand had moved down to the hem of Xerxes's tunic. Evidently it wasn't: I'd rarely seen her so angry.

Arruntius, too, was surprised. His mouth opened then shut tight as a clam's.

Silia turned to me. 'Titus, it's been a lovely evening but I really do think we'd better leave.' Her eyes flicked back to Arruntius. 'Come on, darling. Now.'

Arruntius grunted and slipped tamely off his couch.

'Very well,' he said. ''Night, Petronius. Lovely evening. Lovely ostrich, lovely wine.' Deliberately he bent forwards and kissed Xerxes on the lips. 'Lovely boy. Yum! Buy him from you?'

'Not at present, dear. He still has novelty value. Perhaps later.'

He nodded. 'Look forward to it. Sorry about the . . .' He waved his right hand vaguely, realised he was still holding his wine-cup, drained it and set it mouth down on the table. 'Sorry about the spiel. Got carried away.'

'Don't mention it.'

'Mum's the word, eh?'

Silia reached over and tucked his arm firmly beneath her own.

'Good night, Titus!' she said.

I thought, when they'd gone, about what Arruntius had said. Or almost said. I knew of Decius Romanus. He was a narrow-striper like myself, a notorious fortune-hunter who kept just one jump ahead of the bailiffs. Not long after Octavia's murder he'd gone to Lucius privately (rumour had it with Tigellinus's blessing) and told him he had proof that Seneca was involved in a plot with several notable senators, including the aristocratic Gnaeus

Calpurnius Piso. Luckily the poor dear went about things in such a ham-fisted way that not even Lucius believed him. Seneca provided clear proof of his innocence, and Romanus was exiled to Spain for bringing a malicious charge.

Now. Piso might feel resentment against Romanus for bringing the charge, but he couldn't – as Arruntius had implied – harbour any specially bad feelings for Lucius, who'd thrown it out. But wouldn't it be curious if Romanus was right after all, for the wrong reasons?

I wouldn't've given it a moment's thought if it hadn't been for Silia's behaviour. She'd been on edge as soon as Arruntius had brought the subject of Lucius up, and when he mentioned Seneca she'd come down on him like a ton of ice and whisked him home. Did Silia know something I didn't? And if so why should she be so desperate for me not to find out? This secrecy wasn't like her. It wasn't like her at all.

I was worried. Very worried indeed.

37

In late January of the next year Poppaea gave birth at Antium to a daughter. The baby was named Claudia. Lucius was delighted.

'She's the spitting image of her daddy, Titus!' he beamed. 'Bright red fuzz on top and the loveliest hazel eyes.'

I'd been wondering, with quite a few others, whether the hair wouldn't be dark and curly and the eyes black, but Poppaea wasn't that stupid, and nor was Tigellinus.

'Congratulations.' I sipped my beaker of hot honeyed wine: Lucius had a cold, which meant his guests had to drink medicinally as well. 'When can we see this young paragon?'

'Not for two or three months yet.' Lucius popped a raw garlic clove into his mouth. 'Especially in this weather. She's very delicate. And Poppy gets terribly seasick, poor girl. It's just not worth the risk.'

'She's fine?' I hoped the question sounded reasonably sincere. Personally I wouldn't've mourned too much if darling Poppy had died horribly of complications. I wouldn't've been alone, either.

'Strong as a horse.' He made a face as he chewed. 'Oh, and I'm giving her the title of Empress. Her and the little one both.'

'That's nice.' I tried to hide my shock. The title 'Augusta' carries tremendous weight. By producing Lucius's first child Poppaea had moved straight to the topmost imperial niche.

A slave came in with a charcoal brazier and set it down between us. I moved my chair back – the room was stifling already – but Lucius leaned forward and held his hands over the coals.

'I'm sorry, Titus, but I can't get warm,' he said. 'It's this beastly cold. Do you never get them?'

'Not often. A doctor I met once in Smyrna advised me to eat lemons whenever I felt one coming on. That seems to do the trick.'

'Lemons?'

'An Indian fruit, very sour. You boil them up with honey and spices to kill the taste.' I paused and then said delicately: 'Do the Senate know yet? About the new titles?'

Lucius chuckled, then broke into a fit of coughing. He lifted the silver bowl beside his chair and I waited politely while he spat out a gobbet of phlegm.

'Fuck the Senate, darling.' He grinned, wiping his lips on a napkin. 'Yes, they know. They're thrilled, of course. In public at least. We're to have a new temple to the goddess Fertility. And a special athletics event. They do seem to enjoy their physical exercise nowadays, don't they, the dears?'

I didn't know whether to take that as sarcasm or not. Over the past year Lucius had been going out of his way to encourage senators and narrow-stripers to appear in the arena and the athletic stadium. The younger, wilder set had done it willingly, but he'd made it clear that a token participation was expected from anyone who wasn't totally unfit if they wanted to stay in his good books; which had made him even less popular with the traditionalists.

Lucius was watching me carefully, an odd expression on his face.

'You don't think very much of me these days, do you?' he said.

My stomach turned to ice. 'I'm sorry?'

'You heard, darling. I mean, it's obvious. Don't think I haven't noticed. You don't like the way I'm handling things any more.'

'You're the emperor.' Serapis! 'You don't need my approval.'

He sipped his hot wine, his eyes on mine over the rim of the cup.

'I used to think you were like me,' he said quietly. 'An idealist in a world of barbarians. Now I'm not so sure we're on the same side.'

'It may not be a question of sides.'

'You see?' He set the cup down. 'You're beginning to sound like Seneca. He said that once, do you remember? To me it is. The Senate would make me into their own image if I let them. When they say "Compromise" they mean "Behave yourself, do it our way". I can't let that happen because their way's narrow and wrong. That's why I need Tiggy, to put the fear of God into them.'

'He certainly does that very well.' I was temporising desperately.

'Inspiring fear's his function. I can't do it myself, however much I'd like to.' The words came out quite naturally, as if Lucius really believed them. Perhaps he did. 'It's silly, but there you are. I'm too good-natured. Tiggy's a pragmatic bastard who likes frightening people. Besides, the Senate love being slapped around, it gives them a chance to bumsuck in public and grizzle in private.' He paused. 'Titus, say something. I'm being serious now.'

What could I say?

'Being both emperor and artist can't be easy, my dear.' Ah, weak, weak! But I meant it: it was true enough and always had been. At that moment I felt more sympathetic towards Lucius than I had for months.

He laughed and coughed. 'Tell me something I don't know! No, it isn't easy. But it may get easier now that Poppy's popped because I mean to settle down and be a family man from now on, and family men are respectable. Maybe the Senate'll bend a bit in return.'

This was good news. Lucius was mellowing at last: I hesitated to use the phrase growing up. It was on the tip of my tongue to warn him about Piso, but I didn't. I'd no real proof (if there was anything to have proof of), and besides it was none of my concern.

'You haven't any children yourself, have you?' He was rubbing his hands again over the flames.

'No. Not that I'm aware of.'

'You should. It changes your perspective. And of course it's a tremendous responsibility. I'll have to be careful with little Claudia. I don't want her growing up with the same problems as . . .' He stopped. 'With any problems.'

'I'm sure she won't,' I said.

'No.' He wasn't looking at me now, but staring fixedly into the brazier. 'No. Poppy'll be a marvellous mother. Marvellous.'

I didn't answer. The silence lengthened, and I sat very still. Lucius's eyes were still fixed on the flames. He seemed to have forgotten that I was there.

Suddenly he blinked and sat back.

'I'm sorry, Titus,' he said. 'I was wool-gathering. What was I saying?'

'That Poppaea Sabina would be a marvellous mother.' I tried a smile and hoped that it didn't look too false. 'I don't doubt that she will.'

'Of course not!' He grinned. 'Of course she will! Now that's enough seriousness for one day. Where can I get hold of these lemon things you mentioned?'

I told him – there is a shop in the Velabrum which specialises in luxury fruits – and we began chatting in a more relaxed way than we had for months. When I left we were almost back on our old footing. Almost, but not quite. As Arruntius had said, there'd been too many deaths and too much grief for that. I might still sympathise – Lucius and I were too similar in nature for sympathy ever to vanish – but I couldn't bring myself any more to like the poor darling, even allowing for this new mellowness of his. And without liking friendship is impossible.

In any case, Lucius never did have his chance of becoming a family man, because four months later the baby was dead.

She died of a fever, still at Antium, and Lucius was totally devastated. It didn't endear him any further to the old guard in the Senate.

'The way he went on you'd think he was a woman!' Arruntius complained bitterly to me after the senatorial deputation had offered their official condolences at the palace. 'Tears, torn clothes, the lot! In public, too! I was disgusted, Petronius, simply disgusted! But that's these nancy-boy actors all over, they've no sense of proportion. Jupiter, the little basket wasn't even a boy!'

I didn't agree. Lucius's grief may have been theatrical, but it was real. Certainly he was less guilty of hypocrisy than Arruntius and his senatorial cronies, who immediately declared Claudia a goddess.

I was at the palace offering my own condolences when the news arrived.

'You see, Titus?' Lucius said, giving me a ghastly smile (he hadn't slept or eaten for four days, and his private room was even more of a pit than usual). 'They think I'm a child myself, to be kept sweet with nonsense. How could the poor mite possibly be a goddess just on their say-so? It's silly.'

'Then tell them it's silly. Use your veto.'

He shrugged. 'Why bother? It wouldn't do any good. They're despicable and there's an end of it. Anyway, I'm finished with them. From now on they can take me as I am or leave me alone.'

This sounded ominous, but I didn't pursue the matter.

'How's the empress?'

'Taking it very badly. What mother wouldn't?' He hid his face in his hands. I thought he was going to cry but it was only tiredness: he was slumped against the back of his chair. 'We'll try again of course, but not immediately. The poor girl's inconsolable. Absolutely inconsolable.'

Privately I doubted it: Poppaea's powers of resilience were considerable, and she'd never struck me as the maternal type.

'Is she coming back to Rome?' I avoided the awkward pause.

'In a few days, yes. After the embalmers have . . .' He stopped. His shoulders began to shake and he raised his hands again. This time there was no question about the reason. I wondered whether to leave, but that would have been impolite, so I sat in silence until he'd finished and blown his nose into a napkin. 'We'll bury the child in the family mausoleum. I've never seen a goddess buried before, Titus. What are the rites, do you know?'

'No,' I said quietly.

'It doesn't matter. We'll leave that up to the Senate as well. They'll be . . . impressive, I'm sure. We can trust them for that much.' He fell silent, staring into space, until I thought he'd forgotten me. Then, suddenly, he laughed; a harsh sound with no humour in it.

'I was just thinking, my dear,' he said. 'Old Julius is a god. My great-great-grandfather Augustus is a god. Even poor old idiot Claudius is a god. The Senate was responsible for all of them. Maybe the slimy bastards have got some sort of power after all.'

I said nothing.

'So if little Claudia really is a goddess, then what does that make me? Can a mortal father a goddess and still be only mortal? Come on, my dear, you call yourself an educated man. What's your answer? The father would have to be divine himself to begin with, surely?'

I held my breath. He was sounding (and looking, for that matter) far too much like his Uncle Gaius for my liking, or for the good of Rome. One reigning god-emperor had been enough in a generation, we didn't want two. Mentally I cursed the Senate for a pack of interfering, shit-stirring fools. If we were witnessing the birth of another Caligula then they'd only themselves to blame.

He must have noticed the look on my face, because he stopped laughing.

'Titus,' he said gently. 'It was a joke.'

I let the breath out slowly. If Lucius hadn't been aware of the tension before he was aware of it now. He was looking grave; very grave indeed.

'You thought I was serious, didn't you?' he said.

Wordlessly, I nodded.

'But I told you, dear, the whole thing's silly! You can't dignify it by any other term, it's just silly!'

'I know that.'

His clenched fist came down hard on the chair-arm. I was surprised that the wood didn't snap.

'Then stop treating me like a fool! You're as bad as the bloody Senate! I'm as mortal as you are!'

'You're sure, dear?' The flippancy was out of place, of course, but I was too relieved to care.

Lucius didn't smile.

'I'm not mad, Titus,' he said. 'I'm no god, and if it's left to the Senate I never will be. Not that I care, because being human's difficult enough. It's more than these fuckers can manage half the time, anyway.'

*　　*　　*

Being human's difficult enough.

I thought about that on the way home. I still think about it. Leaving the question of madness to one side (I'd've been surprised if he'd admitted to *that*), what exactly did he mean? Oh, the first part's clear enough. When he goes – however he goes – it's unlikely the Senate will deify him, at least not willingly. But the bit about finding it difficult to be human, well, that I don't understand at all. Perhaps he was only talking about quality of life. When Rome burned and he began his splendid new palace he remarked in my hearing: 'At last I can live like a human being!'

That would make sense, and it would fit with his character. But then again there was something else, something else.

Oh, I don't know, and I never will, now. But I left him feeling . . . well, unsettled is the word. Perhaps I'd've felt better if the poor dear had gone divine on me after all. It would've made things much simpler.

I'm getting philosophical again. Stop it, Petronius, you old fart! Have another slice of pheasant.

38

Lucius had meant what he said about being finished with the
Senate. Over the next twelve months relations were stretched
to breaking point. Poor silly Petronius, of course, was caught in
the middle. I could see what Lucius was after for Rome and to
a certain extent – personalities aside – I sympathised. On the
other hand I also understood the attitude of Arruntius and his
cronies. You can't change eight hundred years of conditioning
just by telling people they're wrong and then ignoring them. Not
unless you're asking for trouble; and that was just what Lucius
was doing.

That June, I was in the garden at the back of the house deciding
where to put a statue I'd just had made when a slave came out to
say that Thrasea Paetus had dropped by.

I was surprised. Thrasea wasn't even an acquaintance, let
alone a friend. Nevertheless, we might not have had much
time for each other, but I'd a certain respect for him: unlike
most senators he had standards and wasn't afraid to stick to
them. Lucius, of course, hated the poor dear's guts; but then as I
said elsewhere Lucius never could abide genuinely moral people.
Thrasea's colleagues weren't altogether happy in his company
either, and for much the same reasons.

So what, I wondered, did this moral paragon want with
me?

The boy showed him through. Thrasea was in his late fifties,
big, very florid, with the look of a Gaul: his family came from
Patavium, beyond the Po.

'Good of you to see me, Petronius,' he said. 'What a lovely
garden you have.'

He was nervous – I could see that straight away, although I didn't know why – so we chatted for a while about rose arbours and topiary, on which he was an expert. Finally I got him to come to the point.

'Petronius, we need your help,' he said.

'We?'

'The Senate.' A momentary hesitation: Thrasea was a truthful soul. 'Or anyway the thinking members of it.'

'Are there any of those?' He frowned. 'Oh, I'm sorry, darling, I'm being flippant. It's just I'm not used to being consulted on anything more vital than what wine to serve with roast flamingo. And certainly not by the Senate.'

The frown deepened. It covered, I realised, embarrassment, not anger.

'Yes, I can understand that.' Ouch, my dear! 'But we need someone close to the emperor who is, let's say, an impartial moderate. And we need him urgently.'

I steered him across to the garden seat next to the box hedge. This sounded complicated and not a little ominous, and if I had to discuss serious matters on a lovely day like this I preferred to do it in comfort.

'I'm afraid you may be wasting your time with me, then.' I sat. Thrasea did the same. 'We get on well enough but I wouldn't describe the relationship as close. Not any more. Not since Tigellinus.'

Thrasea's mouth twisted.

'I appreciate that too,' he said. 'Believe me, if we could find someone more suitable we would.'

I was beginning to see why the man got up so many people's noses. Honest and truthful he might be, but he had as much sensitivity as a brick.

'Oh, how terribly flattering.'

He looked at me; any politician recognises sarcasm when they hear it, even an insensitive one.

'I said an impartial moderate, Petronius, and I meant it,' he said slowly. 'We know you're not one of us. However you're no Tigellinus either, and that's what matters.'

I sighed. 'All right. So tell me what you want. If it's within the bounds of my moderate impartiality I'll do it with pleasure.'

'We want you to help heal the breach between us and the emperor.'

'What?' I laughed. Not the politest of reactions, but I couldn't help myself. 'Is that all? And after dinner perhaps I might persuade the Parthians to let us keep Armenia.'

'Certainly, if you can manage that too.' I hadn't expected humour from Thrasea, not even dead-pan humour. It made him a little more human. 'It'll take time and effort, I know, but . . .'

'It'll take a lot more than that, my dear! It'll take a minor miracle. Or is Tigellinus dead?'

'Petronius, you must understand my position. I deal with these people – I mean the Senate – every day. They could take a tyrant in their stride. They could even take a madman like Caligula or a suspicious fool like Claudius. But they can't and won't take Nero because they don't understand him. And before very long that lack of understanding is going to lead to trouble.'

He was right, of course. Lucius's public stage debut at Naples earlier in the year had scandalised the Senate. Then, more recently, had come his 'marriage' in full bridal dress to the ex-slave Pythagoras, which parodied the ancient wedding rites. I'd missed that, being in Capua on business at the time, but the emperor's theatrical screams and groans from behind the closed doors of the marriage chamber had been widely reported. Lucius had taken the dignity out of the principate, and if the Senate valued anything in their masters, hypocrites though they might be themselves, it was dignity.

'So what do you want me to do?' I said.

'Talk to Nero. Explain. His private life's his own concern, but he must control these . . .' – Thrasea hesitated – 'these public excesses. They're doing terrible harm. Terrible.'

'Enough to make some of your colleagues consider removing him?' That was too direct, even for Thrasea. He coloured up and his mouth shut like a trap. 'Oh, come on, my dear! That's what you're saying, isn't it?'

'There are . . . rumours.' He was cautious.

'Rumours be damned. You wouldn't be desperate enough to come round here if it were only a case of rumours. I don't expect you to give me names, that would be unreasonable.'

'That's just as well. I'm not here to betray my friends, Petronius.'

'I wouldn't expect you to. Anyway, I could name a few front runners myself.' I remembered what Arruntius had said at our ostrich dinner. 'Calpurnius Piso, for one.' He looked startled but said nothing. Bull's-eye. 'So you want me to help take the lid off the pot, dear, before the soup boils over?'

'It would ease matters considerably. These men aren't revolutionaries, they can give and take. But Nero's pushing them too far, and they won't suffer much more of it.'

'Wait a moment, Thrasea. I told you, we're no longer friends, the emperor and I. Not close friends.' I pulled a twig from the hedge and rolled it between my palms. 'Tigellinus is the only one he'll listen to now. And not only on matters of state. I may still be asked to imperial parties but I don't even advise on them all that often now.'

His eyes flickered. We moved in different worlds and this, it seemed, was news.

'You mean the emperor's Adviser on Taste has been retired?' he said. I detected a faint trace of malice.

'Call it superseded.' I tossed the twig aside and wiped the crushed leaves from my hands. 'Nero has found someone better, my dear. Or rather worse.' For a moment I thought of Seneca's charioteer. 'I understand why, of course. Tigellinus is a very clever man. He knows that the emperor needs someone to be bad for him.' I smiled. 'Besides, he's far more inventive than I am.'

'A dreadful admission for an Adviser on Taste to make.' The malice was more open now, although Thrasea was polite enough to try to hide it. Not that I was angry, or even annoyed: we were different people, and Thrasea simply didn't understand that.

'Oh, my dear!' I said gently. 'I didn't say Tiggy had more taste! I said he was more inventive.'

'I see.' He didn't – his lips were drawn in a disapproving line – but it didn't matter. 'So you will help, Petronius? As much as you can? For the good of Rome.'

'For the good of Rome.' I got up and held out my hand. He rose and took it, after the barest hesitation. 'Although I doubt, honestly, if I can do very much.'

'Anything would be better than nothing.'

'I'll bear that in mind, darling.'

I was sorry, when he'd gone, that he hadn't seen the statue. That would really have merited his disapproval.

39

I was at a party on the Caelian the evening of 18 July; alone, since Silia was holidaying with Arruntius in Baiae. When I left my friends' house about two in the morning it was a beautiful night, with a full moon and a clear sky.

Halfway down Staurus Incline the litter stopped. I could hear the slaves chattering together, but since the poor dears were Gauls that didn't help terribly much.

'Rufillus!' I shouted. 'What's going on?'

My head litter slave opened the curtain.

'Fire, sir,' he said. Gauls don't waste words. Latin ones, anyway.

I got out, a little unsteadily and more than a little angry, prepared to do murder: fires were too common in Rome to merit gawping, and I wanted home to bed.

Then I saw what Rufillus had meant.

The city was burning.

It was burning from beneath where we stood to almost halfway to the river, and even from here I could hear the screaming. Once alight, tenements burn like torches, and when they fall they block the surrounding streets and alleyways. The Racetrack District, where the fire was, was one of the most densely populated in Rome, and packed tight with tenements. The gods knew how many were dying down there. Hundreds, certainly. Probably thousands. And the fire was spreading, blown by the wind towards the city centre, destroying and killing as it went. As I watched, a long, low warehouse on the north side of the blaze collapsed in on itself. Tongues of flame leaped up and curved northwards, licking against a new line of buildings no more than a few hundred yards from the Palatine.

'Oh, Serapis!' I whispered. 'Oh, sweet Serapis!'

We weren't alone. People were streaming past us towards the higher ground, filthy, soot-streaked and stinking of smoke and sweat: one man carried a pig, another a bronze cooking stove. There was a child clutching a three-legged toy horse, and a woman with a string of onions. These were the lucky ones. None of them paid us any attention.

I turned back to the Gauls and tried to keep my voice steady. 'Home, dears. And quickly, please.'

We fought our way down Staurus Incline and on to the Septizonium. It was choked solid with traffic and pedestrians, moving at a snail's pace. There was no panic, but it was like being in a captured city surrounded by refugees. Behind us the whole sky was a huge livid bruise; the wind at our backs carried a drift of oily black specks and the stench of charred wood and, horribly, roasted meat. I'd seen fires before, of course, but nothing on this scale. The only way to stop it now would be to form fire-breaks by knocking down great swathes of the city in its path. That would take time, and probably more authority than even the consuls might care to exert without the emperor's approval. And Lucius was away in Antium.

Once we were clear of the Tenth District the crowds began to thin. Cuprius Street was no busier than it would've been during the day, and by the time we reached the Quirinal if it hadn't been for the lurid sky behind I could have believed everything was normal. My front gate was open, and the door slave was standing outside gaping at the sky.

I left the litter in the courtyard and hurried indoors. Crito, the head slave, was waiting in the hall.

'The baths are hot, sir,' he said. 'And I've given instructions for the more valuable items of furniture to be crated.'

'Well done, my dear.' I felt unutterably weary as I stripped off my soot-streaked party mantle. 'Very sensible of you.'

We were halfway across Rome from the fire, but if Crito thought we should be ready to evacuate it was as well to be safe.

'Also, –' Crito took the mantle – 'there was a message from Laecanius Bassus.'

I paused. 'The junior consul?'

'Yes, sir. He asks if you could possibly meet him at your earliest convenience at Maecenas Tower.'

'Did he say what he wanted?'

'It's not only you, sir. I believe he's calling on the help of several gentlemen outside the Senate. The authorities are very short-handed at the moment, as you'll appreciate.'

That made sense. In July and August most broad-stripers left the city for their villas in the Alban Hills or on the Campanian coast. And Bassus, unlike his senior consular colleague, had more between his ears than bone.

I dozed in the steam room of the baths for an hour or so, had my masseur coax the wine from my tired muscles, and set off for the Esquiline.

The tower was part of Maecenas Gardens, built into the line of the old Servian Wall. The last time I'd been inside was at one of Lucius's all-night parties, in the more circumspect days before Tigellinus when he held his orgies in private. It was eighty feet high, taller than the tallest tenement but far more strongly built, of good stone with oak beams supporting each floor and a solid internal staircase. From the parapeted roof you could see the whole of Rome.

'Petronius! You're the first! Well done, my dear fellow!' Bassus, usually an elegant dresser, looked like he'd slept in his clothes. If he'd slept at all.

I didn't answer. I was staring out over the city. Or what had been the city. The whole southern section from Palatine to Aventine and all the way to the river was hidden by a thick pall of smoke lit with flames. It'd been bad enough from down below. From here it was mind-numbing.

Bassus was standing at my elbow.

'Dreadful, isn't it?' he said quietly. 'The whole Eleventh District's ashes. The Palatine'll be next, including the palace itself. Nothing we can do about that.'

Thank the gods Silia was in Baiae; her house was on the Palatine's northern slopes. I was sure that her head slave would've given orders to evacuate all the movable valuables, but the house itself would burn. 'You've sent word to the emperor?'

'The courier left hours ago. I've prayed to Jupiter that Nero comes at once.' Bassus was that rarity in Rome, a pious man who believed prayers had some effect.

'How did it start? Do you know?'

He shrugged. 'Probably in one of the oil shops behind the racetrack. It doesn't matter. What with the dry weather, if we don't stop it now we could lose the whole city.'

I knew that, of course; how could I not, standing there on the tower roof with Rome dying beneath me? It was chilling, though, hearing Bassus put the thought into words.

'What do you want me to do?'

'Come over to the table. I'll show you.'

The 'table' was a number of planks laid over trestles, on which was a scale model of the city.

'Isn't it beautiful?' Bassus said.

'Lovely.' The hills were sculpted in clay, and the river was a line of glass. Public buildings had been carved from ivory, and although the other buildings were simple wooden blocks they were in the right places. There was no sign of the Temple of Claudius, let alone anything more recent, so I guessed the thing was a dozen years old at least, probably more.

'I brought it from the palace.' Bassus signalled to a slave to bring over one of the torches. 'The emperor won't mind, it would've burned anyway. So, Petronius. These're our problem districts.' His finger drew lines in the air above the minia- ture Rome. 'Isis and Serapis. The Subura, from Palatine to Viminal. The centre itself between the river, the Palatine and the Capitol.'

I nodded. The parts he'd indicated were the fire's natural routes, heavily built-up areas that followed the low ground between the more sparsely populated hill slopes where ten- ements gave way to middle- and upper-class housing.

'That's a lot of ground, my dear.'

'Tell me something I don't know.' Bassus rubbed his eyes. 'It's the minimum to keep the blaze contained, but we're stretched thin already and the situation's getting worse. Co-ordination's the problem. We haven't enough men. We need responsible people at ground level, as many as we can get. Organising water supplies, allocating manpower where and when it's needed, clearing buildings, giving the order for demolition.' He paused. 'Well? Will you help?'

'You flatter me,' I said.

He gave a weary grin. 'True, Titus. But then I'm desperate.'

I laughed. When he wasn't being super-efficient Bassus was excellent company, unlike the aristocratic Licinius Crassus Frugi, who was a bore of quite staggering proportions. Which reminded me . . .

'By the way, where is your esteemed colleague?'

'At his villa in Tusculum, as far as I know.' Bassus's brows came down. 'Where the bastard can stay, as far as I'm concerned. I may be desperate, but not that much. I'll handle this myself. And carry the can, until Nero gets here.'

'In that case, darling,' I said, 'I'll be delighted to help.'

40

We fought the fire for six days, and lost. Bassus had put me in charge of part of the section between the Pullian Incline and the Caelian, although by the end that was a burned desert and we'd moved east almost as far as the Querquetulan Gate. If I close my eyes I can still see the flames and taste the acrid smoke at the back of my throat, and hear the slipping rumble of masonry and the screams that went with it. I see other things, too, that are worse: the half-charred corpse I trod on in an alleyway, that I thought was a dog and which turned out to be a child. The woman who jumped from the roof of a tenement I'd ordered cleared for demolition, just before it fell. The fear-crazed mule, broken jars dangling from its sides, that ran past us soaked in blazing oil. There was never enough time, never enough help. Never enough water, either: the nearest mains supply was the Claudian Aqueduct, a mile away on the Caelian, and we had to make do with the public standpipes and fountains. Even if one happened to be nearby and clear of rubble a full bucket moved down the chain with nightmare slowness. When I got home at night – if I got home at night – to the false peace of the Quirinal the first thing I noticed was the obscene sound of water splashing into my ornamental pool.

The fire ate Rome's heart out. On the second day the wind shifted, blowing the flames away from the Market Square and the Capitol but driving them across the northern slopes of the Palatine. By the third day, everything south of the Sacred Way was ablaze, and by the fourth there was nothing left there but blackened masonry, charred beams and a silting of ash. The House of the Kings. Vesta's temple and grove. The Temple of

Jupiter Stayer of the Host, which Romulus had founded eight hundred years before. Gone. All gone. To the east, where I was, the flames raced between Caelian and Esquiline, gutting Isis and Serapis as far as the Servian Wall. By the sixth day between the river and Mount Caeliolus to the west and east and the Sacred Way and the Aventine to the north and south Rome was a ruin, stinking of sour smoke and half-burned corpses.

Lucius had come as soon as he'd got Bassus's message. He threw open the public buildings on Mars Field in the north-west of the city and his own Vatican Gardens beyond to the refugees, organised emergency accommodation and an extra grain supply from the Ostian granaries and the towns outside Rome, cutting the price to a sixteenth of its value. All this, however, I heard at second-hand. I only saw him once, on the fourth day, when I went to the Tower of Maecenas to beg Bassus for more men.

The first thing that struck me was the quiet. Although it was nothing compared to the screaming hell of the Third District, Maecenas Tower, being the operations centre, was always noisy. The ground floor, where most of the routine reports were made, was even fuller than usual, but there was no movement, only a terrible stillness. I shoved my way inside and grabbed the nearest clerk by the shoulder.

'Where's Bassus?' I said.

'What?' His eyes hadn't followed the rest of his body round. They were still turned towards the base of the staircase.

'The consul, you fool! Is he here?'

'Yes.' He had finally given me his full attention, but it had cost an effort. I knew him now: he was one of Bassus's best freedmen, a clever Asian Greek from the Public Works Department. 'Yes, he's on the roof. But he's got . . .'

I didn't stop to listen. Pushing past I began to climb the stair. That was crowded, too; but again no one was moving. The whole tower seemed, for some reason, to be frozen, listening.

I heard the first notes just before I squeezed through the final group on to the roof itself and saw the reason for the stillness.

Lucius was standing with his back to me, facing out over the burning city. He was wearing a tragic gown, sewn with pearls and sequins that flashed and glittered in the light of the flames. In the crook of his left arm he held a cithara, the heavy eleven-string

harp used for concert performances. As I watched he drew the
plectrum across the strings and began to sing:

> Muse, tell of the wrath of the Greeks, when the wooden
> horse gave birth,
> Tumbling to earth her bronze-clad foals
> Terrible in their anger,
> Bringing death to Ilium . . .

I stood as if nailed to the roof's floor. The song was Lucius's 'Sack
of Troy', which he'd written the year before and had intended for
his cancelled Greek tour. Under and above it came the sounds of
the dying city far below; in my ears, and in my head, too. Men
shouting. Women and children screaming. The sliding crash of
falling buildings and the terrible, constant crackling of the flames.
Over to the left, against the southern parapet, I saw Bassus in the
middle of a knot of others. He was weeping. I put my fingers to
my own cheeks and they came away wet and dark with soot.

At last the thing ended. Lucius struck a final chord and held
his pose, waiting for the applause. It came. Scattered, yet it came.
I couldn't bring myself to join in. I was thinking of the corpse in
the alleyway, that I'd thought was a dog's.

The emperor turned and made his bow. I was about to slip
away, but he saw me.

'Titus, darling! What're you doing here?' He handed the
cithara to a waiting slave and came towards me. His gown –
purple-dyed – was dull as old blood in the firelight. 'Did you
enjoy that?'

'Very nice,' I said.

'My dear, you look like a half-burned scarecrow!' He hugged
me. 'And you absolutely stink! What've you been doing to
yourself?'

'Oh, this and that.' I could've hit him. 'Taking part in the sack
of Rome, mostly.'

'It's terrible, isn't it?' For a moment – but only for a moment
– his face clouded. 'Bassus was telling me three districts've gone
already. Including the palace, of course. Such a shame. We'd just
had the decorators in.'

'At least the fire's had its uses.' I gestured towards the slave with the cithara. I don't think I'd ever been so angry. 'It makes for such marvellous theatre.'

'Yes, doesn't it?' He nodded, and beamed. His arm was still round my shoulders and he smelled of scent. 'I couldn't waste the opportunity, could I? Such drama, my dear! Such excitement! It's almost worth everything.'

'Almost.' As unobtrusively as I could I moved out of his grip. Not unobtrusively enough. He frowned.

'I do care, Titus,' he said. 'I've done my best. And what can it possibly matter to anyone?'

'What indeed?' I glanced across at Bassus. His face, and the faces of the others around him – I noticed they were all senators – were hard as stone.

'You'll see.' Lucius was talking to me as if to a child. 'Once we get this terrible fire under control I'll build a proper city. Wide streets with covered walks. Proper fire precautions. Lots of new public buildings. Grants, of course, for private citizens who've lost their property. It'll be a blessing in disguise, Rome was such a dump.' He paused. 'Oh, and a proper palace as well. Not just for me. For Rome. Something we can all be proud of.'

'I'll look forward to that,' I said. 'And now, if you'll excuse me . . .'

I moved away, towards Bassus. Lucius didn't stop me; but I couldn't help noticing his sudden look of hurt, as if I had actually hit him after all. In a way he was right; that was the dreadful thing. Performing his 'Sack of Troy' to the backdrop of the blazing city meant nothing; as I'd said myself, a marvellous bit of theatre. It didn't matter a straw, especially set against all the good he'd done since he'd got back to Rome. He was sincere, too, about his plans for the city. I knew that. Lucius would move heaven and earth to make sure that Rome after the fire was a better and a safer place to live in.

But what would they remember, the Romans of a hundred years' time, when all of us were dead? That the Emperor Nero had rebuilt the city, much of it at his own expense? Or that he played the cithara and sang while the old Rome burned below him? You, my readers, know the answer as well as I do. And so will your children, and your children's children.

Lucius's tragedy was that he couldn't even ask himself the question.

41

We thought, on the sixth day, that it was all over. In the Third, Tenth and Eleventh Districts there was nothing left to burn, and where the alleys gave way on the slopes of the hills to stone-built houses and more open ground the fire had burned itself out or been brought under control. Then reports came in of a fresh outbreak to the north, in the Seventh District, the largely residential region beyond the Servian Wall. From there the fire spread westward into the Flaminian Racetrack District. It burned for three more days, not stopping until it reached the river. By the morning of 28 July, when everything was finally over, half the city was a blackened cinder and half its population homeless or dead.

I don't know when the rumours started, or who started them; no one had had any time for gossip up to then. I heard them first from Bassus, who was staying with me temporarily: being consul, instead of going off to his villa in the Alban Hills while the damage to his own house was being repaired, the poor fellow was stuck in Rome (or what was left of it) organising the clearing-up operation.

It had taken my bath slaves the whole day, plus two pounds of pumice and a gallon of rosewater, to stop me looking and smelling like a lump of charcoal. When I came into the solar for a pre-dinner drink to complete the transformation Bassus was inspecting the fluorspar wine dipper I'd just bought.

'Nice,' he said.

'So it ought to be for three hundred thousand.' I reclined. The slave busied himself with the cups and strainer.

'Jupiter!' He set the thing down carefully on its napkin. 'That's the price of a decent work slave!'

You have to make allowances: Bassus was from Patavium, and his family were farmers.

'The emperor paid a million for his,' I said.

'Then he's got more money than sense. And so have you.'

He meant it. I laughed. 'Not at all, my dear. There's a difference. Mine's worth every penny. They saw poor Nero coming.'

'I'd rather have the slave, in any case. Still' – he sipped his wine – 'I suppose it's a matter of priorities.'

'Indeed. Have you seen him recently? The emperor?'

'We'd an interview this morning, Frugi and I.' The senior consul was back in Rome. He'd arrived shortly after Lucius, but since his own house was on the Caelian and under threat from the fire we hadn't seen much of him. 'A remarkably productive interview, really. Nero came up with a lot of good ideas.'

'You sound surprised.' The slave had gone. I filled my own cup.

'Well, it's just . . .' He frowned. 'You were there that night at Maecenas Tower. You saw him yourself. You know what I mean.'

'I know exactly what you mean, my dear. Very dramatic, of course, but just a little ill-advised under the circumstances.'

'Ill-advised be damned, it was stupid.' He hesitated. 'You know the emperor's being blamed for starting the fire himself?'

'What?' I almost dropped the wine dipper, but caught myself in time and replaced it carefully.

'The Maecenas Tower story's gone the rounds. People are saying he burned the city just for the sake of the performance.'

'That's nonsense! It's worse than nonsense, it's absolute stupidity!'

'I didn't say I believed it.' Bassus was looking uncomfortable. 'I said that was what people are saying.'

'What people?'

'The ordinary citizens. Even a few of the better classes.'

'But Lucius was in Antium when the fire started! Everyone knows that!'

'They say he arranged things before he left. And there are reports of gangs stopping firemen from doing their job, claiming they were acting under the emperor's orders.'

'I had trouble with a few of those myself. They were looters, trying it on.' I hadn't thought twice about it at the time, with so much else to do. 'Bassus, believe me, Nero just isn't capable of something like this. And what reason could he possibly have?' Bassus shook his head, but he didn't look convinced. I was seriously worried. The mob was one thing – the average Roman citizen with a third-floor tenement room will blame anyone for anything at the drop of a corn-dole ticket – but reasonable men like Bassus were another matter. 'That business at the tower was just a piece of silliness. You know how the emperor is. Where art's concerned he just doesn't think.'

'Did he mention his new palace to you?'

The sudden change of direction took me by surprise. 'He said something about it, yes.'

'What exactly?'

I was cautious. 'Nothing much. Only that he wanted it to be impressive.'

Bassus laughed. 'It's to be impressive, all right. It'll take in everything from the Palatine to Maecenas Gardens.'

'I'm sorry, my dear, but that's nonsense. Something that big would stretch halfway across the city. It'd mean demolishing . . .' I stopped, suddenly cold. No demolition was necessary; there was nothing between the Palatine and the Esquiline to demolish. Not now. 'He's serious?'

'He had it all worked out. What it would look like. The decoration. Even some idea of the cost. As if he'd been planning it for months.'

I said nothing. I simply could not believe that Lucius would be so cold-blooded. Performing his 'Sack of Troy' with Rome burning around him, yes, that was in character. But to start a fire that would kill thousands just to clear space for his own building plans – no, not even Lucius was that much of an egotist. Besides, he'd said himself that he'd just had the palace redecorated, and money aside he would never have done that if he'd known it wouldn't last the year out. Never.

'There's another thing.' Bassus was staring into his cup. 'The second fire, in the Broad Street District. You know where that started?'

'Tell me.'

'North-west of the Sanquatis Gate. On an estate owned by Ofonius Tigellinus.'

I set my wine-cup down. It was still more than half full, and I'd almost forgotten I was holding it. 'Coincidence, my dear. Any fire has to start somewhere. And Tigellinus was out of Rome at the time.'

'As the emperor was ten days ago?' Bassus came as close to a sneer as he was capable of. 'How very convenient. Besides, the fire wasn't reported until it was well out of control.'

'Was there anyone on the estate to report it?'

'The house was staffed, yes. And it isn't that big. One of Tiggy's more modest properties.' Bassus set his own cup down. 'Titus, don't get me wrong. I said I didn't necessarily believe the emperor was involved, and I meant it. In any event what you and I think isn't important. People are blaming him, and even if they don't all claim he started the fire they're accusing him of keeping it going for his own purposes. And they've got evidence to back them.' I'd forgotten that Bassus was a lawyer, and a good one. 'Whatever the truth of the matter, Nero has a case to answer.'

'Even although the whole thing was an accident?' I was stubborn. 'You were in charge. You know the situation better than anyone. Could he have done more to help than he did?'

'Perhaps not, but . . .'

'Or been more concerned? Genuinely concerned? Forget the histrionics on the tower roof, they meant nothing, not in his terms, anyway. Believe me, Nero may be guilty of a lot of things but burning Rome isn't one of them.'

He sighed. 'Well, you may be right. He's not in my court anyway, and never likely to be. But if I were the emperor, guilty or innocent, I'd be very worried indeed, because he can't ignore public opinion, and accident or not people are looking for a scapegoat. If he wants to slide out of this one with his credibility intact he'd better come up with one soon.'

At that point the slave came back to say that dinner was served. I can't say I enjoyed it.

42

I was going over my accounts in the study a few days later when my head slave edged his way round the door.

'Yes, Crito?' I said. No answer. The man was shifting nervously from foot to foot.

'Well?' I stared at him. 'Is it a visitor?'

'No, sir.'

'What, then?'

Crito cleared his throat.

'I wanted . . . that is, sir, I was wondering whether . . . If you could possibly . . .' He stopped dead.

I put my pen down. I'd had him for twenty years and never seen the old dear so much as blush. Even at parties.

'Don't tell me,' I said. 'The cook's screwing one of the kitchen girls on the doorstep and the neighbours are complaining.'

'No, sir!' That was more like his usual style. 'I wished to ask you a favour, sir. On a personal matter.'

'All right.' I indicated a chair. 'Sit down and let's hear it.' He hesitated. 'Crito, sit! You're making me feel nervous, dear.' He sat as if the chair seat had spikes. 'Now what's all this about?'

'Will you be seeing the emperor soon?'

Normally I'd have told him to mind his own business, but I bit my tongue. 'I might. Why?'

'Then, sir, I was wondering if perhaps you might consider talking to a . . . friend of mine first. At least, not a friend exactly, more of a . . .' He stopped again. He was bright red.

This was getting more intriguing by the minute. A lover? Crito was over sixty and ugly as sin. The idea was obscene. 'More of a what?'

He ducked the question. 'Someone I respect very much, sir.'

'Does this paragon have a name?'

'Yes. Of course. His name's Paullus.'

'And he wants me to put something before the emperor?' I was beginning to understand. This Paullus was obviously a slave or a freedman in trouble who'd asked Crito for help. And it must be serious for Crito to come to me.

'Yes, sir. But not for himself. For all of us.'

'For all of who?' I was lost again.

Crito squirmed in his chair and turned an even deeper red.

'The city's Christians, sir,' he said.

I got it out of him at last. Lucius, so the rumour went, was about to blame the fire on Rome's Christian community to which, seemingly, my head slave belonged. I didn't know much about the cult, apart from the fact that it was a Jewish heresy currently popular among the domestic slave population, but I was surprised that Crito was an initiate. At his age and with his intelligence I'd've thought the old dear would've had more sense.

'So who is this Paullus?' I asked. 'A slave? Or a freedman?'

'Neither, sir.' Crito spoke with a curious pride. 'Paullus is a citizen.'

'He's what?' The name was Latin, of course, but that meant nothing. I hadn't expected citizenship, though. 'A Roman?'

'No, not a Roman, sir. A Cilician, from Tarsus.' Crito was fidgeting again.

'And what exactly does this gentleman want me to do?'

'I'd rather he told you that himself.' That was said politely but firmly, in the tone Crito used for turning away unwanted guests. I knew from experience that he wouldn't budge an inch further.

I gave in.

'All right. I'll be seeing the emperor in two days' time. Bring this Paullus of yours round tomorrow and we'll . . .'

'He can't come here. He's under house arrest.'

That stopped me. House arrest wasn't usual, not for an ordinary citizen. 'What the hell for?'

'Rabble-rousing, sir.'

I laughed. Crito had the grace to blush; he'd never, so far as I knew, been in trouble with the law in his life, and he'd no time for criminals. This Paullus must be special indeed.

'So you want me to go to him, do you? Crito, my dear, I'm sorry, but really . . .'

'Please, sir!' He was almost crying. 'It's desperately important!'

'Oh, don't worry, I'll go! It sounds like fun.' I put the wax tablets into the desk and locked it. 'Where does this rabble-rouser live?'

'He has a house near the Praetorian Camp.'

Another surprise. I'd expected the Aventine or the Trans-Tiber region. First citizenship, now money. 'A good address. All right. Order up the litter. We'll go there now.'

The house wasn't a grand one but it looked comfortable enough from the outside: an old property behind a mud-brick wall on a pleasant tree-lined street. Someone must've been looking out for us because the door opened even before Crito knocked. The door slave stood aside to let us in.

'Welcome,' he said. 'Go straight through. He's in the garden.'

He. Not the master. The slave kissed Crito on both cheeks, which was also unusual. But, as I was about to find out for myself, it was an odd household altogether.

I followed Crito through the house and into the garden at the back. It was a pleasant place, simple but carefully looked after with a fig tree against the wall, rose bushes and terracotta pots of basil, thyme and rosemary. The small courtyard was full of people. Two of them, I noticed, were Praetorians. They were sitting on a stone bench chatting to each other quite naturally, as if they were at home and off duty. Only when they saw me did they stand up and come to attention.

In the shade of the fig tree sat a man in his sixties, dressed in a simple woollen tunic; smallish, balding, unremarkable in any way, except that he managed somehow to be the focal point of the garden. As we came out through the porch he looked in our direction. His eyes were sharp under massive eyebrows.

'Crito!' he said. 'God be praised!'

He was speaking Greek; good Greek, too, with an educated accent. I began to revise my opinions. He stood up. the younger man who'd been standing next to his chair – a slim, serious-looking man in a finer tunic than his – bent over and whispered in his ear, but he waved him aside.

'No, Loukas, I'm fine. Don't fuss, we have a guest.' The crowd parted respectfully to let him through. 'Welcome, sir. It's good of you to come. Justin, my friend, a little wine for the gentleman, please.'

The last request – it wasn't an order – was in Latin. The door slave who had followed us out smiled and left.

Paullus – this had to be Paullus – took my arm. Standing, he was even shorter than I'd thought, scarcely the height of my shoulder. His legs were bent, almost crippled.

'My Latin's dreadful, I'm afraid,' he said. 'We'll speak Greek, if you don't mind.'

'Not in the slightest.' Someone had brought another chair and set it down under the fig tree. We sat. The conversation carried on around us, but I had the distinct impression that everyone was listening. Justin came back with a plate of grapes and the wine; one cup only. When he handed me it I noticed a huge discolouration on his lower leg. It was old, and looked like a burn: some childhood accident, perhaps. I sipped. A country wine with a hint of myrtle, and not at all bad.

'Now, sir.' The keen eyes turned towards me. 'You're wondering why I asked Crito to bring you here.'

'He says the emperor intends to blame the fire on the Roman Christians.'

Paullus nodded. 'Yes. We don't know for certain, but it's likely.'

'Is he right?' The old man's calmness annoyed me. 'Did you start it?'

'No.'

That was all. If I'd expected a tirade I was disappointed. At the same time the simple denial was vastly more impressive.

'So what will you do if he does accuse you?' I was intentionally blunt.

'Nothing.'

I frowned. This conversation wasn't going at all as I'd expected. 'But you're the cult's high priest, are you not? You've a responsibility to your people?'

'I'm no priest, sir. High or otherwise.' He smiled. I noticed that there were answering smiles from those around, and even some laughter. 'Just a common-or-garden sinner, worse than most if anything. And ours isn't a cult.'

'So what is it, then?' I was becoming really annoyed with his manner now. 'A philosophy?'

'It's the truth.'

I felt as if someone had thrown a cup of cold water into my face. This wasn't arrogance. It was worse than arrogance, it was complete egotism.

'One truth, surely,' I said.

'No. *The* truth.'

Politeness be damned. 'Your truth is in for a shock, then, if Nero decides he wants rid of you. Perhaps even a fatal shock.'

'The emperor can do as he likes. That doesn't affect the matter one bit.' He laid his hand on my arm. 'Don't be angry, please. I'm not trying to impress you, I'm only stating a fact. Bodily death is irrelevant. If Jesus calls us to be witnesses for him we'll die gladly.'

'Jesus being your god?'

'He's no god. Not in the sense you mean. He died himself, once.'

Sophistry was all very well, but this was too silly for words. 'You worship a dead *man*?'

'Wasn't the Emperor Augustus a man? And Claudius?'

There was a mischievous edge to his voice, and I couldn't help smiling. 'That's different, my dear. They're . . . political gods.'

'True. And neither of them rose.'

'Rose?'

'Returned to life.'

If he hadn't been so obviously serious I would've laughed in his face.

'And this Jesus did?'

'Of course. I've seen him myself. Several times.'

I must have simply stared at him. Despite the calm, rational, lawyer-like tones the old man was mad, completely mad. I looked up at the faces round us, expecting embarrassment, or even amusement. I didn't find either. They were as serious as Paullus's. Even Crito was nodding.

'So you see, sir,' Paullus went on as if we were discussing the price of fish in the market, 'we're not worried for ourselves. Our concern is for Nero.'

'Nero?'

'Oh, yes. He'd be making a terrible mistake, you see. At the moment he rules with God's permission, but if he turns against God's son then he's finished, body and soul. And I wouldn't like that to happen. The emperor's a good man at heart, only lost.'

The old man's egotism was unbelievable; only his insanity could excuse it. The threat, however, was chillingly real. We'd had trouble with Jewish fanatics before. And if Crito could be a Christian then so could any of the palace slaves. I looked for support to the Praetorians. They'd obviously heard, but they were smiling. Perhaps neither of them spoke Greek, or were pretending they didn't.

'You'd order your followers to kill him? Assassinate the emperor?'

Paullus shook his head.

'You misunderstand me. The Lord Jesus gives life, he doesn't take it. He may ask us to die for him but never to do injury. Let alone murder.'

'So what do you want me to do?' I said. 'Tell Nero that if he holds you Christians responsible for the fire he'll be risking some kind of Jewish curse?'

'Not one of our making. And we are not Jews, as you see. Not all of us. Not any longer.'

'He'd laugh in my face, darling. And quite rightly so.'

'Is that such a terrible price to pay for telling the truth and saving a soul?'

'Your truth, not mine. And not my soul either.'

'Are you sure about that?' he said gently. 'Perhaps in telling him you might be saving both your souls.'

I got up. Crito, who had edged to the sidelines while we'd been talking, came forward again. The poor man looked miserable. No doubt he thought I'd failed him; as, indeed, I had.

I turned back to Paullus.

'I can't promise anything.' I said, 'and I certainly won't cross Nero for you. But I'll try my best.'

'None of us can do more.' Paullus stood too. With his age and obvious infirmity he ought to have looked frail, but he didn't, no more than a lump of olive root. 'Thank you. Go with the blessing of the Lord Jesus, Petronius.'

The audience, obviously, was over. I bowed ironically and went with Crito instead. His gratitude was sufficient.

43

The palace, of course, was in ashes along with the rest of the Palatine. Lucius was staying in one of the imperial villas on the Janiculum, near Caesar's Gardens. When I arrived he wasn't alone: Tigellinus was a constant shadow these days. They were in one of the solars, huddled over a large table covered with sheets of paper.

'Titus.' Lucius was in one of his expansive moods. Tigellinus scowled at me, as usual. 'Nice to see you, my dear. Come and join us. Tiggy and I are replanning the city.'

The sheets were architect's sketches: I noticed a temple or two and some other public buildings. The Office of Public Works must've been working flat out to have produced that many so quickly.

'Bassus tells me you did terribly well in Isis and Serapis.' Lucius edged his chair towards Tigellinus's to give me room to move mine in. 'He was most impressed.'

'That was one of the districts that was completely gutted, wasn't it?' Tigellinus said sourly. 'Nice work, Petronius.'

'Now, Tiggy, don't be a cat!' Lucius gave him a fond smile. 'Titus did his best, I'm sure.'

'At least I was in Rome and not Antium,' I snapped; then regretted it. It was a monumentally stupid remark, because of course Lucius had been in Antium too.

Tigellinus grinned. 'True,' he said. 'We can't all be heroes. Eh, Nero?'

'So it would seem.' The emperor was frowning. 'However, we're here now, Titus, and you heroes who let the city burn will need us lesser mortals' assistance to put it back together again.'

I said nothing. Tigellinus winked at me.

'Show him the plans,' he said.

Lucius brightened up immediately. He swept the smaller sketches aside and unrolled a large sheet of paper, weighting it at the corners with the bronze lamps from the table. I remembered Bassus's model – but then that would be useless now, except as a curio.

'We're rebuilding on the grid system,' he said. 'Nice broad streets laid out straight, not the old higgledy-piggledy nonsense there was before. All the buildings detached. And it'll be done properly. A fixed proportion of the materials will be fireproof stone. And I'll have the Senate pass a regulation making it obligatory for householders to keep firefighting equipment to hand.'

'We'll regulate the tenements as well,' Tigellinus added. 'Nothing higher than seventy feet. And the frontages'll be protected by colonnades.'

'Very impressive.' I didn't have to pretend enthusiasm, although I winced at Tigellinus's 'we'. The man's newly acquired air of civic duty made me want to throw up. 'It should be a great improvement.'

'Ah, but this is the best part, Titus!' Lucius's hand swept over the centre of the map. 'The new palace!'

Bassus had warned me, of course, but it still came as a shock. The entire area between Palatine and Esquiline had been blocked in with buildings and formal gardens.

'My Golden House.' Lucius glanced smugly at Tigellinus. 'Isn't it marvellous?'

'It's certainly . . . spacious.'

'Naturally.' Tigellinus gave me a bland look. 'Do you think the Emperor of Rome deserves anything less?'

'No, of course not. But the cost . . .'

Lucius was frowning again. 'Oh, the cost! What does that matter? It's not just for me, it's for Rome. And I'm sure the provinces will be delighted to contribute, especially the eastern ones. After all, if the old Greek kings could build on the grand scale I don't see why I shouldn't. I've asked Severus and Celer to take charge, although of course I've got my own ideas as well.'

'A good choice.' Severus and Celer had worked on Lucius's

last building project, the extension to the palace burned down in the fire. They must be rubbing their hands. The new commission would set them up for life, if Lucius managed to push his plans through the Senate. I could hear the popping of aristocratic blood vessels all the way across the Tiber.

'Now, my dear.' Lucius reached for another stack of sketches. 'Let me show you the plans in more detail.'

The cost aside – and even without the rest of the city to consider it would drain the Treasury dry – Lucius's Golden House was a magnificent concept. The low-lying ground between the Palatine and the Esquiline was to be flooded to form a huge lake, round which the buildings were set in an artificial landscape of fields, vineyards and woodland with wild and domestic animals roaming freely. A mile-long triple colonnade, broken to allow the Sacred Way and the New Way to pass through, linked the old and new palaces. On the Caelian, adjoining the Temple of Claudius, was a complex of colonnades and grottoes with plants and running water, while the main residential block lay on the Oppian spur of the Esquiline. Even in its roughly sketched-out form I could appreciate the impressiveness of the finished work.

'Won't it be beautiful?' Lucius beamed when he'd talked me through its main points. 'I'm commissioning a statue of myself. A big one, a hundred feet high. It'll go there.' He pointed to the area between the lake and the house's huge vestibule. 'Overlooking the Market Square. So people will know I'm looking after them even when I'm out of Rome, and these bastards in the Senate will see I've got my eye on them.'

Tigellinus sniggered. 'We're getting Zenodotus to do it. He's only done gods so far. It'll be a step up for him.'

'Oh, don't be silly, Tiggy!' It was a token protest, and Tigellinus took it as such. He smiled at me. 'But it will be nice. And of course you're invited to the housewarming, Titus. When it's all finished we'll have a real party.'

'Thank you.' I needn't hold my breath; he'd be building for years. 'By the way, my dear, speaking of gods I had an odd bit of news myself the other day.'

'Really? Do tell!'

'It seems my head slave Crito has finally got religion and joined a cult.' I kept my voice light. 'The Christians. Have you ever heard anything so daft?'

'Daft is right.' Tigellinus laughed. 'His timing's imbecilic.'

'Oh?' I turned to him, keeping my expression bland. 'Why so?'

'Let's just say he'd be safer lopping his dangler off and signing up for Attis.'

I played the innocent. 'I didn't know it was a dangerous religion.'

'Oh, it's dangerous all right! Or it soon will be. If your pal hasn't paid his dues yet you can tell him not to bother, he won't be getting the good of them.'

'What's all this about?' I looked at Lucius. He was scowling. 'The whole thing sounded harmless enough to me the way Crito described it.'

'Then you were misinformed,' Lucius said shortly. 'The Christians aren't harmless, darling. They eat human flesh and drink blood, for a start.'

I thought of Paullus and the house near the Praetorian Camp. 'But that's nonsense!'

'Are you contradicting me?' Lucius spoke quietly, but there was an edge to his voice that I recognised. Also Tigellinus was grinning; always a bad sign. I closed my mouth and wished I hadn't brought the subject up. 'Titus, I know these people. They're not a proper cult, they're atheists and criminals, perverts of the worst sort.'

'Oh, how exciting!'

'I'm not joking, my dear. They're the dregs of society. Even the Jews'll have nothing to do with them. And the flesh and blood is right enough. Did Crito tell you about their love feasts?' He used the Greek term.

'No,' I said. 'He never mentioned them.'

'There you are, then. Ask him yourself and see what he says.'

'He didn't tell you his friends were arsonists either, I'll bet.' Tigellinus spat. 'Religious fanatics who'd burn every temple in Rome for the fun of it. Who have burned more than half of them already.'

'And tried to blame it on me.' The emperor's voice was still calm, but his eyes had developed the hot, manic glare I'd seen before. 'They burned my city, Titus. Oh, yes, I have proof, it was a conspiracy. They're animals, fucking animals, and they'll die like animals, every one of them. I won't stop until Rome's clean again.'

Oh, sweet Serapis! Nevertheless, I let the subject drop. I'd done my best as promised and there was nothing more I could do. Besides, to some extent my sympathies lay with Lucius. Although I didn't believe the rubbish about the love feasts – typical gutter rumour; Lucius had probably got it from Tigellinus, along with the whole idea – old Paullus's egotism had annoyed me considerably. Basically he deserved all he got. A bit of persecution would make his Christians appreciate the civilised virtues of tolerance and compromise, and if Lucius had to find a scapegoat for public anger I could think of worse candidates than that sanctimonious crew.

Still, I didn't relish having to tell Crito.

44

Operations against the Christians began a few days later. Lucius and Tigellinus had obviously been compiling a private dossier of the cult members, because several hundred were rounded up at once and confined to the Mamertine Prison and other holding areas for eventual disposal in the arena. Most were pimps, prostitutes, common thieves and street hawkers, city sweepings of no great loss to society. There was a tacit moratorium on privately owned domestic slaves – quite rightly so; it would hardly have been fair for their masters to have suffered for the slaves' idiocies – but just in case I sent Crito off to a villa I owned at Alba. Despite, I must say, his own reluctance to go: either the old dear had shaken a tile loose since his conversion or he'd contracted a dose of uncharacteristic heroism. Whichever it was I didn't see why it should lose me a perfectly good head slave.

I found the savagery of the cult's suppression distasteful, even though I appreciated the depth of feeling that lay behind it: all of Rome after the fire was frustrated and angry, and the frustration and anger needed an outlet. How much of Lucius's own anger was genuine I didn't know. Probably most of it – I'd seen before how when he thought himself threatened he would lash out with unaccustomed cruelty that often had no rational basis. In any case, the mob wanted revenge, and revenge was what he gave them.

Most of the executions took place in the newly built racetrack in the Vatican valley beyond the river. I only went once: sword-fights I enjoy, if the gladiators are professionals, but to my mind there's no real pleasure in seeing unarmed men torn apart by wild beasts. Besides, I found the whole thing curiously unsettling.

There is a special atmosphere about these occasions which you don't get with gladiators, a cheerful hardness totally lacking in sympathy. Natural, of course: the victims are criminals, after all, there to entertain by dying, not by killing. Their terror is part of the fun, and although an agile man will get a round of applause for avoiding the cats he's expected to play the game in the end and die screaming.

The Christians didn't play the game at all.

At first the crowd took it badly: no one likes to be cheated. When the first group were brought in and the beasts were released there was the usual roar that turned to boos and curses when instead of scattering the men and women in the arena knelt down together and waited. Even the beasts, I think, were surprised – they were panthers and female lions, natural runners – although not for long. That first group died quickly. The second and third did the same. With the appearance of the fourth group the crowd was deathly quiet, even the mob in the topmost tiers. You could hear the singing distinctly. It was like watching a sacrifice where the audience keep holy silence as the priest cuts the victims' throats.

As I said, unsettling. I left before the fifth group were brought in. I wasn't the only one, either.

That evening Lucius had a party in the Vatican Gardens. I went alone: Silia was still out of Rome. I'd just got out of the litter and was adjusting my party mantle before going through the gate when someone gripped my arm.

'Petronius, my dear fellow! How are you these days?'

I turned, although I'd already recognised the voice. Seneca's plummy tones were unmistakable.

Seneca himself was not.

I didn't ask him if he was well. Clearly he wasn't, and even allowing for the two-year interval I wouldn't have recognised him. The face above the immaculate mantle was a death mask, all shadows and pits and hollows. The hand was a claw.

'I'm back in Rome as you see, like the proverbial bad penny.' He smiled and let me go, and I handed the guard my invitation.

We walked through the gate together. 'Terrible affair, terrible! I lost the town house and a good fifty million in property besides. Yourself? Not too badly hit, I trust?'

It took me a moment to realise he meant the fire. Of course, that would bring him back. Absentee landlords from all over Italy were coming to the city to check on their investments and do a bit of judicious buying while prices were low.

'The Quirinal was hardly touched,' I said. 'And I've no other property in the city.'

'Lucky man! But take my advice and buy some now. You won't regret it.'

I could see the torches up ahead near the centre of the gardens. The evening breeze carried a delicious smell of cooking.

'Roast pork,' I said. 'How nice.'

'I eat hardly anything myself these days. Mostly vegetables and fruit.' Seneca patted his once-ample stomach; like the rest of him it was shrunk almost to nothing. 'A return to my youth, when I took philosophy seriously.'

I laughed politely, as he expected: from Seneca it had to be a joke.

We were on the fringes of the party now, and it was well under way and quite crowded. The trees and bushes had been hung with glass and metal spangles lit from beneath with hundreds of tiny lamps, but the main area where the crowd was thickest had dozens of huge torches the height of trees. Even at this distance I could smell the pitch-pine resin mingling with the scent of the roasting pigs. Over to the left a flute wailed.

We were almost knocked over by a young man in a wreath and very little else pursuing two giggling dancing-girls. They disappeared together into the shrubbery, the girls already turning and falling, with their arms raised. Delightful. I hoped I wouldn't be saddled with Seneca all evening.

'You've seen the emperor since you got back?' I asked.

'No. But I sent him word from Naples that I was coming, and staying for a few days. The dear boy was good enough to invite —'

Seneca stopped, so suddenly that I thought he'd had a seizure.

'What's wrong?' He was rigid, his mouth open, seemingly

fascinated by the pitch-pine torches immediately ahead of us. 'Seneca, are you ill?'

His head moved from side to side, but not his eyes. They were still fixed on the nearest torch. I allowed my own to follow them.

It wasn't a pitch-pine torch after all, and what I'd smelled wasn't roast pork. The bundle of rags on a stick had been a human being once, nailed by its wrists to a crosspiece, doused with pitch and set alight. There were, as I've said, dozens of the things scattered over the middle of the gardens.

'Oh, Jupiter best and greatest!' I whispered. 'Oh, sweet Serapis!' My throat tightened, and I fought back the nausea.

'There can be slain no sacrifice more acceptable to God,' Seneca murmured. At least I think these were the words. They were Latin, but they sounded like a quotation; a particularly cold-blooded one in the circumstances.

'Indeed,' I said. 'Indeed.' The politeness was a reflex. Neither of us could tear our eyes away from the obscenity on the cross.

I was turning aside, finally, when I caught sight of Lucius staggering through the crowd in our direction, hugging a pair of doe-eyed Persian beauties. He was drunk, and his gilded laurel-leaf garland kept slipping down over one eye. As the girl-child – the Persians were twins, no older than ten – reached up on tiptoe to straighten it, he saw us and changed course like a heavy merchantman fighting its way across a contrary current.

'Titus!' he cried. 'Is that you? Seneca, you old devil! Join the party! How do you like my lanterns, eh?'

Neither of us spoke. I know I couldn't. Seneca looked grey.

Lucius stooped down and kissed first the girl then the boy hard on the mouth, his hands stroking their private parts. Then he looked at us and beamed.

'Serves the fuckers right! Poetic justice! They burn Rome, I burn them. Tit for tat. Economical, too.' He giggled. 'A good Christian'll last you hours, properly oiled.'

'Were they dead before you set them alight?' Seneca's voice was deceptively mild; I could see he was shaking.

'Some of them. We nailed them all up first then went round with the pitch. Most lasted out. The ones that weren't too heavy.'

He giggled again. 'Mind you, the fatsos burn better, so it comes to the same thing in the end.'

'Was this Tigellinus's idea?' I was watching the two children. They were fondling each other's genitals now, completely absorbed. Neither of them paid any attention to us, or to the burning corpses.

'Tiggy's idea? Of course not!' Lucius laughed. 'Why on earth should it be Tiggy's idea, darling?'

'No reason.' I felt empty.

'I mean, give me some credit for originality!' He turned to Seneca. 'That's these self-styled aesthetes all over, my dear. No one's allowed to have any good ideas but them. Tiggy's the same, it's so tiresome sometimes you just wouldn't believe.' Suddenly he sagged against the children's shoulders; they must have been stronger than they looked, because they were supporting most of his weight. 'Anyway, don't let me keep you. Go ahead, darlings, there's tons to eat and drink. Enjoy yourselves.'

The Persians moved off, towards one of the little pergolas that dotted the gardens on the edge of the lamplight. I would've gone home myself, but someone would no doubt have noticed and reported it to Lucius when he was sober. That I couldn't risk.

Nor could Seneca, seemingly. We moved forward to join the party. I noticed that as we passed the first of the human torches he bent down surreptitiously, scooped up a handful of earth and tossed it into the flames. I noticed something else, too. The fire had left the corpse's lower legs intact, and on one of them was a broad discolouration, like a childhood burn.

My slave Crito was safe at Alba. Paullus, with his Roman citizenship, was also safe, for the time being, at least. Justin, who had brought me my wine and had nothing and no one to protect him, was another matter.

I only stayed for a couple of hours, although by that time the crosses with their charred remains still attached had burned themselves out and been replaced with more conventional lighting. Tigellinus was there, drinking alone, but I avoided him, not caring much if he saw me do it. Nor did I search out any more congenial company, despite the fact that there was plenty of it around, both male and female. I don't know whether Seneca had gone by the time I left or not. He was hustled away from me early on by a tight knot of grim-faced senators in uncompromisingly plain mantles, and that was the last I saw of him.

45

I only found out that something out of the usual was happening when I went round by arrangement at the end of April to see how the decoration of the new palace was progressing. The gates were closed and guarded. Even my written invitation had no effect on the Praetorians in the gatehouse.

'Sorry, sir,' the commander said as he handed it back. 'No one goes in or out till further notice.'

'Is there anything wrong?' A pointless question: there were twice the number of troops on duty, including a contingent of heavily armed Germans.

'Couldn't say, sir.' The man was polite enough but firm. 'If you've a message for the emperor I'll see he gets it.'

'No, no message.'

I went away very worried indeed. Trouble had been brewing for months. Lucius's attempts to shift the blame for the fire on to the Christians had failed, and his building schemes had caused fresh outrage. The Treasury was almost empty already, the provincial governors were screaming at the latest tax demands, and to make things worse he'd sent agents out to the eastern provinces to requisition bronzes and other items to stock the rooms and gardens of his Golden House. He was not, to put it mildly, currently popular with anyone.

Instead of going straight home I called in at Silia's newly rebuilt house on the Palatine. I was half hoping that Arruntius would be there, but he wasn't. Silia herself was looking flustered.

'But haven't you heard, Titus?' she said when the slave showed me through into the atrium. It still smelled of fresh paint.

'Heard what?'

'About the plot, of course.' Although it was the middle of the day her hair was still loose and she was wearing no make-up. She looked old, and a little haggard. 'Half the Senate's under arrest, if the rumours are true.'

I sat down. 'Arruntius?'

'No. Gnaeus is in Ostia. At least, I think that's where he is. I haven't seen him for days.'

'What happened?'

Her fingers were twisting the pendant at her throat. At any moment I expected the thin gold chain to break.

'I don't know. Not the details. But it's bad, very bad.'

I reached over, took both her hands and forced them into her lap. They were trembling.

'Now, dear,' I said firmly. 'Tell me.'

As these things go, the plot had been well thought out. The principals seemed to be Calpurnius Piso, the consul-designate Lateranus, two more senators, Scaevinus and Natalis, and one of the Guards commanders. Their plan was simple. At the games that day Lateranus would throw himself at the emperor's feet as if making a petition, grab his knees and bring him down; at which point the others would draw concealed daggers and stab him. Piso wouldn't be directly involved; as their choice of successor he would wait elsewhere with clean hands. The plan would've worked, too, if Scaevinus hadn't given the game away accidentally to one of his freedmen who had immediately warned Lucius.

The most worrying thing was, as Silia said, Lucius's probable reaction. Any threat, especially a personal one, threw him into total panic; and when Lucius panicked he lost all capacity for rational thought. People would die soon, that was certain; a lot of people, innocent and guilty alike. It would be the treason trials all over again.

'The fools,' I said softly, still holding Silia's shaking hands. 'The bloody, bloody fools!'

'He has only himself to blame.' Silia's mouth was set. 'Gnaeus has been saying for months that something like this would happen. I only hope the poor lamb hasn't been silly and kept things from me.'

'He's in Ostia. You said so yourself.'

'Do you think that makes a difference?' she snapped. 'We dine with Piso regularly. And Lateranus gave us the use of his country house last summer. For the emperor that would be enough: More than enough.'

'Did he say when he'd be back?'

'No. But then he never does.'

I got up. 'Come home with me. Now.'

She shook her head; she was on the verge of tears. 'I can't.'

'Get out of Rome, then. Go to Baiae.' Arruntius had a villa there. 'At least until all this blows over.'

'No. It's better if I stay here and behave as if everything was normal. Besides, Gnaeus may be back at any moment. He must've heard the news too.'

I felt as if I was teetering on the brink of a precipice, but Silia was right. There wasn't anything anyone could do but wait, and act as normally as possible.

'Perhaps I can get in to see Lucius,' I said. 'Find out what the situation is.'

'Don't even try, dear. He won't be . . . himself.'

That made sense too. I could imagine from past experience the emperor's present mood. It would be safer to walk unarmed into a tiger's cage.

'Someone else, then.' I remembered the conversation I'd had months before. 'Thrasea Paetus.'

'Titus, don't be a fool! You'll only get hurt! Go straight home and do nothing!'

'Let me know when Gnaeus gets back.' I bent forward to kiss her forehead, and left.

The streets were full of soldiers; not just the Market Square area but every corner between the Palatine and the Quirinal. Otherwise there were few people about; the whole of Rome, it seemed, had become an armed camp empty of civilians. I didn't go to Thrasea's after all. Silia was quite right; visiting him would have been stupid in the extreme. In the end I took her advice. I went home, and waited.

The next month was as bad as anything under Caligula or Claudius. Tigellinus's secret police made dozens of arrests, mostly senators and Guards officers, and the accused were taken in chains to the Servilian Gardens where Lucius, Tigellinus and the egregious Faenius Rufus – now back in favour again – held an ad hoc court. Rumours were rife. The only bright spot was a message from Silia to say that Arruntius was safely home and was not, touch wood, implicated. So far, at least.

There were no parties these days, of course – one was never sure that host or guest mightn't embarrass one by being charged with treason the next morning – so I was in the study reading by the light of an oil lamp when Crito knocked on the door (he was back from the Alban villa, Christian slaves being now almost fashionable).

'A visitor, sir,' he said.

I was surprised; no one, as I say, moved over their own threshold that month even during the hours of daylight.

'Who is it?'

His lips set in a tight line. 'Ofonius Tigellinus, sir.'

I don't think I let my feelings show, which was just as well because Tigellinus had brought himself through and was already standing grinning in the doorway.

'Bring us some wine, boy,' he said to Crito, 'and then fuck off.'

Crito ignored him and looked at me. I nodded. Tigellinus pushed past him and lay down on the spare reading couch. We stared at each other.

'Don't worry, Petronius,' he said at last. 'I haven't come to arrest you. Not yet, anyway.'

'I never thought you had, my dear.' I smiled at him, although my heart was thudding and he must have known it. 'And it's a pleasure to have such a distinguished and cultured guest under my roof.'

The grin didn't falter. 'Thank you. Was that him? Your tame Christian?'

'That was Crito, my head slave, yes. His beliefs are none of my business so long as he keeps them to himself.'

'The emperor would disagree.'

'The emperor knows my feelings quite well. And he's gentleman enough to respect them.'

This time the grin did fade. 'Meaning I'm not?'

'Opinions differ.' I set my book aside. 'You're entitled to think as you like. As am I.'

Crito came back with the tray. We both watched as he poured the wine and left, closing the door behind him. Tigellinus held up his cup.

'To justice,' he said. 'And to the death of all traitors.'

I drank. He watched me through narrowed eyes.

'Now,' I said, lowering the cup. 'If you haven't come to arrest me, just why are you here?'

'Oh, but I'm not here.' He smiled again, with his mouth only. 'At least not officially. But I did want to have a talk with you.'

'Talk, then.'

'You know Seneca's dead?'

It would have been dangerous to have shown the shock I felt. I kept my face expressionless.

'Really?'

'Really. He slit his wrists this morning at his country house, on the emperor's orders.' He took a long, slow drink of his wine while his eyes held mine over the rim of the cup. 'One of his many country houses. I thought you'd like to know.'

'Thank you. I'm obliged.'

'You're most welcome.' He finished the wine and poured himself another cup. 'The old goat should've known better than to try treason at his age. We're well rid of him.'

'Treason? Seneca?'

'Of course. You're surprised?'

'Naturally I'm surprised! Did he confess?'

Tigellinus smiled. 'He didn't need to. Natalis denounced him.' Natalis, if you remember, was one of the conspirators. 'The old bastard was in it from the start.'

I set my wine down untasted.

'Well, my dear,' I said carefully, 'it was very kind of you to come and tell me all this, but it is getting rather late and . . .'

'"There can be slain no sacrifice more acceptable to God,"' Tigellinus murmured.

I froze. 'I beg your pardon?'

'I'm not going yet, Petronius. I haven't finished with you. I haven't even begun. You remember these words?'

'No.' It was a lie; I remembered them quite clearly. Seneca

had spoken them to me, or to himself, that night in the Vatican Gardens.

'Strange. One of my people said you were with him at the time. You're sure you don't remember?' His eyes were boring into me.

'Oh, yes. You're right, of course. He was commenting on the burned Christian. Not the most tasteful of remarks, but we shouldn't speak ill of the dead, should we?'

Tigellinus laughed. 'A good try, Petronius. But not quite good enough. I thought you prided yourself on being a literary man. Surely you recognised the words?'

I was genuinely puzzled, and not a little alarmed. 'My knowledge isn't as exhaustive as your own, darling. No, I'm afraid I did not.'

'They're from one of Seneca's own plays, his *Hercules Mad.*' He was smiling broadly now. 'The full quotation goes – and correct me if I'm wrong – 'There can be slain no sacrifice more acceptable to God than an unjust and wicked king.' You replied – and again I'm speaking subject to your correction – "Indeed."'

We stared at each other in silence. The masks were down. Tigellinus wasn't smiling any longer.

'I told you. He was talking about the dead slave,' I said. 'At least, I thought he was.'

'Your thoughts, my dear, aren't worth a wet fart. I'm interested in words. His were treasonous, and you agreed with them.'

I picked up my wine-cup and drank, proud that my hand didn't shake.

'You said you hadn't come to arrest me,' I said.

'And I added *Not yet*. I want you to suffer for a while first.' Tigellinus was grinning again. 'Darling.'

'Why?'

'Because I don't like you. I've never liked you.'

'And that's your reason?'

He shrugged. 'Do I need a better one?'

I shifted on the couch. 'Supposing I kill myself now?'

'You can please yourself. But you'd be a fool if you did. And who knows? You may be lucky. I might die before you after all.'

'Lucius would never believe I was a traitor. I'm not. You know that yourself.'

'He'll believe what I tell him. The poor bastard can't tell reality from fantasy nowadays anyway.'

That was true enough, although I hadn't expected Tigellinus to state the case so baldly. Lucius had always been convinced that despite all evidence to the contrary everyone loved him. Now, with the conspiracy, he was confronted with proof that they didn't, and his world had collapsed around him.

'What do you want, Tigellinus?' I said softly. 'Power? To be emperor yourself?'

He laughed. 'Fuck that! I told you years ago, when we first met. I only want to enjoy myself. Nero understands. He may be stupid in many ways but he knows I'm loyal.' He stood up. Carefully, deliberately, he poured the rest of his wine over the couch and dropped the cup. It smashed on the marble floor. 'A libation to Seneca's ghost. And to yours, Petronius. Don't bother to see me out.'

I lay for a long time after he had gone, staring at the closed door.

46

The treason trials continued. How many of the fifty-odd accused were actually guilty, and how many were innocent victims of Tigellinus, I didn't know. I wasn't sure even about Seneca. Certainly he was on record as saying that when all else failed it was the good man's duty to kill a tyrant, but then the old ham's actions always had fallen short of his philosophy. Frankly I doubted if he had the guts for revolution. The great surprise was the condemnation of Lucius's and Tigellinus's co-judge Faenius Rufus. Him I have no doubts about at all; Rufus had neither the will nor the energy for treason. God knows what Tigellinus promised Scaevinus if he accused him, but it was never paid. Scaevinus and Rufus both died.

Others died, too. Lots of them, including Lucan, Seneca's nephew. I hadn't much time for Lucan, who wore his hair in the old Republican style (despite his flattery of the emperor) and had a grossly inflated idea of his own skills as a poet; but he didn't deserve death on those counts, poor lad, let alone the reason that was given. Relieving himself of a bout of wind in one of the public privies, he had been stupid enough to quote one of Lucius's own lines to the assembled company:

You might have thought it thundered 'neath the ground.

One of Tigellinus's spies happened to be sitting two beams along. He reported the joke back, and Lucan was condemned.

For his help in suppressing the Great Conspiracy Tigellinus was awarded an honorary triumph and had several statues of himself erected in prominent public places, by grateful vote of the Senate. What there was left of it.

Heigh ho.

It is, by the way (to bring us back to the present, which we've almost reached), almost dawn. The slaves are pulling back the curtains and the light of the lamps is beginning to look somewhat pale. Dion (my secretary, remember?) is yawning; he's done marvellously, poor darling, and I'll give him his freedom for this night's work before we make an end. Promise.

Before we make an end. One more page, Dion, or perhaps two. To clear up a mystery.

Who burned Rome? And why?

Oh, yes. I know. No, it wasn't an accident, or at least not completely. Nor was it Lucius, to make room for his Golden House; nor the poor Christians, out of misguided piety or pure devilment. Other agents were responsible.

What agents, you ask? I found out because Arruntius was drunk. He'd never have told me otherwise.

I'd gone round at Silia's invitation: a housewarming (if that isn't an unfortunate term after the first house has been destroyed by fire) which was also – tacitly – a celebration of Arruntius's having escaped being involved in the Great Conspiracy. We were, of course, in the dining-room, rather depressingly decorated in the old-fashioned style with Europa and the Bull plus a Still Life with Dead Pheasants. It had been an excellent meal: spiced seafood dumplings, celery and calfs' brains with egg sauce, and a truly imperial sturgeon cooked whole in wine and fennel. Arruntius had managed to lay his hands on several gallons of thirty-five-year-old Faustinian (I didn't ask how, but I had the distinct impression that it was a bribe for whatever he'd been engaged in at Ostia), and we'd done our best to make a hole in it. Silia had fallen asleep on one of the couches. Arruntius and I were left looking pop-eyed at each other. We were talking about the fire.

'Terrible thing, Titus. Terrible.' Arruntius tried to lift his wine-cup to his mouth and failed. 'A disaster. A complete disaster.'

'Not for Tigellinus, my dear,' I said. 'It left the emperor vulnerable. Exactly where Tiggy wanted him.'

'That's what I mean. Total miscalc-. Miscalc-.' Arruntius belched, then stumbled carefully through the word. 'Miscalculation. All that for nothing.'

I felt suddenly sober. 'Miscalculation?'

'Idea was. Just the poor areas. Get mob on our side.' Arruntius's head was nodding. 'Nero was too popular. Only it got out of hand, didn't it? Shame, Titus. Crying shame.'

I kept my voice matter-of-fact. 'Bassus said it started by accident. In the oil shops near the racetrack.'

'So it did. Accident. Pure accident. But we kept it going despite the fucker.'

'"We"?'

His eyes opened for a moment and he grinned at me.

'We,' he said, and winked.

I remembered the gangs who'd roamed the burning streets stopping the rescue attempts in the emperor's name. And the senior consul, the aristocrat Crassus Frugi who had been, conveniently, out of Rome at the time. Things could've been a lot worse if Bassus hadn't been so efficient, or less ready to take responsibility.

'The second fire,' I prompted. 'The one that started on Tigellinus's estate. That was the Senate's doing as well?'

He nodded, and held a shaking finger to his lips. 'Not the whole Senate. Just the best of us. But don't say a word, Titus. Not that it matters any longer. It didn't work, and we're all dead anyway. Bastard wriggled out of it.' His head settled on the swelling back of the couch. 'Bastard wriggles out of anything. Even a knife. Shame. Still, give him enough rope he'll hang himself eventually.'

I stayed very still, until Arruntius's eyes were closed and he was snoring softly. Then I got up and left.

So there you are. Believe it if you like. Perhaps it was just the wine talking, and the whole thing was an accident from start to finish. In a way I hope so. I wouldn't like to think that any member of the august Roman Senate would put his personal hatreds above the lives of thousands of his fellow-citizens, let alone countless millions in property, even if it wasn't wholly premediated. But if it is true then the conspirators deserved all they got, and I've less sympathy for them than I do for Lucius. Or even for the animal Tigellinus.

The sky through my dining-room windows is turning red. The Praetorians will be here shortly to check that the emperor's orders have been carried out. Briefly, then.

Poppaea died – pregnant, she was kicked in the stomach by Lucius in a blind fit of rage after he had accused her of conceiving the child by another man. She'd never proved to be the danger Seneca had thought her, and Tigellinus had taught Lucius to trust no one but himself. She was buried in Augustus's mausoleum – not burned in the Roman manner, but embalmed like an Egyptian queen. I wasn't invited to the ceremony: Tigellinus had already persuaded Lucius that I wasn't worthy of the honour.

Not present either was Gaius Cassius Longinus, a descendant of the Cassius who'd killed Julius Caesar. Lucius's reasons (or Tigellinus's, rather) rapidly became clear: Cassius was accused of fomenting a fresh conspiracy with poor Junia Calvina's nephew. Among others implicated was one Titus Petronius Niger, erstwhile friend of the emperor. Lucius signed the order for my death, I am told, while selecting costumes for an up-and-coming concert tour of the Greek city-states. I doubt if I caused enough distraction to make him hesitate between the silver or the gold spangles.

So. Here we are, at the end. Dion looks relieved, as indeed he should: the poor darling's right hand must be aching. The plates and the wine jugs are empty. No more figpeckers. No more wine. All gone.

Ah well.

Silia should be in Marseilles by now, beginning her own exile. That, I am afraid, I cannot forgive Lucius for. He may be a killer and a madman, but I never thought he was spiteful; although perhaps that, too, is Tigellinus's fault. Arruntius survives, but then Arruntius would. Tigellinus, of course, is thriving, and emperor in everything but name.

There's a lesson there, no doubt, if I had the time and the energy to learn it.

Perhaps mad old Paullus was right, and Lucius is cursed. If

so then it's a pity. He meant well enough, in the beginning, whatever happened later. And I'd far rather see Lucius's future for Rome than Paullus's. Whatever his faults, the emperor has good taste. He ought to: I trained him to it myself. And wholesomeness left to itself can be so terribly boring!

The sun has cleared the horizon. We've timed things well.

Dion, the pen, please.

And then, my dear, the tourniquets.

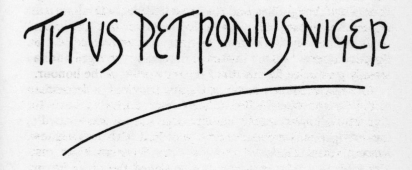